DEADLY PEN PAL

He wrote hundreds of letters from jail—all to women. Carol Spadoni began her pen pal relationship with him believing that there was some good in him. Helen Blair thought her friendship would help him find hope and religion. Shirley Thorp thought her letters would ease his lonely confinement. They ignored his profane, vile, sexually deviant comments, they believed him when he said he was truly sorry for having murdered and raped.

None realized he was lying.

Inside he was a cauldron of burning hatred, wanting nothing more than to kill women, then mutilate and rape their dead bodies.

And when he got out of jail, he would set out to visit each one and make his deadly dreams come true.

DEADLY URGES

Barry Bortnick

Pinnacle Books
Kensington Publishing Corp.

http://www.pinnaclebooks.com

Some names have been changed to protect the privacy of individuals connected to this story.

PINNACLE BOOKS are published by

Kensington Publishing Corp.
850 Third Avenue
New York, NY 10022

First Printing: March, 1997
10 9 8 7 6 5 4 3 2 1

Printed in the United States of America

For my brothers and sisters

ACKNOWLEDGMENTS

I wish to thank the Burlingame Police Department for contributing to the production of this book. I would also like to thank my associates, Nickey Hernandez, George Cline, Kimberly Jolson, Tricia Zabuti, and Kathryn Van Sant for their advice. I must also thank my fellow reporters and staff members at *The Santa Barbara News-Press* who covered for me while I was away researching this story.

Prologue

"My first victim was Fanny Vann, she was five foot, born Sept. 4, 1952. She's 130 pounds, brown eyes, black hair. I met her at the College of the Desert. First time I met her I didn't see much in her, bodywise anyway. Then I started working with her on her car. Then I seen that she had something I wanted—her body.

"When she wore her shorts one day, oh, did she show off that fine little ass and those sweet legs. And I tried to look down the front of her blouse and see those fine medium-sized black breasts.

"I . . . I asked (if) I could take her home, 'cause she was standing around, and she said 'Yes.' I took her home for about three weeks and each night I planned on killing her. So I got a gun, bought a gun at school from a guy I met there. And it was 'bout a week, that Monday night, 22nd of April was her dying night and rape night."

ONE

Death in the Desert

"Sorry sweet thing, can't have no witnesses."

Springtime in the Southern California desert can be a spectacular experience as the dusty brown hills around Palm Springs give way to a lively bloom of color and an enchanting floral fragrance for a few months until the intense heat of summer burns away the new life, leaving the landscape parched and the residents heading for air-conditioned malls or the fine resorts and spas of Indian Hills.

In such a spring, Fathyma "Fanny" Vann sought change. She was already a grandmother at age 38, and a dedicated nurse's aide at a convalescent home in Palm Desert, yet she wanted more and sought extra avenues to express her bubbling personality and boundless energy.

Vann was short and a bit plump, but carried herself well. She loved jewelry and adorned her fingers with rings that caught the sun and played off her beaming smile and cheery manner. The African-American woman favored pinkie bands and never went anywhere without three on the small finger of her right hand. From a 14-carat gold necklace hung a dollar sign made of gold, an indication of the dreams Vann hoped to attain.

Vann even had a gold cap on a front tooth shaped like a clover leaf, so that every smile came with a hint at luck and good fortune.

She favored gold bracelets and wore three on her arms. She had two pairs of pierced earrings, one of which always held a diamond stud. She liked toe rings as well, and often drew attention to her face by clipping a second diamond stud to her nose. Vann's love of shimmering metal was so great she kept the valuables fastened to her body even when she went to work, or while lifting weights.

On other women, this abundance of glitter might have seemed outlandish, but on Vann the look worked.

Like others who have reached the stage where work or socializing no longer fills the spirit or the needs of a hungry mind, Vann sought to better herself by enrolling in night school. She chose the College of the Desert, a community campus of palm trees and groomed lawns in nearby Palm Desert, which offered a variety of courses, including one in basic auto mechanics.

Vann had a limited understanding of the combustion engine, and as a struggling member of the middle class, she could not afford the expense of keeping her 1981 Datsun 280 ZX running in top form.

To save money, Vann signed up for night classes, determined to learn about her car and become proficient enough to take it apart piece by piece.

"That car was her baby," said John Tamulonis one of her teachers.

As the car aged, things naturally fell apart. By 1991, the car needed new valves and a head gasket.

"The [repair] guys downtown were going to harpoon her," Tamulonis said. "An arm and a leg and a left nut, and whatever to fix it. So she went off, took this engine-rebuild class and started taking the stuff apart."

Vann was meticulous in her studies. She cataloged every part of the car she touched, keeping track of the wires and springs as if the auto project were a giant jigsaw puzzle. While the Datsun underwent repairs in class, Vann caught rides with friends or traveled on the bus that ran up and down Highway 111 and connected the desert communities of Palm Springs to the west, and Indio, some 17 miles to the east.

Phillip Carl Jablonski knew the bus route as well. He had often taken the line while making his way from a lonely, one-room apartment in Indio to attend classes at the desert college.

Like Vann, Jablonski was undergoing changes that spring. Just a few months earlier he had been released from the San Luis Obispo Men's Colony, a high-security prison in the middle of the Santa Lucia Range. The prison facility, located near the central coast of California, is home to more than 3,500 state prisoners. Jablonski had been serving time for the 1978 murder of his common-law wife.

Jablonski was a huge man. He stood over six feet, two inches tall. He weighed about 240 pounds and had a thick, fleshy neck, a high forehead, and a slouched posture. With his unkept hair and droopy moustache, the disheveled giant looked like an aging elephant.

"He was an overweight slob," recalled Tina Montez, a street-smart, cigarette-smoking landlord, who owned and managed an apartment house where Jablonski rented a room following his prison release. "His shirt was never tucked in right and his belt was not looped through the loops. He just looked like a big slob, a big gentle man, who was quiet and seemed intelligent."

Montez knew nothing about her new tenant when he first arrived in September 1990. In her line of work, a person's past was not that important. Still, Montez was curious and asked him about his life. Jablonski wasn't bothered by the question, or the answer. In a calm, almost emotionless manner, Jablonski said he had spent years in prison for strangling his wife and leaving her body inside their apartment.

"He said it as casually as if he was telling me his car was parked across the street," Montez said of the revelation.

Because her apartment house is home to many ex-cons, Montez took the news in stride, believing that if the state figured Jablonski had paid his debt for the past murder, it was time to let a dead woman and old memories fade away.

"I never checked up on his past," Montez said. "I tell people who come here that I don't care about yesterday."

Jablonski seemed to have the same attitude and acted like a man who wanted to start anew. In many ways Jablonski was the perfect tenant. He paid his $350-a-month rent on time, organized his room—a common trait among ex-cons all too familiar with the regimen of prison life—and kept to himself.

On occasion, he talked with Montez about old Western movies on television, the actor James Dean, and the success or failure of California sports teams. By day, he went about his business and traveled around Indio on a second-hand 10-speed bike that got him to the grocery store or the Social Security office where he collected a benefits check.

"Phillip did not talk to the people in the hotel. He did not like people," Montez said. "I liked him, because there was something gentle, quiet and sad about him."

Jablonski was always inside the apartment house by nightfall. He usually cooked a simple meal of hot dogs or macaroni and cheese in its community kitchen, then shuffled off to his room at the far end of the first floor and ate by the glow of a 12-inch television set.

On occasion a stray cat Jablonski had named Alex showed up at his door to feast on the scraps left at the bottom of his discarded tuna fish cans.

Montez took pity on Jablonski when he first showed up at her door some nine months before the spring of 1991. He was 44 then and had the look of a burdened animal that had been driven hard most of its life and put to bed wet each evening. Montez has a keen eye for misfits. Years of renting rooms to newly released felons has given her an unusual insight into the underbelly of life and the dark side of the human soul. She could size up these sorry customers at first glance and had Jablonski pegged for a lonely loser from day one.

She gave him a quiet room toward the back that came with a shower. Apartment number nine was not much bigger than the prison cells Jablonski had called home for the past 12 years. The air inside his new dwelling was stale from years of occupancy, but the secluded location gave Jablonski protection from front-desk traffic and kept him away from the community bathrooms.

"I play favorites with people," Montez said in a voice as dry as the parched Indio landscape. "Certain people need more than others. He needed more. He was a big, solitary, lonely, old fat man, who did not need to be walking the hall with a towel wrapped around him."

The loneliness Montez observed may have been triggered by Jablonski's hatred of his new community. He had never wanted to come back to this part of California. There were too many memories. Indio was too close to Jablonski's native San Bernardino; too near Palm Springs and the apartment he once shared with the woman he had killed in 1978; too akin to his parents' old residence in Joshua Tree, where family memories seemed more like nightmares.

But the state said he had to stay in Indio for the duration of his parole, whether he liked it or not. Like so many other cons left broke and bewildered after years inside prison walls, where every aspect of life is dictated and controlled, Jablonski followed the orders and passed his days inside Montez's apartment house, the Indio Tower Manor.

The two-story, 30-room complex was neither tall nor distinguished. The bland-looking monolith is stuck in the middle of Indio's poorest neighborhood, just half a block from the bus station in a district crowded with secondhand stores. Like it or not, Jablonski was here to stay and at first he seemed determined to make a go of things.

"He was supposed to get on with his life," Montez said. "He worked very hard at it."

For a time Jablonski blended into the surroundings. On rare occasions he sought comfort from the prostitutes who worked the streets outside the Manor, an accepted practice with management provided all parties acted like ladies and gentleman, Montez said. Jablonski's only display of emotion during his nine months with Montez occurred during a brief flash of anger when a female neighbor broke into his room and stole his cash.

"It was righteous," Montez said of Jablonski's reaction. "He forgot to lock his door one day and the girl next door, who was not very nice, apparently went in and took his money. He knew who did it, and when he came back and saw her in the hall, he put his hand under her chin and literally lifted her up against the wall."

As the woman stood on her tiptoes and dangled helplessly from Jablonski's meaty paw, he made his feelings clear. "Walk into my room again and I'll kill you,'' he said before releasing his grip.

When Jablonski later expressed an interest in getting a car so he could get to his classes at the College of the Desert, Montez was ready to help. A heroin addict, who also lived in the apartment complex, became desperate as his cash flow dwindled and his craving for the addictive opiate drove him into convulsions and body sweats.

Addicts will do just about anything when it comes time to get a fix and in this case the doper needed $200 to cover the cost of a syringe full of joy. His only bargaining chip was a beat-up 1965 Ford Fairlane given to him by his mother. In desperation, he offered the car to Montez.

By the next day, Jablonski was at the bank, getting $400 to pay Montez for the Fairlane. The addict got his narcotics on time, Jablonski got his ride, and Montez earned a commission.

Jablonski now had a vehicle to get him to school. The aging Fairlane was not fancy, but it was dependable. It also provided Jablonski with a project to tinker with during class and in no time at all, he had stripped off its white paint, coated the vehicle in primer and covered part of the doors and antenna in masking tape in preparation for touching it up at the school.

Tamulonis recalled that when Jablonski showed up for spring registration that year, he was up front about his past. He told the instructor he was on parole and hoped that would not cause a problem for fellow students. The teacher brushed the concern aside, telling Jablonski that as long as he attended classes and quit on time, he could fit in like everyone else.

A "C" student at best, Jablonski kept up with his studies and used a cassette tape recorder to record class lectures. As far as Tamulonis knew, the big man kept to himself and seemed a mellow student trying to learn something new.

But others working inside the auto bays of the community college noticed something odd about the large man. Most could not fully explain their feelings, but many wanted nothing to do with him. One of the leery was Susan Mallony, a classmate who did not like the way Jablonski moved about the room. She felt Jablonski had a chip on his shoulder and seemed to pay too much attention to the women in class.

"It was just the way he carried himself," Mallony said. "I don't know if he did it with everybody, but I've seen him look at a few of the female students, and it wasn't how you would [normally] look at a woman and appreciate her attractiveness. It is hard to describe . . . kind of a hatred."

Maryanne Marco sensed it as well after Jablonski introduced himself one day in class and offered to help tune her car.

"I had seen him watching and he gave me the creeps," she said. "I said 'no thanks' and asked someone else to come over and help me. Even though I didn't need the help, I wanted someone else to be around. I was afraid to make eye contact [with Jablonski] after that."

As the weeks passed, Marco noticed that Jablonski continued to maul her with his eyes from across the room as he stood with his hands in his pockets.

Fanny Vann attended the same class as Jablonski. She caught his fancy when a teaching assistant paired them together after noticing that Vann needed help with the heavy work on her Datsun, while Jablonski seemed to have little else to fiddle with in class.

"When we see people standing around and other people need help, then we get them to pitch in so they could learn a little bit about their stuff," Tamulonis said.

A dangerous seed had been planted, and it would grow into an evil weed, as Jablonski wormed his way into Vann's life while they worked on the Datsun. After gaining her trust in class, Jablonski extended his services by offering Vann a ride home from school at night. Her car was often disabled while she worked to repair the engine's valve system, so Vann accepted her classmate's seemingly generous offer.

To Vann, the ride home was just a simple favor offered by a near stranger. But to Jablonski, the invitation meant more. He had never understood women and over the course of his life mistook innocent looks as something else. Soon he was telling friends that Vann was his girlfriend even though nothing could have been further from the truth. On at least one occasion after driving her home from class, Jablonski tried to talk his way into Vann's apartment, only to be rebuffed at the door.

After Vann was escorted home one night, her daughter, Yolanda, met Jablonski and joked that if anything ever happened to her mother, she would come looking for him. The half-joking retort did not affect the big man, who by then had already plotted Vann's death. In a chilling tape-recorded message, Jablonski outlined his intentions. With a hushed, yet excited tone, he shared his most perverse thoughts on the very machine he used in class to record lectures.

"I met her at the College of the Desert," he told his battery-powered confessor. "First time I met her, I didn't see much in her, bodywise anyway. Then I started working with her on her car. Then I seen that she had something I wanted—her body. When she wore her shorts one day, oh, did she show off that fine little ass and those sweet legs. I tried to look down the front of her blouse and see those fine medium-sized black breasts. Each night I was planning on killing her, but I didn't have everything I needed."

Jablonski did not want to strangle this target, as he had done to other women in the past. Still, he needed a weapon to carry out his mission. A fellow classmate, unfamiliar with Jablonski's past, provided the means through which wrong would be committed.

Warren Dorek worked as a security guard when not attending school. During class on April 14, Dorek fell into conversation with Jablonski and soon the talk centered on a small, steel-blue .22 caliber revolver Dorek owned. He had purchased the gun 10 years before for his first wife to use for self-defense when they lived in Long Beach. After their divorce, Dorek kept the weapon for himself.

Dorek considered Jablonski a friendly classmate who outscored him on a recent pop quiz. He was a little short of money that spring, and thought he could get some cash by selling the old weapon. Jablonski offered Dorek $60.

Now armed, Jablonski filled a small black and gold gym bag with the goods of his trade, stocking the sack with duct tape, a stun gun, and a pair of hand-fashioned wire handcuffs before heading off to class on April 22, 1991.

Vann's day began in typical fashion. She traveled to work at the Manor Care home, went about her duties, and caught a ride home from Carmen Cervantes, a co-worker. They traveled to Vann's residence when their shifts ended at 3 p.m., and Cervantes dropped her off in the parking lot of the apartment Vann shared with her two daughters. Yolanda, the younger child, then 20 years old, had spoken with her mother by phone at about 12:30 that afternoon. When Yolanda returned home later that afternoon, she spotted her mother's stethoscope in the house and reasoned she had returned home during the afternoon and changed into a white outfit before heading off to campus. Vann was taking classes in mechanics, psychology, child development and weight training.

As usual, Vann was noticed by her instructors as she went about her normal evening routine. Gym teacher John Stevens saw her working with weights at about 6 p.m. Louis Ewing, a lab technician in the auto shop class, spoke with Vann about some parts she needed to fix on her vehicle, before she turned her attention to the Datsun's valve springs.

Jablonski had arrived on campus early that afternoon. He met with Tamulonis and told the instructor that he could not attend the next morning's class, because he had to be at a doctor's appointment. Jablonski then came to campus that night and began helping Vann with her repairs.

About 9 p.m., near the end of class, Vann approached Susan Mallory, and asked for a ride home, but she was too busy. Another classmate also declined the request, leaving Vann with Jablonski, who was eager to help out.

"I could not give her a ride that night," Mallory said. "And then she got into his car. I remember looking out, looking over at him, and he just had kind of a strange look on his face. I looked over for a brief moment, then went back to what I was doing."

They drove away from the campus at about 10 p.m. When they hit a darkened spot at the end of Dinah Shore Road, only a mile or so away, Jablonski pulled out the snub-nosed .22 and went to work.

"Time to get raped, sweet thing," he whispered to Vann, whose desperate cries for mercy only excited Jablonski.

He cocked the gun's hammer and told her that she'd better go along or he'd have his way with her corpse. Vann disrobed, taking off her white outfit, white bra and white panties.

"I asked her if she ever sucked a dick," Jablonski said, capturing his desires on the tape recording. "She said 'no.' [I asked] if she ever have it up that fine black ass? I said, 'Tonight's your lucky night, sweet thing. You're gonna get sodomized and you're gonna suck your first dick.'" With his massive hands, Jablonski forced Vann's head into his crotch and made her suck and play with his privates. Not satisfied, he forced her to roll over then—as he put it on the tape recorder—"I rode those fine black cheeks—wham!—right home in that big black ass."

Vann was in agony and began to scream. Her cries were cut short by her tormentor's words. "Ssh, ssh, be quiet girl," Jablonski told her, before he buried his scruffy face in her chest and suckled her breasts.

"God, this woman's fine," he told the tape.

Vann sat traumatized as tears flowed down her face.

"Looked at her," Jablonski said. "I says, 'Sorry sweet thing, can't have no witnesses.'"

The bullet entered the front left side of Vann's head, traveled across her brain at a 45-degree angle, ripped a course through the cerebellum, and left a red-brown powder burn on her skull. Vann's blood spilled across the inside of Jablonski's Fairlane and dripped into the creases of his front seat. Her head rested against the passenger window, blood trickled down and outlined the shape of the dead woman's breast.

"I reached up and got me a handful of that sweet, black breast," Jablonski told the recorder. "I squeezed it again and said, 'Well Fanny, I got what I wanted. Yeah, you sweet little grandmother, you ain't gonna see your grandchildren, honey. Yeah, sweet thing, you're mine, all mine.'"

TWO
Dumping Ground

*"Left her like garbage, what she was after I got done
with her."*

Though the dead end of Dinah Shore Road was secluded,
Jablonski knew this was no place to discard a body. Besides,
he was not yet done with his prize—not by a long shot. He
had been dreaming of this moment for some time and was not
about to let the game end in so staid a fashion. As Vann's body
lay slumped inside the primer-gray Fairlane, Jablonski drove
north out of Palm Desert until he connected with Interstate 10,
a major freeway that shoots like an arrow through the low
desert and into Arizona. The path took him past the familiar
and despised landscape of Indio.

He drove to the edge of town, until the pavement turned into
a dirt road. He steered the Fairlane over an irrigation culvert
and onto a patch of land near an orange grove and little else.
From this spot at the extreme northeast section of town, Jablonski could easily detect any traffic that might head his way,
though few people would be out traveling the barren desert
outskirts this late at night.

After pulling Vann from his car, Jablonski picked the jewelry
from her body and rubbed his hands over her lifeless flesh.
"Run my hands all over that gorgeous fine black ass and those
black legs," he said on the tape. "I turned her over, had a
hard-on. I fucked her in [that] gorgeous black pussy. Yeah, too
bad she didn't feel it this time."

Standing above his victim, Jablonski grabbed her limp arms and dragged her a bit farther, then remained over the corpse and created a terrifying masterpiece using Vann's body as his canvas.

First he stabbed out her eyes. Next he sliced off her ears and cut into her chest, taking the nipples as trophies. He continued the butchery by gouging her sex organs to shreds, and turning her over to carve the words, "I ♥ Jesus," across her shoulders, back and buttocks. The carving was a sick and twisted way of mocking Vann's devotion to God and was likely inspired by the same words that appeared on her key chain, which she had left inside her beloved Datsun.

"Left her there like garbage," Jablonski told his tape recorder. "[That was] what she was after I got done with her. Yeah, she is a sweet-looking loving black woman, that I finally got."

No one knows what compelled the killer to mutilate his victim.

"It may be like the kid who pulls the wings off a fly," observed Martin Murray, a San Mateo County prosecutor who eventually prosecuted Jablonski. "The kid who dissects animals to see what they are made of. Maybe to him, females are such foreign creatures that he has a need to cut them open to see what is inside."

Vann's body was discovered on the afternoon of April 23, by Roanna Doyle, a Desert Hot Springs resident who showed up at the Indio Police Department that afternoon with four Polaroids of the mutilated corpse. Doyle told the police a rambling story about UFO's and CIA plots.

"It was apparent from the start that Doyle was not mentally stable," noted one police report of her meeting with investigators. "She spoke of various religious types, plots, and spoke to what she referred to as her 'friends' who were in the room with her."

She told police that her friends were on hand to sense if she was in any danger. Doyle was kept for questioning. She explained that she went into the Indio desert every so often to search for her identity. She said the desert journeys served as a test to prove herself worthy to God. She said she left her house that afternoon and went to the desolate dirt road where she discovered the body. She brushed the victim's hair aside and saw that the corpse had been sliced up, then took pictures of the remains and went to the police.

Doyle was questioned for two hours. Investigators searched her red Corvette, and her boots were examined for comparison to prints left at the crime scene. Investigators tested her hands for gunpowder residue to determine if she had recently fired a weapon and sent her on her way.

By mid-afternoon, investigators from the Riverside County Sheriff's Department had marked off the crime scene with yellow police tape. Vernon Winte, who lived nearby the desert dumping ground, was questioned. He told police that a motorcycle rider had spotted the body and told him to call authorities that afternoon.

The corpse was found face down, with its arms at each side, and the elbows extended away from the body. Vann's right shoe remained on her foot. The left one, along with her blood-stained white sweatpants, T-shirt and white panties were found scattered 20 feet away.

The police found three strands of synthetic braid, which had fallen off her body as it was dragged across the ground. Her gold charm in the shape of a dollar sign was found near the body among some change, as was a new-looking, blue baseball-styled cap that carried a patch which read: "Vietnam Veteran and Proud of It."

Investigators also found an empty pack of chewing gum, as well as a maintenance book for a Datsun 280 ZX. None of Vann's other personal items of gold were found, nor were the body parts that had been cut off.

As the temperature rose to 80 degrees, and a 15-mph wind kicked up dust from the west, stage one of the investigation came to a close. Detectives photographed the site on the ground, while a California Highway Patrol helicopter captured the scene on film from the air. The body's remains were sealed up and taken to Riverside for an autopsy.

It would take two more days before the body would be

identified after Vann's daughters filed a missing person report about their mother on April 25. A quick match was made after the family members said the missing woman had a gold tooth shaped like a clover leaf.

By the time investigators spoke with Vann's children and learned about her enrollment at the college and her connection with a burly white man who had been giving the nurse rides home from school, Jablonski was long gone. He had left Indio shortly after disposing of Vann's body. Fueled by the success of his kill, Jablonski had set off on a blood binge, determined to settle a few scores with other women—especially those who had crossed him.

On top of the list was Carol Spadoni, a stick-figure anorexic, who lived like a spinster with her 72-year-old mother, Eva Peterson, in the tiny community of Burlingame, a 30-minute drive south of San Francisco. Spadoni had come to know Jablonski nearly 10 years earlier through a pen pal writing association that put prison inmates in touch with those who wished to bring a little cheer to a lonely man's life.

Spadoni was an odd woman, terribly shy, yet possessive of her mother. She had suffered from painful headaches for years and had battled an eating disorder since her teens. By the spring of 1991, the five foot, four inch woman weighed little more than 90 pounds and had cloistered herself inside a cluttered and dirty home on Sanchez Avenue just two miles from Burlingame's quaint downtown.

Spadoni was 46 and had been sick and lonely in recent years. She had been married twice. The relationships had been brief and at times abusive. Despite hard luck with men, she had taken an interest in Jablonski in the early 1980s and had fallen under his spell. Though they made an unusual pair, she petite and wire thin, he thick and mountainous, their relationship continued over the years as they exchanged hundreds of letters while he remained jailed for murder.

The pen pal relationship developed into a romance of sorts and in 1982 they were married at San Quentin State Prison by the facility's chaplain. Jablonski's best man at the service was Archie Fain, a notorious killer who gained infamy and imprison-

ment for murdering a Stanislaus County high school football
star in 1967, then raping two girls.

Some thought Spadoni was out of her mind to court and
finally marry Jablonski. Her brother, Michael Spadoni, told her
she was committing suicide by hooking up with a killer. Still,
Spadoni viewed Jablonski differently, often referring to him as
"bear," and comparing him to a thoughtful college professor.

"What seemed inconceivable to me is that Carol's mother
went along with this," observed Eric Haseleu, a Burlingame
Police Department detective who came to know the killer well.
"She seemed like more of a realist. I don't know if she was
just indulging her daughter. Maybe she thought it would give
Carol a bit of happiness. They also probably thought Jablonski
would never get out of prison."

The marriage continued on paper, as each party flooded the
other with cards and letters. Jablonski's notes started out with
a romantic flair, referring to Spadoni as his "dearest love."
But over time, his writings became perverse and filled with
references to sexual bondage and strangulation. In some of the
missives he even expressed a sexual interest in Spadoni's
elderly mother. "I'll need someone to keep me in line," Jablonski wrote the 72-year-old woman in June of 1982. "But of
course, I'll try to get hold of your big breasts under your nightie.
I would love to feel them and suck them nipples until they get
big and round and hard. I would never go down below your
waist, but I am going to make them free game, OK?"

These letters rightfully scared Spadoni, who later sought to
end the relationship with divorce.

Though she had frequently traveled to the San Luis Obispo
prison to meet Jablonski during family visits while they were
married, she never met with him alone and rejected every
request he made for a conjugal visit. She refused to see him
after his release in 1990 and asked parole officers to forbid
Jablonski from entering San Mateo County where she lived.
The officers agreed, which was one of the reasons why Jablonski
had been exiled to Indio.

Angered by Spadoni's refusal to welcome him, and fueled
by the recent slaughter of Vann, Jablonski spent much of the

night of April 22 behind the wheel of his Fairlane. He drove
north through the center of the Golden State, bound for the
San Francisco Bay and a little payback against that "bitch"
of a wife and his meddling mother-in-law, whom he suspected
had become the mastermind behind Spadoni's interest in seeking a divorce.

On the last day of their lives, mother and daughter were, as
usual, together. The pair rarely separated in public or at home.
They shared a tiny room in the back of their residence, sleeping
in beds no more than two feet apart. The bungalow was filled
with clutter, dust and cobwebs. Their bedroom was in shambles,
with boxes of mail-order clothing piled everywhere and cigarette burns on the bedding and dirty carpet.

The women's lives centered on each other and their interest
in animal rights. When they did venture from home, the pair
went on trips to downtown coffee shops or visits to hospitals
where Spadoni underwent examinations and counseling sessions to deal with her eating disorder.

On April 23, 1991, the pair skipped their regular morning
stops at area coffee shops because Peterson was not feeling
well.

An acquaintance, Frances Leone, a custodian at Peninsula
Hospital where Spadoni received treatment, was supposed to
meet the women that morning in the hospital's restaurant. The
appointment was canceled when Spadoni called Leone at about
7:30 a.m. telling her that her mother's back was hurting and
they would remain home. Instead, she said, they would visit
with her the next day for lunch.

Spadoni and Peterson did not plan to leave the house that
day. Both dressed in casual, loose-fitting garments. Peterson
had on a pair of pants and a blue sweatshirt embossed with a
label, "Defenders of Wildlife." Spadoni wore a colorful, multi-
patterned robe over a green nightgown. Her fingernails were
long and perfect, painted with lavender polish. The left middle
fingernail was painted to look like an American flag. Her right
ring fingernail had the image of a heart.

At about the same time Roanna Doyle was wandering the
desert and pointing her camera at Vann's remains, Jablonski

was pulling into Burlingame. He stopped the Fairlane near a home he had long heard about in Spadoni's letters but had never seen. After leaving the car near the Sanchez Avenue house, he walked past a group of rosebushes toward the front street, saw that two cars were parked in the driveway and stayed clear of the five cats the women kept in cages near the entrance. He moved to a side door just off the driveway that led to the home's garage, which was crammed with boxes of clothes and old newspapers. Jablonski paused, checked his loaded .22 revolver and prepared for part two of his violent mission.

"I walked in, no problem," Jablonski said to the tape recorder afterwards. "And we talked for while. I got up, I hugged Carol. I grabbed her around the waist, around the throat."

He told Peterson to disrobe. The heavyset grandmother tried to calm the intruder down, telling Jablonski not to scare them with the gun. But Jablonski was never the sort to back down from a woman.

"You don't strip, I'm gonna shoot ya between your beautiful breasts," Jablonski said, as he pointed the tiny weapon toward the old woman. He then fired a shot inside the kitchen, catching Peterson in the chest and sending her to the linoleum-tiled floor.

An instant later, Jablonski fired another round at point-blank range above Spadoni's right ear. He let her body fall to the floor, then shot Peterson in the left side of her head. Though mortally wounded, Spadoni continued to breath. To silence her irregular gasps, Jablonski wrapped duct tape around her nose and mouth, nearly obliterating her face behind a silver mask of tape. He rolled the tape around and around, as if he were trying to cut off a leaky pipe.

The force of this constriction closed Spadoni's air supply and flattened her nose to the left side of her face. To make sure the job was done, Jablonski stabbed her throat. Ironically, the wound acted like a tracheotomy and allowed Spadoni's dying body a chance to breath. As she lay helpless, sucking blood into her lungs through the gaping knife wound in her neck, Jablonski turned his attention to satisfying his sexually perverted fantasies. Just as he had done to Vann, he slashed into

Spadoni's right breast, exposing the silicone implant Spadoni had received years before. He next set to work on her sex organs, then cut into her rectum, causing Spadoni's intestines to spill from her body.

Jablonski then turned his attention to Peterson, a woman he had lusted after for years. As Peterson lay dead or near death, Jablonski finally had the chance to fulfill his obscene dreams. He stripped the woman, leaving her jeans and underpants in a pile, pulled up her sweatshirt, fondled her breasts and ran his tongue over her nipples.

"Rolled her over, sodomized that fine big ass she had," he said on the tape. "Ran my hands down her legs, turned her over, fucked her in that fine li'l pussy while fondling those big ole tits. I tried to take her eyes out, [but] they wouldn't come."

He dragged Spadoni from the kitchen, leaving a trail of blood smeared across the floor, and deposited the corpse on its back in the family's living room. He pulled Peterson's body partway into the garage, leaving the remains spilling halfway down the two steps that led from the kitchen.

With a hard afternoon's work complete, Jablonski snacked on some potato chips he found, then he showered and shaved. He left a disposable razor in the bathroom, along with a sink dirtied with bits of beard stubble.

Before departing, Jablonski took Peterson's Unocal 76 card and some checks from her Western Federal Savings and Loan bank book. As a final insult before leaving the home, he stuffed a towel inside Peterson's mouth, causing her upper lip to curl upward in a snarl, and fired a final round from the .22 into the cloth to muffle the sound. The small round shattered one of her teeth and came to rest inside her mouth.

"Well sweet thing, [do you] believe me now? [That] I was gonna rape you," he said on the tape. "The ol' girl cost her her daughter's life. Yeah, I got them both, them bitches. Yeah, got 'em, it was so good to watch 'em fall dead."

No one heard a thing on the quiet street where Peterson and Spadoni had lived for years. The two women had few friends and barely knew their neighbors. There was no one to take any notice of what was happening inside their home.

With three fresh brutal kills, Jablonski must have felt invincible. He certainly was in no hurry to leave Burlingame, or make an effort to cover his presence.

He drove to a bank and forged a signature on Peterson's stolen checks to get a few hundred dollars to finance the rest of his deadly road trip.

After cashing the check at the First Interstate Bank, he made an illegal left-hand turn onto the community's main roadway, El Camino Real. More often than not, an illegal traffic turn would go unnoticed, but on this day, Thomas Ickes, a motorcycle cop and Burlingame Police officer for 26 years, was on patrol.

Ickes saw the Fairlane cut into traffic, nearly colliding with a passing van. He turned on his siren, followed the Fairlane and pulled the car over only one mile from the murder scene. Jablonski stopped right away, as if he had nothing to hide.

Jablonski answered the officer's routine questions about his current address and whether or not he knew why he had been stopped. Nothing about Jablonski indicated he had been under the least bit of stress.

"He seemed normal to me," said Ickes, who asked him about the old car. When Jablonski said he had recently bought it in Indio, Ickes checked out the car's history with a dispatcher at the Burlingame station. Everything checked out just fine.

"I asked him if he had a business address, which is routine," Ickes said. "He told me he did not. We had a slight conversation about where he was from."

Ickes wrote out a ticket, handed it to Jablonski and wished him a nice day. The whole stop took about 10 minutes. Jablonski was on his way out of town by 3 p.m.

It would be three days before anyone noticed that the two reclusive women were missing. Time was on Jablonski's side. He had gone undetected and before anyone could link him to Vann, Spadoni or Peterson, he was out of California, traveling east, bound for Kentucky and Tennessee and two other unsuspecting women, who years before had held pity for Jablonski and sought to ease his prison burden by taking him into their lives through tender letters.

As always, Jablonski saw things differently; to him, these female writers were property to be used and disposed of as he saw fit.

Like a carnivore searching for the weakest prey on the open plains, Jablonski would not be content with just three murders. He planned to hunt down these two Southern women and take out any other female who aroused him as the miles drifted past the window of his Ford.

Just two days after the Burlingame slaughter, Jablonski was in Evanston, Wyoming, a desolate spot in a land of wide-open spaces, where the beast inside him was ready to pounce once more.

THREE
Thompson Springs

"This is what I want. I'm gonna have this woman."

As the bodies of Carol Spadoni and Eva Peterson slowly rotted inside their bungalow, Jablonski drove east, traveling the wide highways between California and the mountains of Wyoming and chattered into the microphone of his trusty cassette recorder. With nothing else of comfort or style inside the Fairlane, he listened to his own voice on the tape, reliving over and over the details of each killing. But the tape was not enough to satisfy his craving. Like many other serial killers who relish the memories of past atrocities by collecting mementos of their victims, Jablonski kept written records of his deeds.

In a small black notebook he had written the names of each victim along with the dates of their deaths. Like a good accountant who does not want to misplace important figures, Jablonski backed up his notes by recording the same information on the inside of a leather belt he had made while in prison. No one had ever seen Jablonski wear the belt, which was shaped in the form of a flattened rattlesnake. The belt buckle looked like a serpent's head, with a metal clasp serving as the reptile's tongue. There was even a piece of leather hand-tooled to look like a rattle on the back end of the belt to lend some dangerous authenticity to the odd accessory.

By April 24, 1991, the belt contained the names of Linda Kimball, the woman he had strangled in 1978, along with Vann,

Spadoni and Peterson. As it turned out, Jablonski would have time to inscribe other names on the sinister-looking death strap.

On April 25, Jacqueline Eadwine, a traveling sales representative for a panty hose company, was on the way to Wyoming from her home in Midvale, Utah, when she pulled over at a rest stop near mile marker 48 on I-80. Typical of road stops in the empty spaces out west, it was a lonely strip of asphalt. There was nothing fancy about the place. No fencing marked it off from the surrounding desert, and aside from Eadwine's van, the area was home to only a couple of garbage cans.

She had been driving for some time that day and stopped her car at about 9 a.m. to let her dog out for a walk. As the animal scampered about, sniffing the ground, Eadwine stayed in the van and read through some work papers. Her concentration was interrupted when a two-door, older model Ford rolled into the deserted rest area.

Eadwine had traveled this stretch of I-80 many times before and had come to know this stop well. She always pulled over here to let her dog do its business, and in all the years she had traveled there, no one had ever pulled in next to her. She watched the old Ford halt in front of her vehicle and noticed it carried California plates.

"It pulled in [and] that's what was real strange," Eadwine recalled. "It drove by real slow from the side of my van. I just glanced, and I thought, 'That is real strange, no one ever pulls in here.'"

When Eadwine's eyes caught sight of Jablonski's hulking, flabby features, a shiver ran through her body. She could not really explain what had spooked her that morning, but by the way he glanced over a shoulder and examined her, she instinctively knew this stranger was bad news.

"[He] wasn't normal," she said. "He was scary."

Eadwine kept a watch on the stranger, then scanned the desert with her eyes and searched for her dog. Jablonski, meanwhile, moved inside the Ford and prepared to step out.

"I looked for my dog and noticed he [Jablonski] was trying to get out of his side of the car," Eadwine said. "He could not get out that way and so he slid across the front seat and got out the passenger side.

"[When] I got out to get my dog, something [inside me] said, 'Don't say anything to this man, just get your dog and leave,' " Eadwine recalled.

But by then the animal had become curious about the burly stranger and scampered over for a closer look. As Jablonski stroked the pet Eadwine kept calling for the dog, hoping it would move away from the big man so she could escape.

"He [the dog] wouldn't come to me," Eadwine said. "And I noticed he [Jablonski] had something in his jeans jacket, and he was fumbling with it."

That "something" was a gun—the same blue-steel .22 revolver Jablonski had used in the past three murders. As he pointed the weapon toward Eadwine, the revolver slipped from his hands, tumbled to the ground and bounced under the Ford.

Eadwine didn't need the voice in her head to tell her what to do next. She spotted the pet at her feet, grabbed it and tossed it into the vehicle, then jumped into her van and sped off. She drove at a frantic rate to the nearest truck stop some 30 miles away.

"I probably made it [there] in three minutes," she said. "I was flying."

Twenty minutes later, Dennis Hutchinson, a deputy with the Uinta County Sheriff's Department, responded to her alert and pulled into the Bingo Truck Stop and listened to her story. With the image fresh in his mind, Hutchinson headed back onto I-80, backtracking toward the rest stop and searching the road for the Ford.

He spotted Jablonski's car near the Lyman Rest Area, not far from where he had encountered Eadwine. Hutchinson turned on his patrol car's flashing red lights and pulled Jablonski over. Jablonski stopped the car immediately. Though gruff with women, Jablonski was always docile around men. He was not about to give Hutchinson any trouble or do anything to raise the deputy's suspicions.

Jablonski told Hutchinson, who was accompanied by a sheriff's sergeant, that his driver's side door was jammed, and that he had to exit the car through the passenger's side. Hutchinson kept a close watch on the large man. The image of the fallen gun that Eadwine had spoken about was clear in his mind.

Jablonski, as usual, acted calm. He did nothing as the deputy and sergeant searched the inside of the Fairlane for the gun. The snub-nose .22 was found underneath the driver's seat. When asked about his presence in these parts, Jablonski played the innocent fool, telling Hutchinson he had been taking a quiet moment at a rest stop a few miles back where he met a woman and her dog. Hutchinson asked Jablonski if he had threatened the woman with the gun, but the calm suspect brushed the question off, admitting he carried the weapon for protection, but saying he never meant to startle the poor woman.

Jablonski apologized to the officers for making the lady nervous, and claimed the entire incident was a harmless mistake that occurred when the gun accidentally fell out of his car after he opened the door. Though the sight of a loaded revolver stashed beneath the seat of a car might have raised eyebrows in the city, here, amid the emptiness of Wyoming where guns are common, Hutchinson believed Jablonski's story. After all, if he pulled over everyone in this part of the county who traveled with a gun at the ready, the jails would be full and the roads would be empty.

After checking Jablonski's license information with his dispatcher and finding out that the traveler was not wanted anywhere for any crime, the deputy was satisfied that the stranger was just passing through the area. There was no reason to delay the man any further.

Before sending Jablonski on his way, Hutchinson advised him to store the weapon in the trunk of his car. For the second time in only two days, Jablonski had brushed shoulders with police in what seemed to be routine traffic stops. Though splotches of blood from Fanny Vann's body could be seen in the dark corners of the Fairlane, neither officer noticed the distinctive brownish red marks. Both lawmen also failed to detect the slightest sign of unease on Jablonski's poker face. Jablonski had always been able to pass himself off as an empty slate when the need arose. That gift of blankness served him well on this road trip.

Before departing, Hutchinson advised Jablonski it might be a good idea to get out of Wyoming. The big traveler took his advice to heart.

"Well, I was making a turn to go out of Wyoming anyway, 'cause I got lost," Jablonski would later recall.

The route change sent Jablonski south through the middle of Utah, where he hooked up with I-70 and drove east. The diversion pushed him into the southeast corner of Utah, where he was destined to leave his familiar calling card on the tiny truck-stop community of Thompson Springs.

Thompson Springs is just a handy place to grab a few gallons of gas or a cup of coffee for those bound to or from Grand Junction, Colorado, some 60 miles to the east. The little community sits amid the high plateau of Utah, where monoliths of towering sandstone shoot up from the desert floor like the high-rises of New York or Los Angeles. The town is a popular stopping point for those who venture into Canyon Lands or Arches National Monument. It is home to a stark and isolated beauty that travelers come from all corners of the earth to see.

Thompson Springs only has two gas stations, a restaurant, a motel and a few trailer homes, but as the last rest stop before the Colorado border, the location catches its share of tourists.

Les Rogers is the man who pretty much put Thompson Springs on the map. His father, Clarence W. Rogers, settled in these parts during the Great Depression and set up a pool hall in the little town. When the highway department carved a road nearby in the mid-1930s, the family patriarch built a cafe and grocery store to accommodate those who would soon drive past. By the time Clarence Rogers died in a car wreck in 1937, the family owned 12 acres near the highway. Les Rogers, a classic-looking Western outdoorsman with a rich baritone voice and a taste for cowboy boots, bought more surrounding land in subsequent years and became the chief proprietor in town.

By the spring of 1991, Les Rogers owned 450 acres around I-70 and virtually ran the entire community, which consisted of about 50 people, a boardinghouse called The Half Moon

Hotel, a cafe, a trailer park on the main drag, and a convenience store he and his wife ran out of a double-wide trailer on the edge of town.

Les Rogers' life had always been prosperous, especially after he caught the fancy of a Moab girl named Margie Stocks, whom he first met while attending a community dance in 1950.

"Everyone and their dog came to those dances," Rogers said, as he reminisced about the day he first saw his future bride. "In between dances you had to go out and slug at a bottle to get the courage to ask a girl to dance."

One night in 1950, Rogers found the nerve to approach a 19-year-old, black-haired beauty, whose tight black curls and voluptuous figure had caught his eye. After a six-month courtship, the two married and set to building a life together in Thompson Springs.

They both loved the outdoors and spent their spare time traveling the land.

"She was a good outdoor lady," Les Rogers said. "A damn fine cook. She liked to make it old-fashioned style, lots of corned beef and cabbage, roast pork and mashed potatoes."

As a teenager growing up in Moab, Margie had taken a shine to writing, and though she'd always said she did not want to work in a diner, after marriage she really had no choice. She began working in Rogers' family restaurant, first as a waitress and later as a cook.

Together, Les and Margie Rogers raised two boys and two girls and became the bedrock of their little town. As their children grew, the couple concentrated on their convenience store, which offered passing motorists gas, coffee, snacks and an assortment of local trinkets, some made from rattlesnake tails. Because Margie was a day person, she always rose early and worked the morning shift at the well-kept store.

By springtime 1991, the Rogerses were looking toward their retirement. He was 63 and she was 58. Their children were grown and working in solid jobs and the grandkids were a happy lot. After a lifetime of work, it was time for them to enjoy the fruits of their labor. To celebrate the good times to come, the couple had recently purchased a new trailer and

Chevy Suburban to take them around the back country in style. Margie had also planned for a June trip to England and had already purchased their plane tickets.

Margie Rogers awoke tired on the morning of April 27, but rejected her husband's offer to open the store so she could stay at home and relax.

"No, you don't clean that well," she told her husband that morning, as she prepared to leave for the day. "That is my job."

She dressed in black jeans, pink socks, a blue long-sleeved sweatshirt and a red smock that carried a label from Phillips 66. A button proclaiming her a "VIP" at a community Grandparent's Day was pinned to her outfit. The gold wedding band her husband had given her some 40 years before was on her finger and a trusty Timex watch on her left wrist.

After arriving at work at about 6:30 a.m., she went about her regular cleaning routine. She also brewed a pot of coffee, preparing to meet the day's demand.

As Margie Rogers prepared for a typical day at work, Jablonski was traveling in from the west on I-70, and like others who pass through this stark Utah landscape, he spotted a distinctive sign alerting him that Thompson Springs was the last chance for gas for nearly 60 miles. It was early morning when he approached the convenience store and gas station known as Rogers' Roost.

"I'm leaving Utah at about six in the morning," Jablonski noted on his tape recorder. "A sign saying gas and diesel at the truck stop ahead, so I pulled off and went in."

He entered the little store at about 7 a.m. and noticed Rogers behind a small cash register counter. He examined the room, bought a can of soda and chips, then walked out to assess his next move. It had been nearly four days since Jablonski had tasted blood and the need to slaughter and maul a woman had become too much for him to control.

"Yeah, this is what I want," he told the tape recorder afterwards. "I'm gonna have this woman."

He walked from Rogers' Roost to his Fairlane and waited as a passing car and two buses came near the lot. When they continued on, he checked the gun, stuffed it inside his pants, then went inside the store to buy a cup of freshly-brewed coffee. Margie Rogers sat at the front counter with her back to him.

With her typical politeness, Margie turned to ask the customer if he wanted anything else before ringing up a charge of 64 cents for the coffee.

For an instant, Jablonski leaned his body toward the door, only to turn back and reach for the hidden weapon. It was about 7:16 a.m. when he began firing.

"I shot her in the body somewhere," he said on the tape. "She goes 'ahh,' and I shot her in the head. She fell to the floor. I walked around, opened up the cash register and took all the bills out. Looked underneath to see if there was any extra money. Ripped open her blouse, pulled her bra up over her big gorgeous big breasts."

As he fondled the bleeding woman's chest, Rogers' eyes flickered and rolled around in her head. To put an end to her dying glance, Jablonski fired into her temple at point-blank range.

"The blood oozed out the side of her nose," Jablonski told his tape recorder. "Yeah, old girl, I got your life."

Before he could completely desecrate her body as he had done with his other victims, another car pulled near the convenience store, sending Jablonski on his way. His total take from the register was $156.

Kathy Knight and her husband, Walt, pulled into the store's parking lot at 7:25. They had spent the night camped in their car about three miles away while on a road trip to Las Vegas. Kathy was behind the wheel that morning when they spotted the Thompson Springs exit sign. Walt had just awakened and asked his wife to pull over so he could use the bathroom and grab a cup of coffee.

Exiting the highway, the couple spotted Rogers' Roost and the closed Texaco station across the street. Walt was still drowsy at this hour of the morning. He was not wearing a shirt, nor shoes, so he sent his wife in for supplies. Kathy parked the car at a slight angle, walked into the quaint store and noticed the place seemed deserted. She scanned for coffee pots and noticed a few on the left side of the store. She recalled her husband's long-standing advice that gas stations usually keep the fresher coffee brewing on the bottom heater. She grabbed a large cup from a nearby stack, and reached for the bottom coffee pot.

As she pulled the steaming container from the counter, Kathy noticed it was still perking. A small stream of black water spilled from the coffee maker and sizzled as the drops danced across the heating coil the pot had been resting upon. After filling her husband's cup, she walked toward the front counter. A display of Carmex caught her eye and reminded her about the dry desert air. As she reached for the moisturizer, Kathy saw what she took to be a man sleeping on the floor by the cash register.

"Oh, great," she thought. "Asleep on the job. I'm going to have to wake him up so I can pay."

The horror of what she was really looking at quickly set in after Kathy saw blood gathered in a pool around the sleeping person's head. In an instant, what had happened registered clearly in her mind and she ran from the store to get her husband.

Terrified, Walt drove with his wife toward a nearby road crew shed, but found it deserted. He traveled into the heart of Thompson Springs and ran inside the town's cafe to alert police.

The victim's daughter-in-law, Kris Rogers, got to the convenience store before police arrived to block off the small shop.

Sheriff's Deputy John McGann knew the family well, just like everyone else in this tight-knit community. After getting the emergency call at his home in Castle Valley, Utah, some 25 miles east of Moab and about 60 miles away from the crime scene, he covered the distance in his patrol car in well under an hour.

When McGann arrived at Rogers' Roost, he found Margie Rogers' body face up with her head turned to the right side. Several buttons from her blouse were scattered on the floor, indicating her clothes had been pulled off after she was shot. There was a visible contact wound near her left ear. No other useful evidence was located inside the store and McGann concluded that the killer had caught his victim by surprise, since there was no sign that a struggle had taken place.

Thompson Springs does not see much violence. There had not been a killing in the town for nearly 10 years. Still, McGann had a few suspects for this crime.

Suspicion first fell on Rick Lennox a drifter from Grand Junction, Colorado, who had arrived in town about one month earlier. He had apparently come to Utah with the intention of venturing into the desert and committing suicide. Unable to summon the nerve to kill his dogs as well as himself, however, he ended up abandoning his plans. He next landed in Thompson Springs and began working for Les Rogers as a clerk at the convenience store.

The deputy was suspicious of Lennox's behavior because he seemed too helpful at the crime scene and even offered to clean up the mess inside the store.

Les Rogers assured the investigator that Lennox was a good man who had nothing to do with the crime. He suggested that perhaps another man, a clerk Rogers had fired about a year ago, might be responsible.

None of the initial leads paid off, however, leaving authorities puzzled at what could have brought this upon so innocent a person.

As Les Rogers prepared the memorial service for his wife to be held three days later, he thought about their last moments together on that terrible morning, with his wife feeling ill, but still—as always—ready to do a day's work.

"We did not have a proper goodbye," Les Rogers said. "That has made me understand that you better be kind to the people you love all the time."

Utah investigators summarized the case and sent out a tele-type about the crime and the victim on April 28, hoping that the manner in which Margie Rogers had died might strike a familiar cord with investigators in other areas.

As the message went out over fax machines and police infor-mation lines, Phillip Jablonski etched another mark onto his death belt, this time scribbling in his usual misspelled way "elderly lady, Utah, April 27, 1991," next to the names of Kimball, Spadoni and Peterson.

As always, he shared his true feelings with the tape recorder, a faithful companion that now carried the tales of four senseless murders.

While authorities in Indio, Burlingame and Thompson Springs had yet to discover that they were after the same serial killer, Jablonski continued driving, stopping at rest areas, then watching and waiting for his next chance while giving a play-by-play description of his quest, like a broadcaster calling a game.

"Hoping this woman ahead of me is my next victim," he told the tape, as the sounds of highway traffic moved past his hidden position at some unknown rest stop. "She's got some great big ole tits, nice big ole ass. Has got a little kid with her. I'm gonna fuck this one alive if I can. God look at that ass! Gorgeous big woman. God, would I like to fuck this. Oh, what an ass. What a set of tits. Well, I'm losing her. She's getting ready to leave. Man, would I give anything to fuck that, then kill it, and fondle those big ole, big tits. God, then kill the little boy. I get a chance, I am kidnapping this woman. I'll put her in my car with the kid. Put her in the back seat. Make her lay down and shoot her. I don't care what I have to do to get this baby. She's mine!"

Fortunately, several truck drivers appeared at the unknown rest stop and foiled Jablonski's plans. Still, he kept the faith.

". . . Lost her, but there's two more that just went into the bathroom. [If] these two guys [outside] would leave, I'd have these two. I'd just walk in and shoot 'em, and do what I want with 'em. Well, I gotta move along. I hope I get one soon."

FOUR
Eva and Carol

"My family came to view them as two loving eccentrics."

Ralph Galindau rose early on Friday, April 26, 1991 inside his cozy second-floor apartment which stood less than half a mile from Burlingame's downtown district. At 79, the retired San Francisco firefighter was still feisty and active. He pumped iron several times a week and rode a stationary bike at a local gym to stay fit. Beyond the athletic regimen, his weekly routine included morning walks to the city center and stops at the Royal Donut shop where he had enjoyed maple bars and cups of coffee with his friends, Eva Peterson and Carol Spadoni.

The early-morning coffee meetings had begun two years earlier when Galindau fell into conversation with Peterson and Spadoni as they sat in a line at the counter, watching a grill cook push pounds of hash browns across a greased stove top while the small city's business district came to life.

Ever since that first encounter, Galindau continued to meet the women on Monday, Wednesday and Friday mornings, to discuss the day's events. As the months passed, the trio moved from the counter to a booth far in the back of the breakfast shop.

Their conversations were always fairly routine and usually centered on politics or the mundane events of everyday life.

"They would tell me about their troubles and so on," Galindau recalled.

Their morning gatherings would usually last 45 minutes to an hour, and the only time the talk turned tense was the one occasion when Galindau mentioned that his daughter had recently bought a fur coat. Staunch animal rights activists, both women took issue with that news. The idea of fur coats sickened the women and they made sure Galindau understood how wrong it was to own such garments.

The barrel-chested and good-natured firefighter took their criticisms in stride and suggested they save their shock and contempt for someone else, since he was not going to pass it on to his daughter.

Over time, Galindau became a close friend to the women—at least as close as the semi-reclusive pair would allow. Though Peterson and Spadoni left their home often to meet other acquaintances for lunch or coffee, the pair remained wrapped in a blanket of secrecy, with their lives as shut as the curtains in their home. Though friendly in public, the two rarely allowed anyone—even family members—to enter their residence, and they certainly did not let people know their inner thoughts.

Eva Peterson was born in Denmark in 1919, and became a popular high school girl with an interest in dance and acrobatics after her family arrived in San Francisco in 1930. The well-built young foreigner participated in city parades and often caught the attention of newspaper photographers, according to her son, Michael.

She married a butcher in 1939 and began raising a family. Michael was born in 1942. Carol followed three years later.

The marriage did not go well and ended with divorce in 1947. Eva and her young children moved into an apartment house her parents owned in the Marina District of San Francisco, where she met Henry Peterson, a young Merchant Marine officer. They all moved to Burlingame after he and Eva married.

Henry Peterson was a good provider and fine father to Michael and Carol. He often urged the young boy to consider a life at sea. The oceans had been good to him, Henry Peterson would say. The waves took him to ports across the globe as he worked his way up the ranks and eventually became a captain.

Eva stayed in Burlingame and enjoyed a 1950s housewife's life. She devoted her time to her children and her home, and pursued outside interests such as bowling leagues and bridge clubs.

Because Eva had loved to dance and show off her acrobatic skills as a youth, she pushed Carol toward the same interests. At the start of high school, Carol weighed about 130 pounds, fairly average for a girl five feet, four inches tall. But at about age 15, she became obsessed with the idea that she was fat. At one point her weight dropped to 75 pounds and she was hospitalized with an ailment no one understood in the 1950s.

Now it is recognized as a potentially fatal disorder which claims thousands of lives each year. The vast majority of its victims are women, young women, though some males also suffer from this mental illness. The victims are unable to see their body rationally and realistically, seeking to change it through excessive control of food. It was not until the 1970s, that awareness of anorexia as an illness came to the foreground.

Carol began controlling not only her body and food intake but the family dynamics.

"In those days no one knew what anorexia was," recalled Carol's cousin, Kres Daphne. "She never got the proper help and it just got worse."

Carol's illness concerned Eva, who grew obsessively close to her daughter. The bond between mother and daughter led to a split in the family. While Carol suffered through headaches and constant health complaints, Michael behaved as if nothing was wrong. He dated his sister's friends, married and had children. His sister used her eating disorder to control their mother's life and ultimately monopolized the older woman's time and energy to the point where Michael and his new family rarely saw them.

"I did not know what was wrong with my sister," Michael said. "I just thought she was obnoxious. She was someone I did not want to be around."

He took a hands-off approach to the strange relationship that had developed between mother and sister and went on with his life. Carol, meanwhile, went through two brief marriages that ended in divorce.

Through all the ups and downs, Henry Peterson stood firm. He had always treated Carol as his own, but as he moved up the ranks and got into a position that enabled him to have more leave time, he wanted to share the world with his wife. But Eva was afraid of leaving her daughter. Whenever the topic of travel came up, Carol would get sick or threaten suicide.

"My attitude was laissez-faire," Michael Spadoni said. "If she wanted to commit suicide, I told my mother to confront the issue, to kick Carol out of the house and let her try living on her own. I told my mom, 'The hell with Carol.' She could have left Carol and been having fun. I told her that she would lose her husband if she did not watch out."

By 1975, Henry Peterson was tired of waiting at sea alone. He divorced and sought better prospects, leaving Eva and Carol with only each other inside their Sanchez Avenue home. Having alienated the men in their lives, mother and daughter melded into almost a single person. They rarely separated.

To get by, Eva cleaned homes. She became interested in the rights of animals and wrote frequent letters to government officials and newspapers in an effort to spread the word about animal abuse. During holidays, Eva and Carol served food at homeless shelters and, to others, their lives seemed to be normal.

In reality, this was not the case and this contrast was reflected in the home they shared. On the outside, the Sanchez Avenue residence looked neat and proper, with its lines of rosebushes. But beyond the closed curtains, the house was a disaster.

"Everyone knew them superficially," Michael said. "That was how they were. You could have a great conversation with my mother, but you would not find out a thing about her. Maybe there was not much to find out, because they had already given it all up."

Carol's life continued to deteriorate as her eating disorder worsened. She was frequently admitted to hospitals for treatment and at one point her weight fell to 67 pounds.

In this respect, Carol was not a typical anorexia patient. Most people who suffer from it are, by adulthood, cured of or dead from the ravaging disease. She was the sad exception, taking that illness with her through her entire life.

In every other way, however, Carol was typical of anorexics. Most victims feel a harrowing sense of shame and outright disgust with their appearance.

Obsessed and upset with her looks, Carol avoided cameras and whenever one was pointed her way at family gatherings, she turned her face at the last moment, letting the lens see only the back of her head.

With two short marriages behind her and a life restricted by headaches and illness, Carol could do little more than watch television and order products through the mail. Mother and daughter favored sweaters and had scores of them piled in the house. They also bought earrings and junk jewelry.

Their home soon became cluttered with boxes of items ordered from Avon or the Home Shopping Network. The house became a massive storage shed. It became so bad that the women formed aisles between the debris just to move about the home.

"Despite Carol's obvious chronic health problems, they managed to function OK," her cousin, Laurel Daphne, told the *San Francisco Chronicle*. "They were enormously kind but vulnerable people who lived in their own naive reality. My family came to view them as two loving eccentrics."

Michael's wife, Judy, said Carol had an odd view of reality and saw the world as if everything took place within the borders of a Hallmark greeting card.

"When I would try to talk to Carol I would get what I considered to be a 9-year-old's response," Judy Spadoni said. "Like everything is sweet, that kind of world. She would just not go any deeper than that. She was really affected by her mental illness."

Carol was often heavily drugged as part of her treatment for anorexia. The physical and emotional drains from the medicines and her illness often left Carol detached. That behavior pushed the mother and daughter further together and increased their isolation, Judy Spadoni said.

Eventually, Carol connected with the outside world by signing up with a church organization's effort to bring hope and positive friendship into the cells of convicted men. Among the names on the church's 1980 list was Phillip Carl Jablonski, who was then serving time in state prison for the murder of his wife, Linda Kimball.

Soon Carol was writing Jablonski on a regular basis. He responded to the letters in earnest, often sending her three or more notes a week.

As with most things in their lives, Carol and Eva kept the correspondence hidden. On occasion they discussed Jablonski, but after family members chided them for wasting time on a convicted killer, the women fell silent.

"I never saw the letters, she never showed them to anyone," said cousin, Kres Daphne. "All of us were appalled by it, it was nothing that any one of us would have done and that is probably why Carol and Eva stopped talking about it. They got the idea that none of us understood and so they pretty much clammed up about it."

When confronted, Carol told people that they did not understand Phillip.

Over time, the letter writing increased and soon mother and daughter were making trips to the Men's Colony in San Luis Obispo, a three-hour drive south along Highway 101, to visit a man Carol described to others as charming, kind and intelligent.

Jablonski was able to come across as a gregarious soul with a gift for clever conversation. His letters, though filled with grammatical errors and misspellings, contained, at times, the flowery prose of a love-struck teenager.

"Every time I receive your letter, I am walking on cloud nine," began one missive Jablonski wrote to Carol in June 1981. "That is how much I enjoy your letters. And I know the letter is [from] a beautiful young lady that cares and takes time out of her day to write me."

In that same letter, Jablonski explained why he had killed his first wife in words that, on paper at least, seemed sincere:

"I wasn't drunk or drinking at the time I committed my crime. She hurt me so deeply that I want to do nothing but kill her. Her last words really bother me. She begged me not to kill her as she loved me and wanted to live to raise her baby. I told her that she was dying and that was all she needed to know.

"What hurts me the most is I took her from her husband and married her for one reason: her mother had money. She was a lady with respect in the community, but she fell for an outlaw. I guess she was turned on cause I was out of prison and would protect her, where her husband wouldn't. You could say she was, like, all her life kept in a shell. Everything was done for her. I showed her how to enjoy the common things of life and there was more to sex than just spreading her legs. Like a nut, I fell deeply in love with her. I never met a decent woman who just cared for a man cause she loved him. All the women I [have] known walked the streets or were con artists.

". . . Sometimes I feel like I should stay away from all women and find a hole to climb into, but I know that's crazy.

". . . I can sense you are looking for a strong man that is willing to give you a lot of tender loving care. I mean a deep down inner love. Not just someone to say I love you, but someone who hurts when Carol hurts, cries when Carol cries and holds her during this time. . . . If you are hurting deeply just sit down and let me know what is bothering you. I am a good sounding board. You can even cry on my shoulders if you like."

But amid the adolescent-like affection of Jablonski's writings were obvious signs of deviance. From the very beginning of his correspondence with Carol, the inmate dwelled on his hunger for sex.

"I love to perform oral sex on a woman," he wrote in the June 1981 letter. "Maybe it's the look she has on her face when I am finished doing the act. I love to see my lady with my manhood run off into her mouth. It shows me she is completely mine."

The pattern of puppy-love intimacy, graphic sexual references and hints at control would appear again and again throughout the 10 years Jablonski wrote to his pen pal.

What caught Carol's attention in his first letter and the hundreds that followed can never be known. Perhaps she started out trying to do a good deed for a troubled soul and lost herself in Jablonski's love letter ramblings. Her view on life was limited due to her failed marriages and her cloistered existence near her mother's side. But she also had a naive and kind manner and may have truly thought she could change the poor convict's life.

"I think at first the letter writing was a fun distraction," Michael said. "Most people would agree that you can present yourself any way you want to in correspondence. You don't have to commit to anything and it is a distraction from being in the house. It is also pretty exciting to get mail everyday."

Jablonski was excited, too, but concerned as well, telling a prison psychiatrist during a 90-day period of observation in San Quentin State Prison about his plans to marry Carol in June of 1982. Jablonski's mood about the marriage changed over the evaluation stay. At first he expressed worry that a second marriage could bring pressure to his life and perhaps force him to lash out as he had done against his common law wife in 1978.

"Can I deal with getting married after the crime I committed?" he asked staff doctor, M. E. Roudebush just weeks before the scheduled marriage to Carol. "I could probably do it [murder] again—I am trying not to do it again."

Whether Jablonski's frankness was a legitimate attempt to address his real fears, or merely his way of fooling staff doctors into thinking that he had made progress through counseling cannot be determined.

As the evaluation period passed, the inmate continued to open up, telling Roudebush that he and Carol were straight with each other. He said he had grown through therapy and had learned to get involved in hobbies, rather than act out in a violent way when pressures mounted.

"He thinks now he would be able to talk out such situations, and reports he has had several heated differences with his current fiancée and that they have been able to resolve these by talking,'' Roudebush wrote in a May 12, 1982 report. "He states his fiancée likes having her neck massaged and [said] 'Every time I feel like I want to squeeze—wrap her hair around her neck and squeeze—it's a weird feeling. I shouldn't have it.'"

Jablonski also told the psychiatrist that he had discussed his feelings with Carol, who reportedly told him not to worry. According to Roudebush's report, the staff recommended Jablonski allow himself more time to work out his inner troubles and put off the marriage. But by the end of his 90-day stay, Jablonski had changed his tune, telling Roudebush that he had planned to marry in June and that Carol and Eva felt comfortable about the idea.

"In regard to his general tendency of a need to hurt his partner during sex, he states, 'I've grown out of it,' " Roudebush wrote.

The marriage went on as planned and took place inside San Quentin. The news shocked the rest of Carol's family, especially Michael, who thought his sister had thrown her life away on a crazy man.

"She would always tell me that 'he is just dying to meet you,' " Michael said. "My position was simple. I said the guy is in there for murdering a wife. Do you think he doesn't do that any more?"

Why Carol chose to marry a man she hardly knew will never be known. Michael would later say his sister may have been captivated by an altruistic mood, or simply caught up in the novelty of having an inmate for a husband. Perhaps, he said, the move was Carol's way of appearing normal and showing the world she could get a man and maintain a relationship.

"Maybe it was just another way for my sister to have control over something in her life," Michael said. "Maybe she thought this was a safe marriage. It allowed her to stay with my mother and yet say she had a husband."

It is also possible that Carol never expected Jablonski would ever leave prison. She certainly had serious concerns about being alone with him and never visited the convict without her

mother. Though Jablonski set up 13 conjugal visits, a practice
allowed under California law, she never kept the date and
always complained of being sick whenever her husband
appeared ready to consummate their marriage.

Jablonski became so frustrated at Carol's reluctance to share
his bed that he attacked his own mother in a furious rage after
she told him during a family visit that Carol had again refused
to see him alone. Jablonski's father had to pull his son away
from Mrs. Jablonski after the convict tried to strangle her with
shoelaces and drag her toward a bedroom.

That 1985 assault inside a Men's Colony family trailer came
a year before Jablonski was set to be paroled and it eventually
added several years to his prison sentence.

The attempt to rape his mother should have been a clear
warning sign to Carol and Eva. Other hints at danger came in
the mailbox. The bizarre sexual references in Jablonski's letters
never let up. After several years of marriage, Carol seemed
tired of the notes that not only mentioned her husband's interest
in strangling her with her long hair, but of having sex with Eva
as well.

"Dear sweet mother-in-law," one letter began. "Hi my sexy
lady. So you are having sexy dreams. I told you [that] you
need a boyfriend," Jablonski wrote Eva. "[If] you lose more
weight you are going to look real sexy and with your big breasts
you will have all the men chasing you."

In another letter addressed to Carol, Jablonski wrote about
his "drunkard" father, who beat his mother through 60 years
of marriage. As always, he mentioned his intentions to hug and
kiss his bride, and promised that upon his release from prison,
he, Carol and Eva would be happy together in Burlingame.

"My object in life is to make you happy for the rest of our
lives together," Jablonski wrote. "Honey, there are two things
I hate a woman to do," he continued. "[First] is to tell [me]
I can't come into [the] bedroom cause she [is] mad at me. Or
using or withholding sex to get something from me. My woman
has everything coming and we can talk everything out in the
bedroom. . . . Even when we have our disagreements, I will
come and make up to you in love. I come bearing a peace

offering . . . I'll never raise my hand toward you in anger. Anytime I touch you, it will be in a loving way."

Most clear-thinking women would never have responded to any of Jablonski's letters, let alone continue to write back for years and eventually marry him. But Carol was hardly clear of mind and Eva was apparently too weak-willed to put a stop to their odd relationship.

"You can't deny that there was a disconnection from the reality we all seem to share," Judy Spadoni said of the women. "Their reclusiveness reinforced a sense of isolation and that led to pen pal relationships. These [women] were not normal people."

By the mid to late 1980s Carol considered divorcing the man she once called intelligent and gentle. But as always, Carol's sickness kept her down. She became combative with her mother, which led to frequent visits with doctors at Peninsula Hospital in Burlingame. In September of 1986, her weight fell to 67 pounds and the doctors feared for Carol's life.

Dr. Colin L. Fox wrote:

"The patient's history is one of severe and extreme self-destructiveness which is manifested in many ways. The current way of destroying herself is through not eating. Another example is the fact that she married a convicted murderer while he was still in prison. It is only after he attacked his own mother in a prison setting that she became fearful enough to file for divorce.

"The patient is currently depressed. She has suicidal ideation. She is very conflicted over eating. On one hand, she wants to eat, gain weight and be healthy. On the other hand, she becomes extremely fearful over the possibility that she will get fat. At home the patient blackmails the mother by telling her that she will eat if the mother will eat certain quantities of certain kinds of food. In effect, the patient ends up not eating anything and the mother has consumed large amounts of food and has gained considerable weight over the last several months."

The situation had hardly improved a year later, despite Carol's telling her doctors she was aware her weight was dangerously low. The disorder kept her in constant motion and led to a three-pack-a-day cigarette habit.

In describing her past marriages, Carol once said her first husband drank excessively and beat her. The second marriage was "destroyed" by her husband's neglect and physical abuse.

Carol told her doctors that she had no idea why she married Jablonski. She continued to write him, however, and do little favors for him, including contacting the Disabled American Veterans organization to ask if he could receive the extra monthly benefits owed him for serving a tour of duty in Korea a generation before. She also had a television delivered to his cell so he could watch educational programs.

As Jablonski's release date approached in the fall of 1990, Carol expressed her fear to whomever would listen. Michael suggested she and Eva get a gun, or leave town and stay with relatives in Lake Tahoe. Instead, Carol and Eva contacted prison officials and arranged that when Jablonski was released, he would be prevented from traveling to San Mateo County. Apparently, they had hoped the threat of being returned to prison on a parole violation would keep him at bay.

Jablonski continued to flood their home with letters and fill their minds with promises.

Jablonski wrote in January of 1989:

"Dearest Wife:

"Called tonight, but you were out. Honey, remember marriage is love in spite of if we hurt each other or break the trust between each other. Love is there in spite of what happened. If you fear me in any way then there is no love. Then there is no marriage. But I don't think you fear me. Maybe your mother does and don't want me to live there with her and you. All I know is I love you so much. . . . I love you too much to hurt you in any way."

By the time Jablonski set up camp inside the Indio Towers Manor following his release, Carol's health was in crisis again.

Sleep had become a luxury her body did not allow, as headaches and body pains kept her up most of the night. She recorded her ailments in handwritten notes in a small pad she kept near her bed. The palm-sized tablet indicated that her days ranged from good to very, very bad depending on the extent of her pain and the lack of sleep.

Jablonski continued to write the women. In a March 11, 1990 letter he thanked Eva for sending him books and a puzzle, and enclosed a copy of his resume, which listed his skill with sewing machine repairs and welding as job-worthy accomplishments.

In the spring of 1991, Carol was still keeping her little medical journal. The entries outlined sleepless nights filled with aches and pains.

> "March 16, 1991:
> "Woke up—12:30 a.m. Headache same as yesterday.
> Constant throbbing. Same as yesterday. Drives me nuts."

Jablonski did not ease up on his own form of mental pressure, writing Eva about his hopes for work as a postal carrier in Indio.

Things were coming to a head. Jablonski was free and still writing letters. Carol was growing sicker by the day.

"Woke up—never slept!" she wrote in April 1991. "No sleep—*None!* Can't stand this pain! **HATE IT!!**"

The entry for April 11 was no different: "Headache not so bad. Lying still, throbbed. Was miserable in bed. Driving me crazy. No end!!"

Though in extreme pain, Carol kept that part of her suffering hidden from her good friend Ralph Galindau. In the years the retired San Francisco firefighter had befriended Carol and Eva through their regular chats over coffee, he never knew Carol had married a prison inmate, nor realized both feared the man might one day appear at their door.

In the late spring of 1991, Galindau had no reason to suspect evil would soon envelop their lives. Though Galindau was one of Eva's and Carol's closest friends, he had never seen the inside of their residence. He had traveled to the Sanchez Avenue dwelling on only three occasions and never got past the front door. He knew little about their lives besides their interest in animals and their taste for coffee and casual conversation.

Galindau last saw the two at Royal Donut on April 19. He spoke to them by phone on Monday, April 22, when Carol called at about 6:30 a.m. to say Eva had a bad back which would prevent them from keeping their regular appointment.

Carol penned her last medical diary entry in the early morning hours of April 23, 1991. She had a restless night, as always, but managed to get about three hours of sleep.

"Headache very bad—not quite as bad as yesterday," she wrote. "Still causing dizziness. Very disgusted. No relief. Damn!!!"

Galindau went to the coffee shop that morning, taking a seat in the back booth and expecting to soon greet the women and hear more about Eva's back. As the morning wore on, it became apparent that the women were not going to walk through the door. Galindau was a bit concerned since the women had not called to cancel. He called their home that afternoon and evening, but no one picked up the phone. He tried again on Thursday, but still found no one home.

On Friday morning, Galindau walked to the coffee shop and waited. When the ladies did not show, he figured something had to be wrong. These women might have been eccentric, but they kept to a schedule and were hardly the type to forget an old friend, or the ritual that had been followed for two years.

"The whole thing did not make sense," Galindau said.

After walking home, Galindau got into his Dodge Colt, drove to the women's bungalow and noticed three days worth of newspapers on the ground in front of their garage. As he piled them on the hood of one of the cars, he spotted a couple of packages that had also been left outside, apparently for days.

Galindau went to the front door and saw that the five cats Eva and Carol kept in a large cage were without food and water.

Now he knew for certain there was trouble. These women might miss a coffee meeting once in a while, but they loved animals far too much to let their pets suffer from hunger or thirst.

"I knew something was wrong because they would feed the cats before they fed themselves," Galindau said. "It did not take an Einstein to figure this out. You see the papers out front and both cars by the garage, and notice that the animals have not been fed.

"I knew there were two bodies inside the house, that was the only solution I could come to."

FIVE

The Connection

"My God, this is unbelievable."

After 30 years with the San Francisco Fire Department, Galindau knew enough about police work and crime scenes not to touch anything near the Sanchez Avenue home. Though he was certain that disaster lay just inside the doorway, he did not try to peek through the women's curtains, or make any effort to force his way inside.

"I really did not know what to expect," Galindau said. "I figured something was wrong, whether they had killed themselves or what, I really had no idea. I just figured there were bodies in there."

Careful not to panic, Galindau returned to the coffee shop and asked the grill cook if he had seen the women that morning. After learning they had not arrived that day, he drove straight to the Burlingame Police Department and bluntly shared his suspicions with a desk officer.

"You will find two bodies," he announced before returning to the home.

A police officer was sent to the scene. He waited outside the home while a dispatcher at the department's headquarters telephoned the women's residence. From outside the bungalow, the officer could hear the phone ring. He could also detect the sounds of a barking dog from inside the house. The policeman let the phone ring about 10 times before he approached the building and knocked on the door.

The officer then snooped around the home's outside, looking for an open window or some other way in. All the windows and doors seemed secured. There were no broken windows to suggest that someone had forced his way inside.

The officer found an unlocked side garage door and went inside for a look. He backed away a moment later after seeing a body inside the dark garage.

Having verifed Galindau's claim, the officer sealed off the home. Detectives and crime scene experts began to arrive. By 8 a.m. the investigation started. Among the cops on duty was Sergeant Eric Haseleu, a stocky detective with a round, friendly face and an earnest interest in the profession he had practiced for 20 years. At his side stood Robert Morse, a gravel-voiced investigator with the San Mateo County District Attorney's Office, and a former county sheriff's detective who has worked on hundreds of murder investigations during his 20-plus years on the beat.

Morse stood just a tad over five feet, 10 inches. His nickname was "Bones," a fitting moniker given Morse's slender build. Haseleu, by contrast, was over six feet tall and had a solid belly that spilled over his belt.

Armed with flashlights, Morse and Haseleu led the way into the dark garage as crime scene technicians followed. Haseleu glanced at the boxes the women had stacked from floor to ceiling inside the garage, then focused the light on Eva Peterson's body.

"I saw this elderly lady laying there, naked from the neck down, with a sweatshirt or something pulled up," Haseleu said. "She is all black and blue and I walked into the kitchen and saw where she had been dragged across the floor and left on the steps of the garage."

Carol Spadoni's remains were even more horrifying.

"She was laying there in a nightie and the nightie comes down to just above her pubic area," Haseleu said. "There was duct tape so tight around her face that her face was just flattened. No nose, no nothing. Only two eyes. Everything else was just a flat line all the way across. There was blood coming down from her breasts, her stomach. You start thinking: 'Oh man, what caused this? Where is this person? My God, this is unbelievable.' ''

The home's condition drew their attention as well. It was so filled with clutter that Haseleu mentioned it in his police report. ''Every room, closet, drawer, and cupboard I looked in was full of boxes. The living room had several hundred pieces of clothing neatly packaged and neatly stacked on the floor. The back bedroom had no beds set up, but was full of boxes and furniture. And the carpet in the bedroom was filthy with dirt, dust and animal hair.''

As the detectives moved past the bodies, Spadoni and Peterson's pet dogs, a Chihuahua mix that had once belonged to Jablonski's mother, and a mixed breed of unknown heritage, barked and ran about the home. Both were collected by officers from the county Humane Society before either animal ventured near the bodies and contaminated the evidence.

The crime scene was by far the worst Haseleu had ever experienced. Burlingame, which is home to many elderly women and well-off families, does not see many murders. Up to that time, Haseleu had investigated only five homicides and had never taken the lead on any such investigation.

''The brutality of the murders, the totality of it really was just awful,'' Haseleu said. ''The cuts, the breast removed . . . that was a bad day in my life. I've seen some other murders where people have been shot or people have been poisoned, but I've never seen one where they've been cut to pieces. And one was an older woman! I mean, there is no reason to kill her, strip her and leave her there for everybody to find. This was brutal, savage.''

Though more seasoned, Morse was equally shocked by the images before him. He recognized the slaughter for what it appeared to be: the wild act of a sadistic mind, driven by the need for perverted sex and violence. In simple terms, this was a classic lust killing.

''I've seen 300 or 400 homicides,'' Morse said. ''You think you have seen it all, but this was gruesome.''

During the initial moments of the investigation, the officers suspected Galindau had something to do with the crime. It was a fair assumption given that he was familiar with the women, and had predicted police would find bodies within the house even though he had never looked inside. One investigator threatened to arrest Galindau that day, claiming police had found evidence that proved he had been inside the home.

The claim took Galindau by surprise and filled him with anger. He scoffed at the accusations and immediately offered to take a lie detector test.

"They said they had proof," Galindau recalled of his brief interrogation with Burlingame police. "I told them, 'Let me meet my accuser.' I was disgusted with them and told them that the next time I discover anything like this, I would just walk away."

Better clues to the real killer lay inside the victims' home, where evidence team officers were able to lift fingerprints from a garage door. The best evidence turned up inside the bedroom Peterson and Spadoni shared. Amid the clutter, the dirt and cobwebs, rested two hand-written letters and envelopes marked with a curious post office box number that began with a "C."

Several days later during a different search, the investigators would find a partial left palm print left on a bathroom sink. From within the drain they uncovered what looked like bits of razor stubble. But for now, the letter served as a smoking gun. To the untrained eye, the numerical sequence might have meant nothing, but Morse recognized the distinctive marking immediately as the post box number for a state prison inmate.

"Oh shit!" Morse said as he looked at the envelopes and letters, and first saw the name Phillip Jablonski.

A short time later, investigators with the Riverside County Sheriff's Department, half a state away in Indio, would speak the same name as they put together the last days of Fanny Vann. The two agencies had no idea the cases were linked, but that changed when Burlingame police examined Jablonski's criminal record to learn if the inmate was still behind bars or on parole.

When word came that Jablonski had been paroled several months earlier to Indio after serving time for murdering a women in 1978, Morse and Haseleu figured they had their man. They contacted Jablonski's parole officer in Indio and discovered he had married Spadoni nine years earlier, but was forbidden to be in San Mateo County. Haseleu ran a computer check on Jablonski to see if, by chance, he had been seen in the area. The traffic stop made by Thomas Ickes on April 23 appeared on a Burlingame Police Department computer screen.

"Well, now we've got him," Haseleu thought.

It was the kind of evidence prosecutors drool over, but things would soon get better.

As officers from the coroner's department went about the job of photographing the bodies and videotaping the crime scene, the phone inside Spadoni and Peterson's home rang. Frances Leone, an acquaintance who often met the women for coffee at Peninsula Hospital, was on the line checking up on her friends and trying to find out why they had missed their regular lunch date that day. When Burlingame detectives asked her about Spadoni's husband, Leone remembered that her friends said they were afraid of the man because he acted strange. She told police that Spadoni did not want to see him again.

Jablonski's parole officer, Robert Paredes, backed up the account. He told the Burlingame detectives that Jablonski disliked Indio and had wanted to stay with his wife and mother-in-law in San Mateo County. He said Spadoni specifically requested he be kept from her, a fact the parole officer had kept hidden from the former inmate.

The dominoes of evidence were falling in line and the tumbling continued after Haseleu spoke to officers with the Palm Springs Police Department and learned more about the murder of Linda Kimball—a crime which was strikingly similar to the ones now being investigated. The detectives in Palm Springs knew about Vann's murder and mentioned the crime to Haseleu.

"The detectives down there had just read a teletype from the Riverside County Sheriff's Department about a terrible murder where they found a body in the desert," Haseleu said. "She'd been strangled, shot in the head, mutilated, breasts cut off, eyes cut out and I realized it was pretty similar."

Tom Barton, a Palm Springs police detective worked the Kimball murder in 1978 and knew Jablonski well.

"I was very familiar with Jablonski and I thought he was supposed to be in prison for all the crap he had done before," Barton recalled. "I got on the phone with the officers in Burlingame and learned how he killed his wife and his mother-in-law. When they told me he was a student at the College of the Desert, I thought, He probably killed that lady they found in the desert! I tried to call the Riverside Sheriff's Department to tell them that the guy would kill more people. As far as I was concerned, they could not cut him off at the pass fast enough."

By nightfall, investigators from Burlingame and Riverside County were comparing notes. A search of Jablonski's apartment in Indio turned up bloody clothes and letters sent to Jablonski from Spadoni and Peterson.

Less than 12 hours after Galindau had notified police about the possible tragedy on Sanchez Avenue, an arrest warrant was issued on Jablonski and the alert sent out across the nation. The warning was too late to save Margie Rogers, but it came in time to prevent Jablonski from adding more names to his ominous snake belt.

Morse had Jablonski pegged as a lust killer, and based on his knowledge of such men, the veteran investigator figured the man was on the road, hunting for his next victim. He and Haseleu worried about the women Jablonski might encounter on the wide-open highway, but there was nothing they could do until the predator slipped up.

The break they sought came one day after Jablonski left Rogers dead on the floor of her roadside convenience store in Utah, while he traveled south through the flat Kansas countryside bound for Texas. His gray Ford, though old and odd looking with its primer paint, still chugged along. It was Sunday night, April 28, and Kansas Highway Patrol Officer John C. Smith was on duty, cruising near a rest stop close to the town of McPherson, when he spotted the Fairlane stopped at the side of the road with its hood up.

Smith pulled alongside the car and scanned the rest area for its owner. Jablonski approached the officer and made small talk. He told the officer that he had been on the road for some time and had come through Utah, Colorado and Nebraska, while bound for Texas.

In past encounters with curious law officers in California and Wyoming, Jablonski's luck had held, but this time the dice came up craps. Smith eyed the car and wondered to himself why it was coated in primer paint. He thought the car might be stolen and that the thief had tried to cover his tracks by repainting it. Besides, there was something about the car's owner that just didn't sit well with Smith.

"I got the impression he didn't want to talk to me," Smith noted in his police report. His suspicions proved true when he ran the license plate number on the Ford and learned from his dispatcher that the driver was wanted on suspicion of multiple murders and was to be considered armed and dangerous. He was advised that back-up officers were on the way, and instructed to keep an eye on the driver, but to stay out of his sight.

Smith let Jablonski drive away from the rest area, but followed at a safe distance. When two back-up patrol cars arrived, Smith turned on his siren and red lights. Jablonski immediately pulled to the shoulder, stopped, and was handcuffed without protest.

The officers found an identification card that belonged to Vann and more than $700 inside Jablonski's wallet. Jablonski was booked and held in a small jail cell, while his car was sealed with police tape and locked inside a garage to preserve whatever evidence remained within.

As soon as news of Jablonski's capture reached Burlingame, the detectives received word from Utah investigators about the Rogers murder and Jablonski's encounter at the rest stop in Wyoming.

"We needed to get him to tell us what happened," Haseleu said. "We thought that maybe he killed the woman in Utah and we felt that there might be other victims laying in the desert or someplace. We know he pulled a gun on a woman in Wyoming and I had to wonder how many others were out there. Were their bodies in a car trunk? Dumped in the desert? We did not know.''

The only one who did was the suspect. But to get there before Jablonski got wise enough to find a lawyer, the Burlingame detectives had to coordinate plans with their counterparts in Indio. The men investigating Vann's murder told Haseleu and Morse that they needed to track down their sheriff and use his department's private plane before heading to Kansas. Had Morse agreed to wait for them, Jablonski might have been left to sit unquestioned for days. That was unacceptable.

"I laughed at the idea," Morse said. "I told Eric that we had to talk to this guy before he got arraigned and met with a lawyer."

Morse, who by now had researched Jablonski's past and knew him to be talkative, was not about to let the prime suspect cool his heels in a small city jail, conjuring up alibis, while the deputies in Southern California let key evidence lay uncollected. With the blessings of Burlingame police officials, Morse and Haseleu hopped a plane and headed east.

Morse had seen cop-against-cop competition before. He figured the folks in Riverside County wanted to take the case from Haseleu.

"The worse thing you can do in any case is lose control of it," Morse said. "If you don't have one person in charge, you lose control."

Morris and Haseleu's action prompted action from their counterparts in Indio. They agreed to get to Kansas and compare notes.

Holed up inside a hotel in McPherson, Morse, Haseleu and Mark Barfknecht, the lead investigator from Riverside County, outlined a plan of attack. The lawmen knew all about Jablonski after having been briefed on his military career, his failed marriages and his past crimes.

On May 1, Jablonski was moved from his cell inside the city jail to a McPherson Courthouse conference room. The room had been wired for sound to allow Morse and other officers to record the conversation and listen in on the talks from another adjoining room while Barfknecht and Haseleu probed the suspect's mind.

At 10:35 a.m., Jablonski was brought to the small chamber to meet his questioners.

"He was a big guy and real strong looking," Haseleu recalled about his first face-to-face encounter with Jablonski. "He was a lot taller than me and real heavy; not fat, just big."

The detectives stayed relaxed, not wanting to tip their hand about what they knew. It was time to play poker with the suspect, let him feel comfortable with the scene and speak at his own pace.

"I needed this guy," Haseleu remembered. "I just wanted him to tell us what happened. At that point, we did not know if he had done the crime in Utah, and the people in Riverside did not have any solid evidence to support their case. So we wanted him to talk, and we started pretty cool. He was cool and collected. He knew he was in trouble and he knew he was going back to prison."

Barfknecht broke the ice.

"We are here to obviously talk to you about [what] happened over the last several weeks," Barfknecht said. "And we just want you to be comfortable, and if you need anything, just let us know."

Jablonski complained about being bored with the jail because it had no radio or television. He gave the investigators his name and address and birth date. When Haseleu asked if Jablonski was married, the suspect said no.

Jablonski was willing to talk when the topic was light, but when the conversation drifted toward the crimes, he told the detectives he would not say anything without seeing a lawyer first.

He admitted taking classes in Palm Desert, but said nothing about Vann when Barfknecht brought her name up. When the conversation shifted to Jablonski's war record, the big man's tongue loosened, and so did his imagination. He told the investigators he had been in Vietnam on rescue-and-recovery duty, even though his official army record has no mention of him ever having seen action in Saigon.

Haseleu again returned to the pertinent subject and made a play for Jablonski's emotions, knowing that a guilty mind can often compel suspects into giving up the truth.

"I would think if I was in your position, I'd certainly like to get some of this stuff off my chest," Haseleu began. "I understand you have got some problems and you're gonna have to deal with them. Maybe we can help you out."

Jablonski was not the type to listen to or even experience a guilty conscience.

"No comment," was his response to all matters dealing with the victims.

After dancing around the issues with talk about Jablonski's life in Indio and the travel route he took though the West, Haseleu returned with a frontal assault. He offered to turn the tape recorders off, in order to get some straight answers about Carol Spadoni and Eva Peterson.

"I am not judging you for what you did," he told Jablonski. "What you did is what you did. You gotta live with that yourself. You seem to be a good guy to me. You're calm, relaxed and all that, and I'd sure appreciate it if you'd help me out a little bit."

Jablonski was unmoved.

"Well, I gotta go to stand trial there, so I'd rather wait and talk to a lawyer," Jablonski replied.

Haseleu did not back off.

"What did Carol do that made you mad? I can't figure that out. I've read your letters to her. I've read her letters to you. I can't understand why you'd be so mad at Carol and Eva. I'm trying to figure it out. And I need your help. Did she say something to you that pissed you off?"

"No comment."

The interview continued into the afternoon, with Jablonski retelling bits and pieces of his life's story. The detectives learned about his past marriages, his parents' deaths in 1986 and his pen pal friendship with Spadoni.

By 2 p.m. the conversation was winding down. The detectives had placed some of their cards on the table, but had received little in return. Jablonski knew he was in trouble, but was not about to lend the officers a hand at pushing him toward the gas chamber in California. The rock had been bled for all it was worth.

Before leaving, Haseleu asked Jablonski what he thought this investigation meant.

"I'm going back to prison for life or death row," he told them.

Before the day ended, James Bayne, a district attorney investigator from Riverside County, began to write a search warrant affidavit for Jablonski's Ford. Morse figured the car contained a treasure trove of evidence, but held off going inside the vehicle until a judge had given the OK. Bayne had high hopes for what lay inside. Among the items he expected to find were Fanny Vann's missing jewelry and body parts.

Morse and Haseleu had already glanced through the car's windows and seen the tape recorder in the back seat. Though Jablonski was in no mood to talk to detectives, Morse figured he had been less shy with the machine.

"When I saw the tape recorder, there was no doubt in my mind," Morse said. "I knew we needed to get at the tape. I knew what was on it. It is a classic situation. Killers keep tapes to tell you what is happening and what they are going to do. It happens a lot."

When the detectives unsealed the car on May 3, they discovered a loaded .22 caliber revolver that had hair stuck to its barrel. A roll of blood-stained duct tape was found by the right rear floorboard. They also spotted a black and gold gym bag which held the snake belt. When the investigators unrolled the belt, they found the murder victims' names written in ink, along with the names of Jablonski's mother, as well as the names of Elizabeth Fisher, Helen Blair and Shirley Thorp—women whose identities and fates were then unknown to the detectives.

"It's chilling, it's a death belt," said Martin Murray, the soft-spoken San Mateo County deputy district attorney, who supervised the murder investigation and later prosecuted Jablonski for the Burlingame killings. "It is chilling to get a glimpse into the mind of someone who not only kills, but has the need to memorialize the killings. Death to him is a very important thing; important enough that it needs to be chronicled. For whatever reason, he needed a permanent record. It is frightening to know there are people like that out there. To them, the killing is an end to itself."

Perhaps the mementos were kept to occupy Jablonski's mind during the down time between murders, or they may have served as special charms he held and coveted to enhance his experiences.

"Death fantasies may live in the minds of killers [like Jablonski] for many, many years before the crimes are actually committed," Murray said. "The items may be their hook to reality, something that reminds them that they really did this stuff, so they know the killing was not just something in their minds."

But the best lucky charm, not only for Jablonski, but for the investigators, was the tape recorder which contained a detailed recounting of the murders, spoken in his own words.

"I was happy and overjoyed when I saw all that," Haseleu said. "I knew we had a lot of evidence at the murder scene that would lead to him. But in the car, everywhere we looked there was something. I mean there it was, the whole thing. Everyone was jumping for joy because everything was right there."

It would be days before Haseleu first heard the tape-recorded message. On it, Jablonski can be heard speaking in an excited, soft whisper, as he details the horrible crimes committed and the ones he hopes to perform in the future. There is no pain, sadness or remorse in his words, only the excitement of a man enthralled with the relish he gets by imagining the terror he can inflict on women.

"It sent chills up and down my spine," Haseleu said. "To hear that tape and to hear him huffing and puffing on it and moaning and doing the things he wants to do . . . and you can hear him getting more and more excited as he talks about how he is going to kill a woman outside a restroom.

"What you realize, listening to the tape, is that some unknown woman out there by a rest stop was lucky that a truck driver was nearby, otherwise she would have been dead and probably tortured and brutally murdered and cut up and left like dirt.

"I tell you, my wife will never use a rest stop along the highway anymore. I don't care how bad she has to go. She will go home or hold it until need be. Because this guy, he was just preying on people . . . He is a psychopath, a serial killer, and the only thing that stopped him was that he got caught in Kansas, otherwise, he would have kept on raping and killing."

With the evidence safely secured and Jablonski ready for his trip back to California to face justice, it was time for the detectives to study the suspect's life in order to understand what sent this killer down the deadly road that ended in Kansas.

SIX

Life With Father

"We were more scared of him than anything else."

Some people are said to be born under a bad sign, destined not for greatness, but for infamy. Others evolve into failures and learn evil habits through trial and error or the choices made as they stumble through life. And there are some sorry souls who have vileness thrust upon them, either by nefarious intervention or from the circumstances of their birth and upbringing.

There is no telling what Phillip Carl Jablonski might have become had he known the frequent embrace of loving parents, or the constant, proud smile of a benevolent father who was prepared and willing to guide his child in times of trouble and show him the way to become a man. Stable, open and tender households, be they affluent, middle class, or impoverished, are most often the fertile ground upon which strong, well-adjusted people take root and grow. But that was not the world Jablonski was tossed into. Instead, the fifth child born to Nettie Jablonski and her husband, Phillip, on January 3, 1946, would know all too well the shame and terror of a home ripped to its foundation by an alcoholic father who unleashed hatred upon anyone in his path.

The life and times of young Phillip Jablonski were rough and ugly. It seems only the strongest, or those who ran away early from the house the elder Mr. Jablonski built, would survive.

Though he was reared in the 1950s, a time of promise and

pleasure for many Americans, young Phillip's early years were a far cry from the fresh apple pies and wonderland of Ozzie and Harriet.

There is a good chance Phillip Jablonski might never have acquired a passion for violent sex and developed an intense hatred for women had he not been born the son of a hot-tempered little man from Michigan, who, despite his small stature was strong enough to lift the back end of a car with arms that bulged from years of physical labor. The elder Mr. Jablonski was not only strong for his five-foot, six-inch frame, but he had a temper that was outmatched only by his love of drink. He was said to have practiced rough sex on his wife, and when not beating her, he humiliated his spouse by groping other women in public without shame or apology.

The stories told of Mr. Jablonski seem too cruel and bizarre to be true, except that almost everyone who came to the family's one-bedroom home near the foothills of San Bernardino tells a similar story of a household controlled by a man who drank too much and abused everyone and everything in his path. One of the sons, Louie Jablonski, fled the San Bernardino home while in his teens, after he received one too many blows to the face. One of the daughters ran away at age 13 to live with her older siblings because the stress of returning to the home that the old man ruled like a crazed despot would send shivers down her spine and tie her stomach into knots.

Patsy Jablonski, who was born one year after Phillip, would become the strongest and most rebellious member of the troubled brood. Before running away from home, she watched her older brother, Louie, receive frequent beatings from her father. The sight of blood dripping down Louie's shirt would remain in her mind for over 40 years. So, too, do her recollections of her father's brutal treatment of her mother. She claims to have seen him use a pillow to smother Nettie Jablonski, then ridicule his gasping wife with taunts of "whore" and "slut" while he had sex with her.

Patsy would eventually spend time in Juvenile Hall and California youth camps for delinquents before taking off with a motorcycle gang. The wild and dangerous ride was a small price to pay to escape the physical and mental horrors that went on at the direction of Mr. Jablonski.

Several family members and neighbors who grew up alongside the clan in a poor section of San Bernardino, recalled that little good ever came from the home the family occupied at the far end of Severance Street. It was a home dominated by the elder Mr. Jablonski, who demonstrated his angry, bullheaded view of life while moving from Flint, Michigan to California in 1945 with his wife—then pregnant with young Phillip—and two children, Phyllis and Louie.

Orill Crum knew Mr. Jablonski in those days. His brother had married Nettie Jablonski's sister and the families grew close. Crum was raised on stories about Mr. Jablonski's strange ways. He was fond of telling one tale passed down to him from his father about the odd trip the Jablonski family took after pulling up stakes and heading west to the promised land that stood between the Rockies and the great Pacific.

It is not known why Mr. Jablonski moved his family west, but he did so without his oldest son, Stanley, who had already run away from his parents.

Life with the elder Mr. Jablonski was tough, even by 1945 standards, according to the stories Orill Crum's father passed on to his son. Evidence of Mr. Jablonski's strange way of thinking came to light during that cross-country trip in the family's 1936 Chevrolet. Recalling his father's account, Crum said things did not go well on the road. The trip had been made extra costly because Mr. Jablonski was too stubborn to fix the Chevrolet and its faulty alignment chewed up the vehicle's tires. Rather than make a simple repair, Mr. Jablonski denied any problem existed, according to Crum, thus forcing constant pit stops every time a tire exploded.

The old man's blind stubborness cost the family hundreds of dollars for several sets of new tires, emptying their bank account and forcing them to abandon a trailer in Arizona which contained many of their possessions.

Mr. Crum's father had established himself in San Bernardino, California in 1940 and by 1945 he owned a restaurant, feed store and bar. Being a good sort, he let the Jablonskis live in his home. They eagerly accepted the kind offer and it didn't take long for the family elder to settle into his usual routine. Soon he was spending hours at the bar drinking to excess, and demonstrating his physical strength.

"He [Mr. Jablonski] was kind of a touchy person," Crum said. "I mean, he would always want to arm wrestle [always] lifting things and showing his strength."

Crum recalled that Mr. Jablonski was especially adept at hoisting the back end of a car off the ground with his bare hands. Mr. Jablonski's powerful arms served him well as a wall plasterer and cement finisher.

By the time Phillip Jablonski, Jr. or "Little Phil," as he was called, came into the world weighing four pounds and three ounces, the family had moved from Crum's residence and into a home on Severance Street. The place was modest even by the standards of the poor, rural neighborhood, which sat amid farms, grape orchards and orange groves. The little home had only one bedroom, and as the years passed and more children were born to the Jablonskis, sleeping space became a luxury.

According to Jablonski family lore, Mrs. Jablonski took her marriage vows seriously and considered divorce unacceptable to her Catholic beliefs. Mrs. Jablonski was so loyal that she would drive her husband to the bars at night, then stay inside the car, sometimes in the company of one of her small children, and wait until her husband had had his fill.

Around the time little Phillip's younger siblings, Albert, Patsy, and little Nettie were born, a dining room had been converted into a second bedroom for the boys. Though Orill Crum was in his early 20s when little Phil was an infant and had not spent much time inside the Severance Street home, he did remember that the young boy was always upset. Other family members recall that the young child was sickly and needed goat's milk for nourishment.

"I didn't pay that much particular attention, but every time I saw him, he was crying, sitting in a high chair, very thin and white," Crum said. "I thought he was very ill. Most of the time the kids had to take care of him."

Crum said Mrs. Jablonski was a jolly person, but not much of a housekeeper.

"The kids did most everything," Crum said. "Setting the table, cleaning up the house—whatever cleaning was done—and taking care of the baby."

Right after the Second World War, when California experienced an incredible boom of growth, Mr. Jablonski earned a decent living as a contractor. According to Crum, Mr. Jablonski earned more than $1.25 an hour, a fair wage for the time, but spent little on his family and kept them on the poor side of life.

"I thought that he should have given more towards his family, because they never seemed to have any entertainment that I ever knew of," Crum said. "I mean, outside of going to the grocery store. And they never had a lot of friends."

The few neighborhood kids who did know the Jablonskis viewed the family patriarch as a dictator who beat his kids and wife and carried on a reign of terror that even extended to the animals the household raised either as pets or for food. Statements from family members and neighbors suggest that young Phillip took the most abuse. There was some dispute as to whether Phillip brought on the the whippings and general beatings by "acting up." Phillip's younger brother, Albert, considered his old man stern, but not unduly so in terms of discipline.

"If you messed up, you got spanked," Albert said. "He was an old Polish [guy] and he would get a stick and you would get your butt welted."

But law enforcement officers who investigated the 1991 murder cases agree that the elder Mr. Jablonski was a violent man who set an horrific example for his children.

"I think it is a fair assessment to say that it was a house that from time to time had inappropriate amounts of violence and alcohol abuse," said Murray, San Mateo County prosecutor, who came to know the workings of Phillip Jablonski's mind. "The father had little respect. There were sexual innuendoes and inappropriate touching."

He'd also call his wife and daughters horrible names,

according to Patsy, who listened to her parents having sex and then endured the sound of her father's voice filling their tiny home with profanities and vile accusations against her mother and her aunts.

"He would be having sex with my mother and he would tell her things like, 'I had sex with your mom and I had sex with your sisters. They ran a whorehouse and you're a whore.' And all this time he is supposed to be making love to her.

"My mom would scream and cry and we [kids] didn't know they were having sex, we thought he was still beating her. He would be yelling and screaming. He accused her of sleeping with the milk man, and the insurance man. . . . The whole neighborhood heard it."

According to Patsy, her father would often try to smother his wife, with his hands or a pillow.

"He would come up behind her, grab her, and put both hands in a chokehold. He'd pull her to the bedroom, throw her on the bed and then push his hand across her neck so he could beat her in the face," Patsy said. "He would put a pillow over her head and hold it there. She would be weak and stop fighting. If we got the pillow off my mom, and got my dad out of the bedroom, he would start [beating] on us."

When young Phillip tried to intercede, imploring the old man to "Leave my mom alone!", Mr. Jablonski would unleash his anger at the boy, smashing into the child with his fists, sending him flying across the room. The shouts inside the Severance Street home were loud enough to wake the neighbors, Patsy said.

The biggest dirty little secret of Severance Street and the Jablonski family was not overheard by neighbors. The story remains shrouded in mystery and only surfaced through the dreams, or repressed memories, of Patsy, who claims to have recalled the terrifying event in 1978, after learning that her brother was wanted for murdering his wife, Linda Kimball. Patsy told the story to investigators after her brother was arrested in connection with the murders of Vann, Peterson and Spadoni.

If true, the account could explain why her brother turned into a serial rapist.

According to Patsy, Phillip had been mentally ill most of his life, a fact she attributed to an alleged abduction carried out by two male neighbors who snatched young Phillip at age five or six, then raped the little boy inside their home. Patsy would have only been about three-years-old at the time, so her account should be viewed with some skepticism. She maintains that a neighbor and close friend of Mr. Jablonski, along with a second, unidentified male accomplice, captured Phillip and brought the young boy into the friend's home and forced the child onto a bed. She claims the men brought her into the house first, then decided that she was too young for what they wanted to do.

"So they let me go and they took my brother," she said. "He was screaming and I was pounding at the bedroom door and screaming. I kept trying to tell them I wanted my brother."

Patsy claimed she saw belts and dog chains inside the room, and remembered the men held her brother down.

"I went in and could see they were holding him by the throat," Patsy said. "One man was on the front of the bed, and the other man was at the end of the bed. He [Phillip] just screamed and cried. After it was over, and it didn't happen just once, they both took him in the shower and washed. They took him outside and kept telling him, 'You are a man.' My brother was so upset. I held him, and comforted him, and told him that I loved him."

Patsy said the rape was seen by another neighborhood boy named Dale Rearick, but Rearick contradicted her story, telling investigators that he never saw any such thing. In fact, he considered the neighbor a kind and generous man, who had a girlfriend and treated the children of Severance Street as friends.

Rearick did recall other things, however, and painted a picture of a fractured Jablonski family that witnessed incest, hatred and abuse. The worst offender in the Jablonski household was the old man himself, Rearick recalled. He said that it was common to see police officers pull up to the Jablonski home once a week to look into one disturbance or another.

The sounds of screams and beatings emanating from the Jablonski home were staples of the neighborhood, according to Rearick, who was born in San Bernardino and grew up in a home two doors from the Jablonski residence. As a child, Rearick considered Mr. Jablonski vicious and cruel. Years later, Rearick, who later served two tours of duty in Vietnam, still considered Phillip Jablonski, Sr. the meanest man he ever knew. The old man was especially rough on young Phillip, Rearick said, recalling the sounds of terror that echoed along Severance Street.

When not thumping young Phillip, Mr. Jablonski directed his anger toward his wife. The violence often sent the Jablonski children running from the home in fear toward a nearby flood control canal where the frightened youngsters hid like soldiers hunkered down to escape a bombardment. The children would stay hidden until the yelling inside their home died away. Sometimes the torment would last for hours.

Young Phillip seemed especially traumatized by the brutal beatings his father meted out on his mother.

"He would sit there [in the canal], cry and worry about my mother," Patsy said. "I'd hit him in the mouth and say, 'I'll give you something to cry for, now shut up, because we're not going home. If she wants to stay there and take this shit, she's welcome to it, but we are not.' " Patsy said she developed into a strong child by the time she was in the second grade, and often led her siblings into the canal when her father came home drunk, angry and looking for a fight.

"I just would not let my brothers and sisters go back," Patsy said. "If we'd be in bed and he'd come home, we had to stay there and take the shit. But if he came home at six o'clock, drunk and raising hell, if it was daylight, I was getting the hell out of there."

The worst beatings occurred on Friday nights, and they could last all weekend, according to Patsy. There was never really any reason for the abuse, save for the drink that had turned Mr. Jablonski's mind into a volcano of hate.

"He'd come home after the bar closed and wake the whole household up," Patsy said. "He'd start arguing with my mother, then start beating on her. We would try to get him to stop and he'd end up beating all of us.''

Patsy and her siblings fled into the surrounding hills or the canal. But Phillip usually stayed behind to protect his mother, Patsy said. The children would stay away until the violence had subsided, or their father passed out or went to sleep.

''My mom would turn on the porch light, go out and sit,'' Patsy said of the weekend ritual. ''A lot of times she'd signal with the porch light and we knew we could come home.''

There were even occasions when young Phillip escorted his mother from their home and huddled with her in the ditch while the old man stumbled about, ranting inside the house.

''He used to take her down in the canal once in awhile,'' said Dwayne Meadows, another Severance Street boy, who knew the family and witnessed the abuse. ''It was kind of a steep incline, but he [Phil] would rather see that than see her get slapped around.''

Mr. Jablonski was also cruel to the family's animals, according to the tales that spread along Severance Street. The family raised pigs, goats and chickens and some said Mr. Jablonski took pleasure in decapitating chickens with his hands, then terrorizing his children with their bloody remains. Mr. Jablonski allegedly took the family's pig to a butcher, then cooked the animal and fed it to his children, even though they had come to view the beast as a pet, not a meal.

The children had cared for the animal since it was a piglet and to them it was part of the family.

''It was our friend,'' Patsy said. ''It was our playmate and we couldn't eat it.''

But Mr. Jablonski was not one to waste food or patience, so as usual, he used force to have his way.

''Because we couldn't eat it, our faces would be either shoved into our food and rubbed into it, or the plate would be picked up and rubbed in our face,'' Patsy said.

For a long time after that, Patsy stuck to a diet of vegetables, and avoided meat. Farm animals were not the only beasts to know the burden of life on Severance Street. Rearick said that Mr. Jablonski was also rough with the family's pet Husky. He said his angry neighbor would grab the animal by its collar or lower jaw in a stranglehold and toss it around like a sack of trash, sending the pet scurrying away with a panicked yelp. No one ever tried to stop Mr. Jablonski's rampage, not even Albert Jablonski, who usually tended to the Husky's feeding and general needs.

"He was too afraid to," Rearick said. "Everyone was too afraid to."

Meadows, who rode bicycles and played baseball with the Jablonski children, always felt uneasy about his neighbors. He remembers that Mr. Jablonski preferred to drink himself into a daze rather than take care of his family. Like most of the neighbors, Meadows remembers seeing the Jablonski kids hit with belts. He also recalls the day Mr. Jablonski killed the Meadows' family puppy by running the little pet over with his car and not stopping the vehicle to see what kind of damage he had done.

"We were outside playing whiffle ball and he—I'll never forget it because he just kept on going around the corner, never blinked an eye, or anything," Meadows said of an event that had occurred four decades ago when he was no more than 10.

No one, not even Meadows' father, stepped in to set things right.

"We were more scared of him than anything else," Meadows said of Mr. Jablonski, adding that his family never considered getting even with the vile old man who had claimed their pet's life.

Mr. Jablonski proved so frightening to the neighborhood children that whenever he arrived home, everyone scattered.

"His mother seemed nice," Meadows said of Mrs. Jablonski. "But when the father came [in] everybody was to leave. I would never go up there, I was more or less afraid to go up there because you never know what is going to happen. You never know."

Even family outings to the drive-in theater could be unnerving experiences. On one occasion, Mr. Jablonski loaded up his family into a van and headed out to the movies. He was drunk as usual, and this time armed with a handgun.

"He was shooting the gun out the window and making threats to my family," Patsy recalled. "On the way he was yelling and threatening to shoot us."

After pulling into the drive-in and parking next to a speaker pole, Mr. Jablonski exited the car and urinated in front of his family and all the the others who had gathered to watch the big outdoor screen. When those around him voiced complaints, Mr. Jablonski lost his temper and sped from the drive-in with his terrified children trapped inside the van. He eventually pulled off near a field. The children bailed out and ran for cover, fearing that this time their old man had gone too far and might start firing rounds at them.

As the Jablonski kids lay motionless in the field, their father drove the van back and forth across the darkened landscape using the van's headlights to search for his huddled children.

"That was an example of a typical family day out," said Richard Keyes, a Burlingame defense attorney, one of two co-counsels who represented Jablonski at the trial for the murders of Eva Peterson and Carol Spadoni. The defense attorneys argued that Phillip's fiendish upbringing turned him into a deranged killer.

"To some people, childhood doesn't matter that much because they've had a good childhood and they are independent and mature and confident in approaching the world," Keyes said. "But when you have had a childhood as destructive as this one, you're more ingrained. You're more confused, you're more unable to do anything."

Keyes, a Lincolnesque figure who is well over six feet, five inches tall and rail thin, said Jablonski not only suffered the sins of his father, but he took them to heart and built upon them.

"If anyone had adopted Phillip at a young age there would have been a tremendous difference," the lawyer believes. "They would have fed him spiritually and emotionally. They would not have drained his humanity from him."

Within the nightmare on Severance Street, young Phillip first learned about life. To no one's surprise, he became withdrawn, according to his siblings and the neighbors. He was also a poor student in elementary school who lagged behind Patsy.

"They failed him, put me up, and we started school together," Patsy said. "I advanced and they put him behind because he was insecure. But we knew something was wrong with him because he always felt insecure and he cried a lot."

The young boy's timidity caught the attention of a school counselor who had Phillip tested by a school psychologist when he was nine-years-old, an unusual step in the 1950s. Reports indicate Phillip tested in the dull range on an IQ exam. He was later observed in play-room activities by school counselors. There is no clear record as to what the school professionals thought about the boy. Oddly enough, when Phillip was young, his siblings were considered wild, and he was described as quiet, polite and law-abiding.

"He used to tell us [kids] that we were too wild for him," Patsy said. "He would say that we were bad. We always called him the cop because, even from that age, he was always going to be the policeman when he grew up. He was the best one of us all. He was a really good kid."

Others recall Phillip as a shy student, who kept to himself and walked the halls of Pacific High School with his shoulders slumped. His grades were always poor, but he showed an early interest in photography, law enforcement and the military. He took part in the school's ROTC program and seemed to enjoy the regimen that included marching and mock drills with toy guns.

"My memory of him is that he was tall and skinny. He kept to himself and was sort of slumped-shouldered, looking at the ground mostly and walking from class to class hunched," recalled fellow Pacific High student, Stephen Crane. "He was definitely on the social fringe. He didn't fit in."

High school photography teacher Charles Painter remembered Phillip as a loner who dressed badly and never said anything to anyone. The boy seemed at home in the dark room. The teacher never urged Phillip to go out and take pictures of events or clubs, because he did not feel the painfully withdrawn teenager could handle interacting with others.

Somewhere along the way, Phillip changed from the obedient, shy soldier-to-be. He became interested in sex at a young age. The stories of Phillip's exploits vary. Some people say he engaged in an incestuous affair with Patsy, and raped his youngest sister, Nettie. Other claims have him exposing himself to young female relatives, or molesting young girls. There are even accounts of Phillip bragging about his exploits to high school chums.

Rearick later testified to having seen Phillip and Patsy having sex on at least two occasions when they were teenagers. He said they boasted about their deeds, not just to him, but to others in the neighborhood. Patsy has always denied such stories, but said her brother did force himself on Nettie by knocking the younger girl out and raping her when he was nearly 18. Patsy also contended in court that her brother tried to rape her in their high school years.

"We were going on a beach outing with our church. I was in the bathroom wearing my pajamas and robe. I was ironing the outfit I was going to wear and he came up behind me with a rope and put it around my neck," Patsy said. "I caught him behind my back and I put my hands up. He put me on the bed, got on top of me and had me pinned down. He said, 'I'm going to get some of that off you.' I only weighed 89 pounds. He was already tall and his weight held me down. I kept pushing him 'cause my hands were free, but he kept holding the rope. All of a sudden he looked at me and he said, 'What am I doing?' He told me he loved me and broke down and cried hysterically."

As children, Patsy and Phillip had "played doctor," but this assault with a weapon was quite different. Though Phillip had halted his attack, Patsy was filled with panic, even after her brother left the room and continued to sob on the front porch.

"I was afraid of him," Patsy later said. "I was getting ready for a bath. He reached his hand in [the bathroom] and got the little flip lock open. I ran into the bedroom, locked the door and shoved a dresser up against it. He tried to get in from the window. He had already gotten my robe off and all I was wearing was a pink shortie nightgown and underwear, and he was coming in the window.''

Patsy fled for the safety of her front yard before her brother made it inside.

"I knew to get the hell out of there," she said. "I knew if I was outside, he wouldn't hurt me because people could see me."

Later that day, Phillip attempted to put a good face on the episode.

"He came to me and he said he wanted to buy me a present," she recalled. "Now after everything that he's ever done, every time [in the past] he lashed out at me when I was little, he bought me a present, an ice cream, a vase, flowers. He wanted to tell me he was sorry. I told him I knew he was sorry, but that I did not want to get close to him. I stayed out by the street in case I needed to run."

That evening Patsy, who by then was living full-time with her older sister, reported the attack to her mother.

"I said, 'Mama, I can't come back to visit you anymore. I became hysterical and told her."

Later that evening when Phillip returned to the home, his father stood waiting and beat his son so badly that Mrs. Jablonski had to pull her husband off the child in order to save his life.

"He beat my brother, instead of getting him the help that I asked them to get for him," Patsy said. "We knew something was wrong with Phillip, I don't know why, but we knew something was wrong."

SEVEN

Rose

"I was scared of him. I was afraid of what he was going to do next."

Despite years of abuse at home, low grades in class and an escalating hunger for sex, Phillip made it through high school and became the first member of the Jablonski household to earn a degree. Though shy, stoop-shouldered and ill at ease in a crowd, Phillip maintained a dating relationship with his classmate, Rose Ludwig, who considered the tall photography student to be a normal guy, not unlike all the other boys attending school. They dated on and off at Pacific High, hung out and went to dances.

"He seemed like a regular person," Ludwig recalled of the young man who began courting her when they were 16. "He had an average amount of friends. He was not real, real popular, but he still had friends."

Though sister Patsy recalled that Phillip dated several girls in school, Ludwig had no recollection of the competition. The other women were of little importance to Phillip, at least according to Patsy, who recalled that Ludwig was the only girlfriend Phillip ever introduced to his family. Mrs. Jablonski did not like Ludwig, who had seen tough times after having been bounced from various foster homes in Oregon and Washington before landing in San Bernardino.

"She was a peculiar girl," Mrs. Jablonski once said of Ludwig. "She was into the dog clubs and she would run around with other kids, while Phillip went with his church group. He was more of a homebody boy; he did not go out with a gang of kids, or anything like that.''

If the two were ill-matched, Patsy did not see any conflict. Despite her past troubles with Phillip, Patsy became friends with Ludwig and went out with her brother and his new girl on double dates after the couple had graduated high school.

While he romanced Ludwig, Phillip considered his exciting future and dreamed about a career he had coveted for years. As a boy, he had seen himself wrapped in battlefield glory or standing up for the community as a cop. After a brief stint in junior college following his high school graduation, Phillip pursued his gung-ho interests and volunteered for the army in 1966. After the sweat and pain of boot camp came a tour of duty in Korea, where he was trained as a dog handler.

Phillip played on his knowledge of military jargon to lend credence to the exaggerated stories he concocted to create an heroic image. Over time, Phillip claimed to friends and relatives that he had seen action in Vietnam where he used his skills with dogs on search and destroy missions to hunt Viet Cong. At other times, he claimed to have been a door gunner on a helicopter where he saw a chopper pilot take enemy rounds in the chest before the brave soldier died in his arms.

Years later, investigators with the San Mateo County District Attorney's Office discovered that not only was the pilot in Phillip's story alive, but Phillip had never even been to Vietnam.

As Phillip aged, he frequently returned to the Vietnam theme, claiming that the atrocities he had witnessed there triggered his emotional outbursts toward women. In later years, Mr. and Mrs. Jablonski would use a similar rationale to explain their son's bizarre behavior toward his first wife. Before their deaths in 1986, the couple spoke with police officers about their son and blamed his radical change in behavior on his unfortunate experiences in Vietnam.

Phillip told family members that he received a Purple Heart and a Bronze Star for deeds in ''the Nam.'' Though Phillip did receive a ribbon denoting his presence in the armed forces during the Vietnam era, his actual army record gives no indication that he ever took part in the Vietnam conflict. That little fact did not stop Phillip from spinning stories about the horrors he saw in that country. In addition to the "door gunner" fantasy, Phillip claimed that he used his army dogs to help a unit known as the "tunnel rats" root out hidden enemy soldiers. The tunnel rats were a special band of men who crawled into the Viet Cong underground compounds and killed whatever they came across.

At six feet, two inches, Phillip would have towered over the average Vietnamese and his bulk would have made it nearly impossible for him to crawl through the narrow pathways used by the North Vietnamese soldiers. When not pushing the dog story, Phillip claimed to have suffered a serious stomach wound in combat, and to have once carried the body of a fallen buddy for days.

"I started out in Saigon, then I went to Cam-ranh, then I was with the 101st Unit 15th Scouts, then the 249th Medivac for coverage and recovery," he once claimed.

The stories seemed detailed enough to fool some people. Patsy remembers one account bounced around the family where Phillip was said to have carried a decapitated soldier's remains through the jungle for three weeks. The myth and the fantasy mixed into one, and it all became a convenient way for Phillip, or his relatives, to explain the man's deranged behavior. Perhaps they wanted to believe his stories since it would put less blame on themselves and prove an excuse for Phillip's strange ways.

"After he got hurt in the service, when he came home, he was different," Mrs. Jablonski once said.

Phillip would take the line a step further, claiming that he had learned sexual deviance from the whores in Saigon, whom he said liked rough sex and enjoyed being choked during carnal escapades. Time and again, throughout his life, Phillip used his imaginary experiences in Vietnam as a crutch to explain away the rotten seeds that had already been planted in his head.

He even used the Vietnam cover to explain his attack on Fanny Vann, telling one psychologist, following his 1991 arrest, that he "scooped out" the dead woman's eyes in the Indio desert because he had seen a member of his squad in Vietnam do it to the daughter of a village chief.

In reality, Phillip spent much of his three-year army career in Fort Bliss, Texas.

As the war in Vietnam hit full force in 1968, Phillip planned life with his old high school sweetheart. He and Ludwig had kept in touch through letters, and when he returned to San Bernardino on a brief leave in January, the two sped off to Las Vegas and got married. Ludwig recalled that the wedding was a spur-of-the-moment decision. The honeymoon was equally abrupt since the couple had no money. They spent the night in Las Vegas and returned to his parents' house the next day. Ludwig briefly moved in with her in-laws while Phillip traveled back to Fort Bliss and searched for a proper home for his new bride.

At that time, Ludwig was unaware of Phillip's dark side. High school days were still fresh in her head and she thought of him as a quiet, easy-going type, who spoke well of his mother and badly of his father.

The first several days of their marriage passed without incident as the two shared a house with Phillip's parents. Phillip behaved like a considerate husband. He treated his wife well and appeared to be an affectionate lover. All that changed once the two relocated to Fort Bliss, far away from the watchful and protective eyes of Phillip's mother.

"Having Phillip's mother around when they were first together in San Bernardino may have provided a calming influence," said county prosecutor Martin Murray. "But in El Paso, Texas, Ludwig was isolated and there was no one there except for Phillip, who began doing violent things."

By the winter of 1968, Phillip had found his first female captive. Within months of departing California, Ludwig became the unwilling subject in her husband's seemingly insatiable craving for hard sex. The tender man she had known in high school was no more. His attitude toward her had suddenly shifted from the calm affection he had shown her in California, to a frenzied pace that pushed her past the edge.

Life at Fort Bliss was hellish for Ludwig. Phillip now had

the time and opportunity to relive the terrible things his father once practiced on his mother inside the cramped little Severance Street home. The demonic torch lit by the old man years before had been passed to a new generation, one willing to take the violence to new levels.

"He would be mean to me—beat me, try suffocating me with a pillow, choke me. One time he tried to drown me in the bathtub," Ludwig said.

Ludwig said this bathtub attack, as with all the others Phillip launched, came without warning when he entered the bathroom and suddenly shoved her under the warm water. Ludwig is still unsure how she got free from that near-death experience. She remembers being grabbed and pushed down by his great bulk. She does not know if she struggled free, or if Phillip changed his mind and let her up for air.

Phillip, who always had an excuse for his irrational acts, claimed the incident had been brought on by a Vietnam "flashback" that clouded his mind and convinced him Ludwig was a "Viet Cong."

The abuse continued and even escalated as Phillip used other restraints on his wife even after she became pregnant. He would also demand anal sex on a regular basis, despite her hatred of the sexual practice. Her protestations were ignored and only seemed to provoke his wrath. Whenever Ludwig refused him, Phillip would grab her around the neck and choke her until her body went limp, allowing him to have his way.

"There was no loving or foreplay or nothing," Ludwig said. "It was just force. Usually I just gave in and went along with him because I was scared of him. I was afraid of what he was going to do next. . . . When he wanted it, he was going to do it."

Phillip tried to brush the abuse off, telling Patsy that the choking was his way of following orders delivered by his wife's doctor.

"He said that the doctor gave Rose medication and she would not take it," Patsy said. "The doctor showed him how to knock her out so he could inject this syringe into her."

The sexual slavery might have gone on indefinitely had Ludwig not sought the advice of a Fort Bliss doctor who noticed her bruised body and warned the pregnant woman to get away from her husband before he killed her and their unborn child.

"A gynecologist said that by the way I was bruised, that he thought I had been raped," Ludwig said.

Afraid for her life, and that of her unborn child, Ludwig packed up and fled back to California. She stayed with Phillip's parents after her husband was arrested by Fort Bliss military officers for abusing her. After undergoing mental health treatment, army doctors diagnosed Phillip as a schizophrenic—a catch-all determination that may have missed the root of Phillip's twisted being.

"In psych language at that time, the term 'schizophrenic' meant this guy is bizarre but we don't know why," Murray said. "Other doctors in later years would conclude that he had been misdiagnosed. In reality he was a sexual sadist."

The label stuck with Phillip for life and he used the diagnosis for years as an accompanying excuse to the alleged trauma he claimed to have suffered in the rice paddies of Vietnam.

Phillip was not the only one who refused to face real problems. Mrs. Jablonski also overlooked her son's outbursts and appeared to have no idea why his first marriage had fallen to pieces. Her "hear no evil, see no evil" mind-set had been cemented long ago.

"She and him just didn't hit it off," Mrs. Jablonski would tell investigators years later about the collapse of Phillip and Rose's marriage. "We don't know what the background was there. I mean, what their home life was like."

Mrs. Jablonski's denial deepened after Ludwig returned to San Bernardino and explained her troubles to Patsy, who could no doubt relate to the story of her hulking brother manhandling a woman.

"You could tell on Rose's face that something had happened," Patsy said. "When I held her, she hung on to me and she started to cry."

She spilled her guts to Patsy and admitted being afraid for her life.

"He ain't gonna hurt you as long as I'm around you," Patsy assured her.

But the promises proved empty when Phillip went AWOL from Fort Bliss and came back to San Bernardino looking for his estranged wife. Their child had not yet been born, but she had moved into an apartment with a friend, hoping to never see her violent husband again.

Phillip had always feared abandonment and even as a small child he would sit on the front porch of his home and sob uncontrollably whenever his mother left the house. That insecurity grew into rage as the years went by. The frightened tears he once shed for his mother had hardened into something different toward Ludwig and the other women who would try to escape him in years to come.

Phillip surprised Ludwig just outside her new home in San Bernardino a little more than a month after she fled Fort Bliss. He spoke not a word, but rather let his hands do the talking. He grabbed his pregnant wife from behind, wrapped his fingers around her neck and started to squeeze.

Fortunately for Ludwig, Mrs. Jablonski had accompanied her son. She broke off the attack by calling her son's name, causing Phillip to retreat as quickly as he had sprung.

"I was scared to death," Ludwig said. "I didn't know what was going on to begin with, but I think she called his name and he just quit. After that he cried and said he was sorry. He did not know why he did it."

Years later, when she spoke with investigators, Mrs. Jablonski still stood by her boy, telling the lawmen that Phillip had always been a passive child who ran from fights.

"He had never been violent," she insisted. "If there was an argument or a fight in the house, he'd take off; he would not stay there and listen to it. Whenever the kids would get in arguments like kids do when they're playing ball, Phil walked away. He would have nothing to do with it. Even if him and I got into an argument, he'd walk off. He wasn't the kind to argue and fight."

Mrs. Jablonski seemed unable to accept that her son was a

dangerous man. It was far easier for her to blame his strange habits on the women he married.

"To tell you the truth, I think she [Rose] was bad for him," she said. "I caught him trying to smother her face, but . . . it was because she left him."

Ludwig was lucky. After the final attack, she gave birth to a healthy son and sought a divorce, determined to keep the child away from his father. But by then, Phillip had already moved on, seeking his odd brand of comfort from another woman, who had befriended the oversized soldier while he was being treated at an army mental hospital in Fort Bliss.

One lover had escaped the net, but the next one might not be so lucky. A pattern of life that had begun with secret molestations and random attacks on relatives had now moved on to a serious level.

"If you live around violence, you'll be violent-prone. I think there is a possibility Phillip's old man did sadomasochistic things," said Robert Morse, the San Mateo County investigator. "I believe sex criminals start out doing innocuous things like peeking into windows and exposing themselves and then just get worse. It is a power and control thing, like Phillip would say about Fanny, 'You're garbage! You're mine!' "

If Morse is correct, then by 1968, Phillip was firmly planted on the road that would eventually take him to Indio and Burlingame.

"If you have a sexual need to be violent with someone and you don't want to go to jail for it, you have to find a willing partner," Murray said. "This building [sadistic] behavior is not unlike a traditional courtship, where a person might take someone out to a romantic dinner on the first date. By date three, they might try kissing, and that may lead to hugging and down the line, intercourse. But Phillip is different, he may want his women to lie still in bed, or close their eyes. Gradually he will get them to tie their hands or pretend to have their hands tied. Over time, he can bring that person along with the game without frightening them off. After all, if you start out by placing a knife to your date's throat and choking them to the point where they lose consciousness, you lose your partner pretty quick.''

Phillip's aggression had cost him his first marriage and his first partner. His liking for sadistic affairs had been whetted in Fort Bliss, and after Ludwig turned her back on him and fled, his hunger needed replenishing,

''Typically, when one woman leaves Phillip, another will be at risk,'' Murray said.

EIGHT

Ann

*"What he wanted was what he got. He was just so
mean about it."*

Ann Riordan was a naive country girl. She grew up in the
little town of LaPeer, Michigan, home to a general store, a post
office, two gas stations and three churches. It was small-town
America at it finest. A place devoid of much public trouble
and ruled by the strict guidelines of the Baptist faith. Like most
youngsters raised in such a narrowly defined world, Riordan
wanted to know more than the familiar settings of her own
backyard. She chose the army as her escape route, and after
serving basic training in Anson, Alabama, transferred to Fort
Bliss, Texas, where she worked as a psychiatric technician at
William Beaumont Hospital in nearby El Paso.

She was only 18 and knew nothing about the world, or the
types of men who inhabit it. She had never had a date. All that
would change when she ran across Jablonski in the hospital's
halls.

In spite of her inexperience, Riordan should have known
better, since she understood that Jablonski was in the hospital
for mental health treatment. After his arrest, army authorities
had let Jablonski decide whether he needed time in the stockade
for the past attacks on his wife, or required psychological help
from army doctors. Jablonski opted for the help of medical
men, not jailers.

By November 1968, Jablonski was coming to the end of his

treatment. As an outpatient at the hospital, he had the freedom to move about the base. Sometime around the beginning of December, Riordan spotted Jablonski walking the halls dressed in a military police uniform. As a staff technician, Riordan had access to Jablonski's records and knew that he had been diagnosed as a schizophrenic. She understood that he had received drug treatments and had reacted violently when given Thorazine. She should have known better than to pay attention to this man, but Riordan, like so many other women Jablonski would run across in his life, found something of interest in the big man.

"When I was in the army, I was very, very backward," Riordan recalled. "I never had a date through high school. I did not know what a man was for. I didn't date when I was first in the army. I was really a kid from a hick town."

Jablonski was always adept at spotting weak females, so it was just a matter of time before he separated Riordan from the others. He embarked on a pattern that had been successful with Ludwig, who also had initially viewed Jablonski as a nice, quiet guy before living under his thumb for months.

"Phillip is a predator," Murray said. "From an early age, his goal was to find people who would engage in this twisted sexuality that he has. He is so wrapped up in suffering and death, and once women are under his control, it leads to domination and violence."

First the hook had to be baited. Jablonski presented himself as a non-threatening, normal man when he first spoke with Riordan. Though she had been warned not to get friendly with hospital patients, Riordan ignored the advice and looked for the good in this troubled soldier.

"When you first meet him, you wouldn't know there's anything wrong with him," Riordan said. "I met him two or three times at the hospital. He seemed like a nice guy. . . . I think he knew I was backward, and that I was vulnerable."

One day in early December, Riordan met Jablonski coming out of the hospital as she headed in for work. After saying hello, Jablonski invited her on a date to the mess hall. He had promised to treat her to a hamburger, but instead he picked

Riordan up at her off-base barracks and drove toward McCulligan's Canyon, a notorious make-out spot for young Texans.

"Well, here's the dumb part," Riordan said. "We were in a car and we went up in the canyon where everybody necks and all that. Stupid me, I didn't know anything about sex. I knew you kissed and necked and all that, but I didn't know what sex was."

Her initiation would be rude, and swift.

"We were talking about the way you introduce each other to each other, and what his background was and what my background was," Riordan said. "He kissed me, put his arm around me, and got me to the side. He was sitting behind the steering wheel. He got out and got in on the passenger side. He pushed me over and put his hand on my leg and pushed up my skirt."

Riordan tried to fight him by moving Jablonski's big hands away, but the brief match was quickly over when he shoved her under the steering wheel. There was no way that Riordan, five-feet, three-inches tall, could budge Jablonski. Trapped beneath the steering column, she tried to distract him by pounding on his chest.

"The next thing I knew, I was lying down and he was doing it and all I could think of was that finally it was happening to me," Riordan said, referring to sexual intercourse. "He did not do anything other than just have straight sex. He didn't do anything to harm me or hit me or anything. I remember the steering wheel was in my gut. I figured I [had] let him go too far, but [at the time] I did not think of it as rape."

Jablonski made a hasty apology after completing the act, and returned her to the base. Riordan was too panicked to even think about reporting the crime. She was too naive to even know she had been victimized.

"He said he was sorry he did it," Riordan recalled. "It's just that he got those kind of urges and he just couldn't control them. He let me go in [the barracks] and didn't try to keep me from going in or anything. I wasn't bright enough to report it."

Days later, Jablonski spotted Riordan on base. Once more

he apologized and asked to take her out for lunch. He sent her flowers and said that the attack was way out of character for him.

"He told me it wasn't his normal behavior," Riordan said. "He said he was sorry and he wouldn't be doing it again, he wouldn't do anything that I didn't want him to do."

Still stunned at the turn of events, Riordan called Jablonski and chided him for not treating her to dinner as he had initially promised.

"I did not know what was going on," she said. "I called him and said, 'Hey, I didn't get a hamburger out of the whole thing.' So I made him come back and take me out to eat. That was stupid."

Jablonski's second big catch was not only on the line, but well landed on the beach. Like a seasoned angler, he understood that his helpless prey was now ready to be stunned into submission.

"He had lost power and control over Ludwig," Murray theorized of Jablonski's quick switch of attention to Riordan. "And as soon as he could, for the sake of his twisted ego, he had to have power and control of someone else."

Soon, the two were living together and Jablonski's strange sexual needs began to emerge. As he did with Ludwig, Jablonski used a pillow to smother Riordan as a prelude to intercourse and choked her with his hands. He added a few new games to the mix, too. According to Riordan, Jablonski threatened her with a gun and occasionally smacked her in the head with the butt of the weapon before engaging in sex. He also added bondage to his repertoire.

In the span of only a few years, Jablonski had made the leap from a fondler of young relatives to a fully-fledged sadomasochist. There was no reason to believe his behavior would slow down.

"A psychiatrist might say that people like Jablonski have [sex] fantasies early in life and that at puberty the fantasies become more involved and the people get hooked," Murray said. "Those daydreams can be enough until the person gets into their early 20s. The progression goes on until the person needs to risk something, such as a rape or perhaps murder. That progression often takes 10 to 15 years.''

Riordan would be at the center of Jablonski's evolution for the next three years. They left the army and moved in with Jablonski's parents in early 1969 after Riordan became pregnant. Following a fight with Jablonski's father which ended with the old man tossing an iron at his son, the young couple relocated to nearby Fontana, where Jablonski found work in a PX shop on an air force base, as a clerk in a liquor store, and as a dog handler for a security firm.

Jobs and fatherhood had not slowed Jablonski's cravings one bit, according to Riordan, who said she could not keep up with his constant demands.

''Well, Phillip likes sex three times a day, seven days a week,'' Riordan said. ''I just can't take it. I am not built for sex three times a day. I mean, I like sex like everyone else, but that was a little much. And when he'd do it, he was cruel about it. He'd get what he wanted and that was it. He didn't want to satisfy me, and he was getting very weird.''

Riordan stayed with him despite other odd acts that included flashes of violence from Jablonski at television shows he did not like and at dogs that were unable, or unwilling, to follow his orders. She recalled one incident early in their California days when Jablonski drove with her on a tour of the desert surroundings. When she complained about his aggressive skills behind the wheel, he pulled over and dumped her amid the sagebrush, forcing her to walk back home.

''I loved Phil at one time,'' Riordan said. ''I really thought I did. I thought I could help him. Maybe it's something that I could do that will bring him out of it. But the more I tried, it seemed the worse it got.

''He was real subtle at first. It was just him wanting sex more and more, and he wanted it in positions I didn't think I could get into. That really did not signal anything to me, because I read that other people would do it in other positions and in places other than the bedroom. That did not faze me.''

As the pendulum of madness swung in a more violent direction, Riordan continued to go along with Jablonski's demands—even when he began hiding a gun under their bed. At times he used the weapon to coerce his mate into sex. Next came other kinky games that centered around Riordan being knocked unconscious, thus providing Jablonski with a limp subject upon whom he could perform any act unchallenged.

But even that was not enough to sate Jablonski's desires. Not long after moving out of his parents' home, Jablonski began staying out late at night. Riordan suspected he had taken a new lover, but there were hints that he was out raping women in the community. It seemed that Jablonski had evolved farther down the continuum of deviance, and had no intention of looking back.

"He'd be having sex with me and he'd be going out at night," Riordan said. "I wouldn't know where he'd be going. He'd say it was work."

Jablonski worked at a liquor store at the time, and one night an underaged girl came into the shop. No one knows for certain what occurred that night, but the event led to violence. Though the girl reported the incident to the police, in those days investigators were less understanding toward rape victims. They doubted the girl's account and warned her that she could be prosecuted for making false accusations. Despite the police's attitude, 17-year-old Noreen Mitchell stuck to her guns, telling San Bernardino County sheriff's detectives that Jablonski had lured her into a back room, then tried to take her clothes off.

The incident took place on Jan. 10, 1970. Mitchell said that she went into the store to make a phone call and talked briefly with the clerk after getting a busy signal. Jablonski invited her to make a second call in the back storage area. Once isolated at the far end of the store, Jablonski pulled out a silver and black handgun and pointed it at Mitchell's face, according to a sheriff's report of the event.

"You stole something and I want to search you," Jablonski told the teenager. "I want you to take all your clothes off."

Mitchell protested, telling Jablonski he could search her, but she was not getting naked. She denied taking anything from the store and pointed out that it would have made no sense for her to steal since he had been nice enough to let her use the telephone.

Jablonski moved toward the girl. He spun her around and made her place her hands on the wall while he remained behind her with the gun in his hand. He next tied her hands behind her back with a belt.

"You stole something and I am going to find out what it was," he promised.

He moved his hands over her body and yanked at her blouse, but suddenly his mood changed and the attack was over just as quickly as it had begun.

"I'm sorry," Jablonski said as the girl clutched her clothes. "Please don't tell anyone."

To appease the girl, Jablonski said she could take anything she wanted in the store, so long as she vowed to be silent. Mitchell told the investigators that she "got smart" and demanded a bottle of Ten High whiskey to buy her silence. Jablonski was eager to please. He tossed in a bottle of 7-Up as a chaser and let Mitchell walk out with a few packs of cigarettes to seal the deal.

Mitchell spilled the story to her brother as soon as she returned home. Minutes later a crew of friends were headed to the liquor store for some old-fashioned street justice.

"I don't like what you've done to my sister," Victor Mitchell said upon seeing Jablonski.

A brawl ensued with Jablonski getting the worst of it.

San Bernardino authorities, however, did not make any arrests. According to a report of the event, detectives found too many holes in the girl's story. They were not impressed with her willingness to take a lie detector test to prove her case. The investigation stalled and Jablonski was never prosecuted.

"He came home one night with a bloody nose and a black eye," Riordan recalled. "He said that this girl had come into the store and that she was young. He went to the back of the store and she ordered some liquor. She followed him into the storeroom and he told her he thought she was too young. He asked for some identification and grabbed for her purse."

Jablonski claimed the girl cried rape to get even with him

for questioning her age. He told Riordan that the girl's brothers returned to the store and beat him up. Riordan took Jablonski's side of the story, but today she believes otherwise.

"He had delusions and his rationalization was off," Riordan recalled. "It was always somebody else's fault. He tried to shift blame onto someone else. . . . I don't know what happened [in the liquor store] but I think he was capable of just about anything."

The bizarre behavior only increased once Jablonski moved Riordan and their young son into a new home in Fontana. In short order, stories spread about a girl being raped and left in the nearby desert in the spring of 1972. Riordan remembers the event well, because the local cops came to her house after the victim gave a good description of her attacker and the type of car he drove.

"The girl got our car down pat, [even] the stain on the front seat. She knew everything," Riordan said.

But Riordan covered for her husband, telling police he had been with her on the night of the desert assault.

"I should have said something then," Riordan admitted. "Maybe it would have stopped."

It didn't and the trouble continued at home and in the community, even after Riordan became pregnant for the second time. By now Jablonski was spending most of his time at his dog handling job, working for a Fontana company that specialized in training and delivering guard dogs. With his military training background, Jablonski fit right into the career. Riordan liked it as well, because the job gave him a way to unleash his aggression, especially when he donned a padded attack suit and worked out with the animals.

But even after Riordan gave birth to a daughter and they moved into a three-bedroom home, Jablonski never let up his strange ways. He became more irritable, tossing things at the television set, and heaving tools if he had trouble making repairs at home. He took his anger out on the dogs he kept as pets, by kicking the animals when they disobeyed him. He even left his infant daughter behind in a department store.

"She was just a couple of weeks old and I let him take her,"

Riordan said. "I did not think anything of it. But he forgot her. I went down to the Woolco store and did a lot of fast talking. I know I just beat the welfare system out of that state or I would have had my kids taken away."

But Riordan could not talk her way out of being an unwilling subject for Jablonski's sexual experimentation. It was common, she said, for him to pull at her clothes and bite her body hard, things she did not want to participate in. He liked intercourse hard and violent.

"It was like he was doing it with a vengeance," she said. "He liked to do it doggie-style, with the woman turned around so he could grab whatever he wanted. He was in control and he knew it, and he would do it just as hard as he could. . . . It was like he was getting back at somebody. It might have been his mother, 'cause from what I understand, she never tried to interfere when his father beat him, or she was afraid to. Back then, what could a woman do?"

Jablonski's lovemaking was devoid of romance, passion and tenderness. He wasn't into hugging or hand-holding. Inflicting pain gave him pleasure, provided he could dictate how much was delivered upon a subject. He also enjoyed receiving oral sex, Riordan said. Jablonski forced his needs upon his woman, no matter what her mood or physical condition. It was always Phil's way or no way at all.

"He was rough with everything," Riordan said. "I thought it was just that he didn't have any manners, didn't know how to do it. But he enjoyed it that way, and he didn't care where he was having it."

Foreplay was also not on Jablonski's list of activities.

"He wanted to get right at it," Riordan said. "It was just too much, all the time, rough. He had to have his satisfaction. When I didn't want to have sex, he would pry them [my legs] apart. He was strong enough to do it. If he wants to do it, it is done. It did not matter what I wanted. What he wanted was what he got. He was just so mean about it."

Over time, Riordan began to adapt her behavior to avoid making the violence worse. She learned how to fake unconsciousness by going limp whenever Jablonski put a pillow over her head or placed his hands on her throat to incapacitate her.

"It didn't seem like he was trying to kill me," she recalled. "It just seemed like he wanted to do it [with me] unconscious. I pretended that I was unconscious. I wanted to see what he was doing, and he'd just have his sex. I mean that way he could bite what he wanted to bite and I wouldn't be fighting him. It just seemed that he enjoyed doing it with a person who was unconscious. He'd go right at it and, oh, it was awful."

The only time the onslaught let up was when Riordan threatened to complain about his behavior to Jablonski's mother. Somehow the family matron, who seemed oblivious to her son's misdeeds, could rein him in.

"The only time I could get away was when someone else was over," Riordan said. "Of course, I could always tattle to his mother. His mother seemed to be a discipline thing in his life. If he did something I did not like, I'd tell his mother. She'd tell him, and he wouldn't do it."

Mrs. Jablonski claimed to have seen no trouble at all with the young couple, at least according to statements she gave police investigators following the 1978 Kimball murder.

"I never question any of them [children], always kept my nose out of their business," Mrs. Jablonski once said. "We never—you can ask any of the kids, if they had any problems they could talk to us. But we never stuck our nose in any of their affairs, in their home life."

As far as Mother Jablonski knew, Riordan was getting along just fine with her boy. Considering what kind of home life she had known, perhaps she had no reason to think otherwise.

"Oh, they didn't seem to get along too bad," Mrs. Jablonski once noted.

Life in the little hell Jablonski made for Riordan was getting intolerable by the fall of 1972. In their years together, she had given birth twice, all the while continuing to endure her husband's perverted sexual predilections. In addition to the pain he liked to inflict during intercourse, he also developed an interest in performing sex in public places, on the off chance that someone might come across the pair and enjoy the way Jablonski handled his woman.

"I remember he rolled over into a cactus and I was picking those little things out of his bottom," Riordan said of one escapade. "He fell off the side of a mountain once, too. He liked having it in weird places. I just think it was the idea of being caught."

Riordan had once enjoyed the excitement of being with a married man. When they first met, Jablonski was still legally married to Ludwig. But by 1972, the thrill was long gone and only the pain remained. Riordan, like Ludwig before her, eventually realized Jablonski was not going to change.

After more than three years of abuse, Riordan was tired of all the unpredictable behavior, including an odd form of torture she called "a swirly"—Jablonski would stick her head in the toilet as the circulating water flushed down.

Riordan had also become sick of his Vietnam stories, which included claims of winning the Congressional Medal of Honor. There was never any point in questioning Jablonski as to why these facts did not appear in the mental hospital records Riordan had once looked through. As usual, Jablonski had answers for everything.

"He says the reason there is no military record on his being in Vietnam is because his records are in Washington and the records are sealed," Riordan said. "And nobody can get a hold of them because the things that he did over there, they don't ever want anybody to know about and if the government thought that he was going to talk about it, they'd come and kill him."

Finally, one day Jablonski went too far. In keeping with his escalating pattern of sadomasochistic experimentation, Jablonski discovered bondage. In the late fall of 1972, Jablonski tied Riordan up, spread-eagled on the bed and went at her.

"He wanted to have sex in a different way and when he was through, he just left me tied up," Riordan said.

He added to the excitement by smothering her with a pillow to the point of unconsciousness.

"I was afraid for my kids," she recalled. "If he were to

actually smother me, my children would be left alone with him.''

On December 7, 1972, just days after the bondage humiliation, the situation came to a head while Riordan was cooking a hamburger for Jablonski in their kitchen. He had frequently complained about her cooking and often ignored her food, saying it was too greasy for his taste. Sometimes he would toss pots and pans about the house if the meal was especially not to his liking.

"He thought the hamburger was too greasy, so he picked up the pan and he threw it at me," Riordan said. "The pan missed, but I got a grease burn all the way down my arm. Well, I got angry and picked up the pan. I threw it back and I didn't miss. I knocked him out."

Fearful about what might happen when Jablonski recovered, Riordan called her mother in Michigan, and had her wire money to California. She collected her children and fled, taking a $48 taxi ride to the Los Angeles Airport, where she caught a plane. They arrived in Chicago at 3 a.m., with little more than the clothes on their backs. By the time the clan had returned to LaPeer, Jablonski had already called his in-laws and begged Riordan to return. Instead of sympathy, Jablonski got an earful from Riordan's mother, who refused to let her daughter speak to him.

"My mother said if he ever came here, she'd kill him," Riordan recalled.

Sometime later, Riordan spoke with Jablonski and told him that as a child living in the closed community of LaPeer, she had witnessed domestic abuse at home from an alcoholic father who battered her mother. Riordan saw history repeating itself with Jablonski and did not want to pass that same legacy on to her young children.

"I can't raise two kids that way," Riordan told Jablonski. "My mother and my dad, they stayed together. My dad is an alcoholic and he used to hit my mother. I can't go through that. My mother stood in and I thought she was stupid. I had to help my father to bed and he'd lay in his puke. I had to clean it up,

I saw it. I said that I was not going to hide it. I'd rather raise the kids alone.''

Jablonski crumbled, just as he had when he was a little boy after his mother left him alone.

"He cried," she said. "If he didn't get his way, he'd cry. It would not be sobbing, it would be tears. He said he wanted me to come back, but I told him the only way I'll come back is if you straighten yourself around and you start seeing a psychiatrist.''

Jablonski cried and complained that he could not handle things alone. For him, the house that had stood witness to the swirling, the bondage, the violence and the insanity crafted by his own uncontrollable need for sex, had become too empty.

"I told him, 'Well, you made it empty by the things you've done. You're the one. You've only yourself to blame,' " Riordan recalled. "For the longest time I took 100 percent of the blame.''

For the second time in three years Jablonski had seen a woman whom he once had under his total control grow wise and escape before losing her life.

"He could manipulate anybody," Riordan said. "He knows what he is doing, and you think he is just a straight person and that there is nothing wrong with him. And yet, he has this whole thing planned out.''

NINE
The Guard Dog

"You're so skinny, I could stifle you out in a minute."

Agnes Robbins was a slender, young blonde with a husband and two youngsters to care for as 1972 came to a close. She had recently moved into a suburban home near San Bernardino, California, and had begun to get acquainted with her new surroundings and her next-door neighbor, Dennis Seton, a 34-year-old air force sergeant. Robbins' husband, Charles, worked in Los Angeles and was often on the road at night, which left the 28-year-old young mother alone and feeling vulnerable after dark. Her fears increased when word spread that a stranger had been seen lurking in the neighborhood.

To assuage his wife's worries and calm his own mind, Charles Robbins bought a large German Shepherd guard dog to watch over his family. It seemed like a prudent move at the time, however, Robbins went to the security company that employed Phillip Carl Jablonski.

The dog Mr. Robbins purchased that winter was a disaster from the start. The stout four-legged sentry looked rough and tough at 125 pounds, but it had bad habits and often disobeyed commands. In short order, the beast had torn down the family's curtains, ripped open a screen door, and had happily accepted food from strangers. Mr. Robbins complained about the animal's behavior to the company's owner and planned to exchange the shepherd for a new one.

Jablonski had been to the Robbins' home on at least five

prior occasions to show them dogs. In all those visits, the animal handler behaved professionally. Mr. Robbins' had been present during those past encounters.

On the night of Dec. 17, 1972, Jablonski called and said it might take a few weeks to find a replacement animal for the rowdy German Shepherd. Mr. Robbins understood. He told the dog handler that he was leaving for work and that his wife would call later if they needed his services.

It had been 10 days since Ann Riordan had fled to her family in Michigan. Jablonski had no one to dominate, and the pressure built inside his sick mind. He had used violence by raping Riordan to deal with an earlier sense of abandonment after Ludwig fled from his grasp. It was time to find someone else to compensate for his renewed feelings of isolation.

One hour after learning that Mr. Robbins would be gone for the night, Jablonski changed into his security guard outfit. He strapped a .38-caliber, six-round Arminius pistol into his belt and placed a seven-inch long knife inside his 1960 Chevy station wagon. After pinning a plastic guard emblem to his tan permapress work shirt, and pulling a 12-point company cap onto his massive head, Jablonski drove away from his home to seek adventure.

He parked his car a short distance from the Robbins home and approached on foot. Agnes Robbins came to the door dressed in a red blouse. Her eight-month-old son was in the living room inside a playpen enjoying a bottle. Mrs. Robbins recognized the dog handler and asked him inside for a cup of coffee. She went over their complaints about the dog's behavior, while Jablonski noted the problems on a pad.

Jablonski assured her that he could handle the situation. He told Mrs. Robbins to remove the animal from the house and tie it to a tree in the backyard so he could watch how the dog responded to commands. While Mrs. Robbins fished around her garage for a dog leash, Jablonski remained seated on the living room couch. The location offered an inviting view of Mrs. Robbins bedroom.

After securing the guard dog to the tree, Mrs. Robbins came back into the living room and followed Jablonski's recommendation to watch the chained animal from her bedroom window while he went outside to discipline the canine. Just a few moments later she heard Jablonski moving around her living room. The coffee cup was gone from his hand and in its place was a knife. He put the cold steel to her throat and brought her into the bedroom.

"You're so skinny, I could stifle you out in one minute," he said after placing a hand on her slender neck.

Shaking and sobbing with fear, Mrs. Robbins complied with his demands that she disrobe quickly. She pulled off her outfit, while Jablonski did the same with his security uniform, all the while babbling about how his girlfriend had just left him days before.

"Shut up! Don't cry, don't do nothing," Jablonski ordered as he cracked the butt of the knife into Mrs. Robbins' face, shattering her left eye socket.

He pulled off her head scarf and shoved it into her mouth to muffle her cries before tossing her on the bed and placing his naked body on top of her trembling one.

"I'm going to get you pregnant," he said. "Am I as good as your husband? Was your husband the first one?"

Jablonski had trouble maintaining an erection and pawed at his own privates to get hard. He flipped the young woman over to enter her from behind.

"Charles didn't work last night," he told Mrs. Robbins, indicating that he had spied on them the night before.

Upon hearing her son's cries from the living room, Mrs. Robbins told her attacker that she needed to take care of the baby before the neighbors heard the infant's wails and became alarmed. Jablonski followed her into the living room, keeping his knife ready in case she made a bolt for freedom. He watched her place the infant in a back bedroom, then motioned for her to return to the master bedroom so he could finish what he had started.

As Jablonski went about his business, he continued to talk to his victim, telling her that he had two guns and would kill her children if she put up a fight. The second attack, however, was interrupted by the loud barks of the chained guard dog.

Though frozen with fear, Mrs. Robbins had enough sense to convince Jablonski that she needed to quiet the dog before her neighbor investigated. He let her up, but warned that if she did not return, he'd slaughter her family long before she had the chance to call the police.

Once outside, Mrs. Robbins untied the dog and hopped a fence, running for Dennis Seton's front door where she pounded away until help arrived. In a hysterical state, the naked woman rambled about a stranger, a rape and the murder of her children, while Seton raced for his bedroom drawer where a loaded .38 lay waiting.

Seton approached his neighbor's front door from a blind side and heard some movement from inside the residence. When he heard the Robbins' front door swing open, he kept out of sight and waited for the enemy to move into the clear. Jablonski appeared a second later. He was naked to the waist and in his arms he held a shirt and his shoes.

"I told him to halt and not to move," Seton said as he leveled the .38 toward the imposing stranger. "I said, 'If you drop those shoes, I'll drop you.'"

Jablonski made a quick move, but Seton was faster and fired off a round toward the ground near the intruder's feet.

"He got real scared and tense and I said that I would blow his head off. I told him to listen to me," Seton said.

Though he had received some combat training in the air force, Seton said he was working on a mixture of adrenaline and the scenes of arrests he had seen in television shows and movies.

"I just reacted," he said.

Jablonski quickly had his hands on top of his head and was squatting Indian-style in the driveway. Seton stayed 10 feet away. Mrs. Seton stood ready at the front door of her home, armed with a rifle also pointed in Jablonski's direction.

"I had just come back from Vietnam and had been to Southeast Asia on two or three other tours," Seton recalled. "At the time, I did not have a lot of fear or anxiety. That came on later when I thought about how I could have been killed. But at that moment, I did not recognize the anxiety. I only recognized that it was a cold night and it seemed to take forever for the police to arrive. I remember my wife was by the door, dressed in a bathrobe and armed with our .22 rifle. She kept telling me to keep an eye on him.''

As Jablonski waited for the law to arrive, he stared off into space, mumbling about how he was sick and needed help. Minutes later, two squad cars raced through the neighborhood, while a police helicopter shined a bright light upon the scene from high above.

Four cops jumped from the car and ran toward Jablonski. One held a shotgun in his outstretched hands. One of the cops placed his foot in Jablonski's back, sending him face first toward the pavement. ''I must need help,'' Jablonski muttered after being handcuffed. ''I don't know what's wrong with me.''

A search of the home turned up Jablonski's revolver, his cap, and guard emblem from inside Mrs. Robbins' bedroom. The knife was found resting between Jablonski's legs.

''I was just glad it was over,'' Seton said. ''We went back inside my house to give the officers our statement and they took Agnes to the hospital.''

Twenty-four hours later, Jablonski was seated inside a Riverside County Jail interview room with Detective L. Venable, who hoped to nail the case shut with a confession.

''Every story has two sides,'' Venable told Jablonski. ''I want to hear your side of it.''

Jablonski was only 26, but he knew the ropes of police interrogations from his past trouble in Ft. Bliss. It was time to lean on the mental health crutch he had clung to years ago. The psycho angle had helped him avoid the stockade once, maybe it would help again.

''I had too many problems that built up, that is what led me to it. I've been trying to get medicine for my nerves. This is what my problem is, my nerves,'' he began before asking the detective what kind of penalty he could face since this was his first offense. He told Venable that Riordan had just left him and that he did not have the money to afford the necessary medicine to quiet his unsteady mind.

''I was living with this woman, really a great woman,''

Jablonski said. "She put up with me for years and I was trying to get my divorce and the lawyers just kept putting it out of court 'cause I didn't have the money to pay 'em," Jablonski said. "This built up, and I've been paying bills, trying to pay the lawyer and trying to pay off my car and trying to pay for the house . . . everything blowin' up."

He told the cops that Riordan's parents had "poisoned" her against him, but that he was going to recapture her love. He said he had earned a Purple Heart and a Bronze Star while serving in Vietnam. The lies continued as he blamed Mrs. Robbins for the attack, claiming she had wanted him all along.

"I've been over their house five or six times with her alone," Jablonski said. "On this night we had a couple cups of coffee and talked about dogs and figured out a way we could do the obedience work without too much money. I guess I just took it that she was leading me on. She kept walking by me real close and asking me this and calling me over to show me the curtains and getting close to me and stuff like that."

When questioned if he asked the woman for sex, Jablonski cut off his narrative and said, "No comment." He denied putting the knife to her throat, but admitted pointing it at the woman.

"I don't know what I was doing at the time," Jablonski said. "Everything was blanked out for me and I just wasn't myself. I figure that under [a] doctor's care and supervision, that it would never happen again."

Months later, Dennis Seton sat outside a Riverside County courtroom waiting to testify against the man he had captured. He figured it was an uncomplicated case that would land the rapist in jail for many years. Instead, the case ended in a plea bargain that sent Jablonski off to prison for four years. In the ensuing time, Mrs. Robbins' marriage collapsed. According to Seton, Mr. Robbins became pained by guilt and suspicion. He felt bad for having purchased the dog and bringing Jablonski into his home. He also held suspicions that his wife had somehow encouraged the rapist.

"The thing that has stayed with me all these years is the tragedy of rape," Seton said of the nightmare he interrupted.

"I think about all the people it has affected. At the time, no one talked to Mr. Robbins except us. He had this beautiful wife and two kids and he thought she was freelancing. There was no education. People did not understand then that this was a crime of opportunity and control."

TEN

Sandra

"Well Sandra, you're alone with the crazy now."

Boredom, inactivity and repetition are the realities of life behind bars and inmates occupy their time in various ways to keep from going insane. Some work out, others read and others take to writing.

Jablonski discovered that letter writing served as an outlet for his building frustrations. While he might not be able to escape from prison, he discovered that a few words scribbled on note paper could affect the lives of family members and even strangers.

In the early stages of his confinement, Jablonski targeted Riordan with hate mail, telling his estranged girlfriend that he had friends inside and outside the prison who could punish her for deserting him.

"He said that I'd be surprised at what he could do while he was still in prison," Riordan recalled of the letters Jablonski sent to her home. "It left me with the idea that he could have people come here and harm the kids or me, or take the kids away where I couldn't see them."

For a brief time, Riordan wrote back and sent Jablonski pictures of their kids.

But as his letters grew more ominous, her replies were less frequent. Eventually, Riordan stopped corresponding altogether. Jablonski finally gave up on her, not necessarily because he had surrendered his dominance, but because he had found a new means to deal with his stress and fantasies. Not long after arriving in state prison, Jablonski learned about a prison pen pal association that offered help to incarcerated men by giving them the chance to pass their time with friendship letters. Most of the organizations had a religious twist—the writers from the outside would try to counsel the inmate into accepting the Lord into their lives.

On paper, the pen pal groups sounded inspiring and there is no doubt that many people benefited from the experience. But Phillip Jablonski was an inmate of a very different stripe. While free on the outside, he could talk a fine game, telling his family that he had found religion inside prison; in truth, Jablonski had used the pen pal organizations to reach unsuspecting women, whom he could lie to by filling his letters with fantasies about his war record, his wrongful conviction and a desire to dedicate his life to Jesus Christ.

As a free man, Jablonski had always found a sympathetic female. He had the skill to mesmerize and draw them into his circle of violence. In prison he found an even larger sphere of influence, courtesy of the brochures that sought out inmates interested in corresponding with religious women from across the country.

There have always been women who are drawn to dangerous men. Serial killers like Ted Bundy, Richard Ramirez and Kenneth Bianchi received countless letters from interested females after their arrests. Why these women find dangerous inmates attractive remains unclear. Some are pulled by the excitement of being in precarious situations, others flock to the warped celebrity often attached to notorious killers, and a few believe they can change the person by their friendship.

Carol Spadoni certainly began her pen pal relationship with Jablonski with altruistic notions. But the power that pulls women toward dangerous men is hardly limited to the pure at heart, according to Robert Morse, the San Mateo County District Attorney's investigator. Before moving up the ranks to become a detective, Morse worked as a sergeant in county jails and saw firsthand the power inmates have over females.

"It is absolutely amazing," he said. "You will see these

ladies come in and take their clothes off for these guys and start masturbating themselves. The visitors will do this for guys they have just met. It is the weirdest stuff you have ever seen.''

The sexual phenomenon is not limited to the inside of jails. It is not uncommon for women to flash prison inmates from outside jailhouse walls.

Jablonski was never fortunate enough to have naked women parade before his cell.

Sandra Norbert was one of the first to discover that Jablonski's written words were not his bond. A deeply religious person, Norbert hoped to spread faith to prison inmates after members of her church group in Indiana joined a prison correspondence group to share the gospel with those trapped behind bars. The idea of spreading God's grace with inmates had germinated in her mind for years after friends at a Bible study group discussed the idea in 1970. By 1973, Norbert had come across a few brochures and picked six names at random. The documents did not contain the inmates' pictures, nor describe the crimes for which they had been convicted. They only contained the subject's name, age, address and prison number.

Jablonski's name jumped right out, Norbert said. Being a good Catholic, she thought his name sounded Polish, and since many Poles are also Catholic, she reasoned he was as good as any other to begin her letter-writing career.

She began writing Jablonski a year before his parole in 1976. Their letters were not intimate and focused on religious prose. Norbert instructed her pen pal about the Good Book and discussed the meaning of certain Bible verses. Jablonski appeared receptive. He wrote her every other day, while she tried to drop him a note each week.

''The first were introductory letters. Like who he is, and how many members [are] in his family and that sort of thing,'' Norbert said. ''. . . They were about religion, about psychology.''

Though Jablonski's letters to other pen pals were often laced with profane comments, he walked a G-rated path in the notes sent to Norbert.

''Phil impressed me in the sense he never talked to me about sex,'' Norbert said. ''He never said anything such as curse words. I got the impression he was a very clean-minded individual.''

Jablonski opened up about his rape conviction, but misled her about the facts, claiming he had attacked the woman on impulse after she had paraded around her home in a bikini. To influence her, he sent Norbert transcripts from his court case.

''He said he was sorry it happened, and that he did not know what came over him,'' Norbert said. ''He said it was the stupidest thing he'd ever done. I was a lot younger then and I was a sheltered person. I thought that a lot of people did things in life and then said that it was stupid. Maybe there was a chance this guy just did a stupid thing, you know?

''He was not saying he was innocent, but he was saying more or less that he was not a criminal,'' Norbert said. ''He said it was more like he was led into it. Well, I did not buy that, but on the other hand, I can see where somebody might do something stupid.''

Court records painted a different picture of the convicted rapist. According to an analysis done in 1973 by Dr. E. Rivlin, a psychologist from the California Department of Corrections, Jablonski demonstrated childish behavior and projected his difficulties on female victims. Rivlin noted that the rape victim represented females in general for Jablonski, especially those who had rejected him in the past.

Rivlin found that the 1972 rape was not done for sexual gratification, but occurred because Jablonski was filled with rage and hostility over Riordan's departure from his life. The attack was carried out to degrade women, Rivlin found, before concluding that Jablonski was consumed by his hostility and certainly dangerous.

But by 1975, Jablonski was inside a state prison and allowed to review pen pal applications and reach out to unsuspecting women. A creature of habit, Jablonski was now traveling upon very familiar ground. In the past, he had used words and glances to attract women; now his letters had grabbed Norbert's interest, and as their correspondence evolved, Jablonski continued to bait the trap with lies about his past and pledges for the future.

Jablonski told Norbert he was Catholic. He claimed to have drifted from the fold, which gave her the opening she needed to guide him back to the loving arms of her Savior.

"I was trying to convince him to go back to the church," she said. "That was two-thirds of his problem, that he didn't have God in his life."

Jablonski's letters also referred to a military career that he said included Green Beret training in Vietnam. By now the war stories had taken on a new spin, with Jablonski telling his pen pal that his combat years had been vicious. By one account she later told investigators, Jablonski claimed to have invaded Vietnamese villages with other warriors. The specially trained troops, he claimed, raped and strangled native women to show the villagers that American forces were more powerful than the Viet Cong.

Jablonski claimed, according to Norbert, that after he got out of the service he was brought back to the United States and "thrown into the streets" without benefit of deprogramming. He offered this yarn as a way of explaining his past difficulties with women. The stories could not have reached a more understanding ear.

"I was young and I was against the war in Vietnam," Norbert said. "I was very sympathetic to people who told me all these atrocious things that they were forced to do in Vietnam."

After his release from prison in 1976, Jablonski telephoned Norbert and shared stories from his boyhood. He gave details about the domestic abuse he witnessed as a child, and made it clear that his father had tortured his mother.

"He said that when he was a little boy his mother suffered so much," Norbert recalled. "I remember he said that he could hear his mother screaming and crying. . . . He said he used to cry because he could not stop it."

Jablonski became very interested in Norbert and hoped to meet her in the flesh. They had to get together, he kept insisting, which meant either she had to travel to Joshua Tree, California where he lived with his parents, or he would have to visit her in the Midwest.

"This was a bad situation I was in," Norbert said. "It was almost like this guy was under some kind of compulsion."

Norbert was reluctant to meet her pen pal at first, but she figured it would be un-Christian to lead this apparently devoted soul to the brink of rebirth, then abandon him at the altar. She had no intention of meeting him on her turf. After speaking with Jablonski's mother on the telephone, Norbert was convinced that the trip would be a great adventure. Mrs. Jablonski assured Norbert that she would be welcomed in her home. She said that her son had really changed under Norbert's guidance.

"He talks different now," Mrs. Jablonski said. "He talks about your letters and some of the stuff about God you're talking to him about. He discusses it with us and we can see that you're making a change in him, by really pounding at this."

"She told me that he would get the Bible out and would compare what I said to what was in there," Norbert said. "And he would even ask her to read the letter I sent, ask her what she thought and they would go over the Bible together. She told me she had never remembered ever seeing Phil read the Bible before, and that I was making an impression, which encouraged me tremendously."

Assured that the family would keep Phillip on his best behavior and faced with a free trip to California, Norbert accepted Mrs. Jablonski's offer to visit their Joshua Tree home in March of 1977. Before departing Indiana, Norbert spoke with Jablonski and made it clear that she was coming out only to advise him on spiritual matters. She had just broken up with a man and had no intention of turning this trip into some kind of romance.

"I told him that his being in prison for rape worried me," Norbert said. "I was not coming there for sex. I wanted it very clear. I didn't want him to think I was misleading him."

Jablonski agreed, making it clear he only wanted to meet the woman who had so changed his life.

"He wasn't the kind of guy who promised you the moon," Norbert said. "He didn't promise you anything. It was just

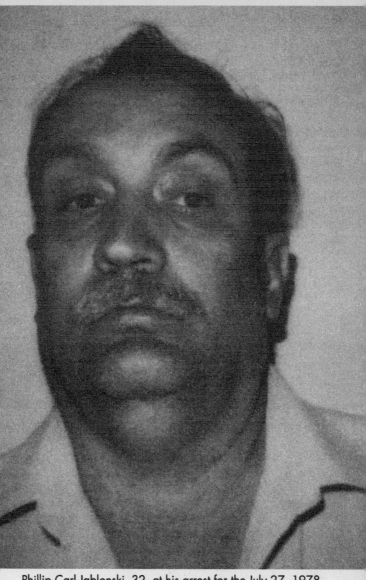

Phillip Carl Jablonski, 32, at his arrest for the July 27, 1978 murder of his common-law wife Linda Kimball. *(Courtesy of Palm Springs, California Police Department)*

Jablonski at San Quentin while serving a 7-year term
for second degree murder during the mid-1980s.
(*Author collection*)

Carol Spadoni picked Jablonski's name from a 1980 church list of incarcerated men looking for pen pals. (*Courtesy of Burlingame, California Police Department*)

Eva Peterson (right) and her daughter Carol Spadoni. (*Courtesy of Burlingame, California Police Department*)

Carol Spadoni on a visit to Jablonski while he was in prison. (*Courtesy of Burlingame, California Police Department*)

Former home of Carol Spadoni and Eva Peterson. (*Courtesy of Burlingame, California Police Department*)

Eva Peterson's body was found amid the boxes of mail-order clothing that filled her house and garage. (Courtesy of Burlingame, California Police Department)

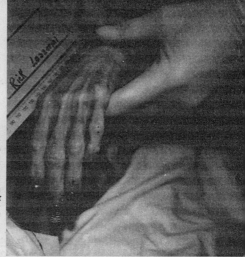

Carol Spadoni's anorexic left hand had an American flag painted on the middle fingernail. (Courtesy of Burlingame, California Police Department)

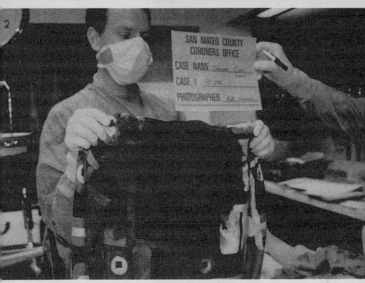

The bloodied clothing Carol Spadoni was wearing on the day she was killed.
(Courtesy of Burlingame, California Police Department)

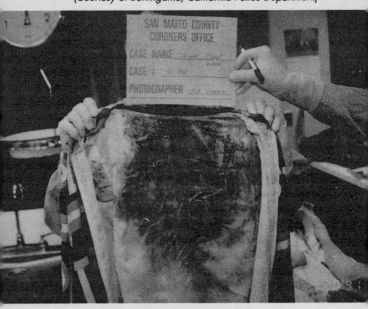

Margie S. Rogers, 58.
(*Courtesy of the family of Margie S. Rogers*)

Jablonski killed Margie Rogers in Rogers' Roost, the convenience store she owned and operated with her husband.
(*Courtesy of Burlingame, California Police Department*)

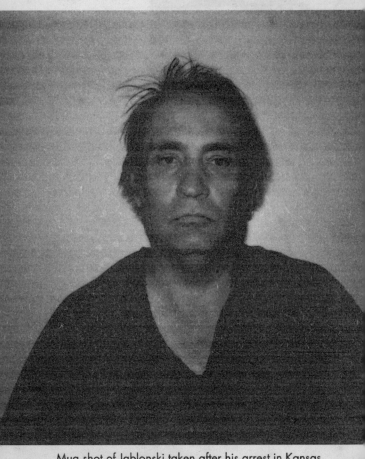

Mug shot of Jablonski taken after his arrest in Kansas
on April 28, 1991.
(Courtesy of Burlingame, California Police Department)

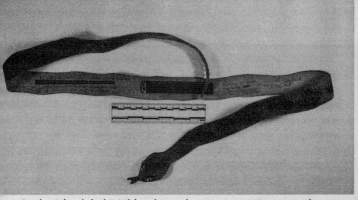

Snake "death belt" Jablonski made in prison. Written inside are the death dates and names of the women he killed and the names of the female pen pals he intended to kill. (Courtesy of Joanne Del Bene, San Mateo County Sheriff's Office)

The .22 caliber gun Jablonski used to shoot his victims. (Courtesy of Burlingame, California Police Department)

Phillip Carl Jablonski at his 1994 trial for the murders of
Carol Spadoni and Eva Peterson.   (*Courtesy of John Green*)

Defense attorney Richard Keyes. *(Courtesy of John Green)*

San Mateo County, California prosecutor Martin Murray.
(Courtesy of John Green)

Burlingame, California police sergeant Eric Haseleu.
(*Courtesy of Eric Haseleu*)

like, 'You really helped me and I'm really mesmerized by the kind of person you are and I've got to meet you.' ''

The stage was set for Norbert's first visit to California. When she arrived in Los Angeles, Jablonski, his youngest sister Nettie, and her husband were there to greet her.

"I'll never forget, Nettie made the comment to me," Norbert said. "She said, 'Well, Sandra, you're alone with the crazy now.' ''

At the time, Norbert did not know what to make of the strange statement. She was nervous enough about heading west to meet a family of strangers.

"I thought, is she giving me a hint or is she just joking?" Norbert said. "So I got in the car and we conversed. I was just talking to him [Jablonski] and we got to his mama's house without any incident."

But the ride toward Palm Springs and Joshua Tree had been unusual. For most of the three-hour trip Jablonski, stared out the car window, as if he did not notice Norbert, or had no idea who she was. Norbert was not sure how to react to his indifference. At first, she thought he was a deep thinker, transfixed by a heavy notion. She also feared he was disappointed in a woman he had come to know on paper.

Jablonski sat hunched for most of the road trip, barely responding to the questions Norbert asked.

After a shopping tour in Palm Springs, the group headed toward Joshua Tree and pulled up before the family's two-bedroom home where Norbert met Jablonski's parents. Despite the horror stories she had heard about the family's home life, Norbert considered Mrs. Jablonski a dear woman. But any thoughts of lasting peace with her new friends ended that first evening, when Phillip Jablonski cornered her in a bathroom. He kissed Norbert, then put a big hand over her mouth and nose until she struggled for air. He did not release his grip and Norbert feared he'd smother her.

"I was kind of mumbling and trying to catch my breath," she said. "And then he started laughing like it was a joke. I did not think it was very funny."

On the first night of her stay, Norbert slept alone in the

family's spare bedroom while Jablonski bedded down on the living room couch. The next morning, Mrs. Jablonski discussed traveling away from the home on errands, while her son said he'd keep Norbert company. After Norbert objected to the idea, telling Mrs. Jablonski that she did not want to be alone with Phillip, they all went sightseeing and visited several parks. While traveling inside the Joshua Tree National Park, the family pulled off near a rest area where Phillip related a tragic story about a six-year-old girl, who had disappeared near the site and had never been found.

It was a somber thought, but Jablonski found the whole tragedy quite funny.

"He started chuckling when he said that no one had seen anybody," Norbert recalled. "I said to myself, 'Why are you chuckling?' His mom and dad and I are talking about how sorry we feel for that family and he thinks that's funny. In my mind I was saying that this guy is sick."

Despite the warning signs Norbert did not want to be rude to her hosts. She was afraid of offending Jablonski's parents, whom she felt had treated her very well by paying for her visit to California. Her trip was almost over anyway, so there seemed no reason to spoil it by running away.

After they'd all turned in for the night, Jablonski got up from the couch and went into the guest bedroom. He awakened Norbert with a brisk shake and demanded sex. Norbert tried to be logical, telling Jablonski that she was not on the Pill and feared becoming pregnant. She warned that his parents were asleep only a few feet away in the next room.

"He was explaining that he was in love with me and all this stuff," Norbert said. "He said he'd be happy if I just let him tie me up. I thought I was dealing with a nut and I know it is stupid if I let him tie me up. I [thought] there was no doubt he was going to rape me, but I can live through that."

Norbert did not cry out for help, because she feared causing a scene, she told investigators. She was also afraid that any outburst might cause Jablonski to lash out and kill her in an effort to silence her protest.

"I did not know how nuts he was," she said. "He is liable

to kill me. He's liable to kill all of us. Who knows how nuts this guy is? So I halfway must have consented.''

Jablonski lured her into his game with a combination of fear, dominance and assurance that he wasn't going to tie her up real tight, or use any kind of restraint she could not escape from, and that he would not demand sex.

He fetched some string and demonstrated how fragile the line was.

"See, you could break that if you wanted to," he assured her. "I just want to tie your hands and feet."

Panicked, Norbert calculated her options.

"I was thinking, if that will do, then what can that hurt?" she said. "His parents are in the next room. He said he would leave me alone if I played this little game. I believed him and I also thought the string didn't look hard to break."

Jablonski wound the thread around her legs and secured them to the bed. He pulled her arms behind her head and fastened them before leaving the room. When he returned, Norbert noticed there was something in his hand.

"There was a ray of light coming into the bedroom from somewhere, I think from an outside lamppost and I seen the shiny thing," Norbert recalled. "I remembered saying, 'What are you doing?' And he said, 'It's a razor, I'm going to shave you.' That was the most terrifying thing, to see that light making that blade shine. I was laying there thinking, I can scream, but I don't know if they [Mr. and Mrs. Jablonski] will come to my rescue. And if I scream, this could trigger this nut off, and to shut me up, he'll cut my throat.

"I was in absolute fear of my life. The only thing I was thinking was, I don't think he is going to kill me unless he is totally nuts because he's going to have to explain the blood on the bed and everything."

She remained silent and accepted Jablonski's will.

"Phil, your mom and dad are in the other room," she told him. "If you cut me when you're shaving me, nick me or something, we're going to get blood on the bed and I'm a guest in your house. What is your mom going to think?"

But Jablonski was in his own world now, playing out a fantasy.

"I'll be careful. I won't cut you," he said and moved closer.

Norbert feared that her frightened commentary might put thoughts of blood into Jablonski's excited mind, so again she remained still as he pulled her nightgown above her waist and shaved the area clean without spilling a drop of Norbert's blood.

As Norbert lay spread across the bed, Jablonski left and then returned with a Polaroid camera and fired away. As the picture slowly developed, he moved closer to his victim and pulled a pillow from beneath her head, placed it across her face and applied pressure, pushing so hard that Norbert could not breathe or scream for help.

"I was trying to move and wriggle as best I could," Norbert said. "And finally it crossed my mind that this was a game. So if I acted like he won, maybe the game would end."

She went limp, hoping that her play-acting would stop Jablonski. He continued to lean into the pillow with the full force of his body for a few more seconds, before he ripped the pillow aside and walked out of the room.

"I was so terrified that night [that] I can't describe it," she said. "It was like I was in God's hands. It was like if I die, I'm meant to die. That was the attitude I took."

Norbert remained motionless in the bed for several minutes, fearing that any movement might alert Jablonski and bring him back into the room.

"I was shaking so bad from head to toe," Norbert said. "My teeth were chattering . . . and I could not stop. I thought that he was going to hear my teeth chattering and come back."

But Jablonski did not returned that night. The next morning. Norbert found the Polaroid picture on a shelf in the bedroom and tore it to pieces. She was now ready to bid farewell to this hellish trip west.

"I got up, got dressed and thought, 'I'm out of here today,' " she said.

But as other women had already found out, leaving Jablonski was never an easy task. Jablonski begged her to remain, again saying he was too attached to her to say goodbye so suddenly.

Norbert kept silent about the nocturnal attack, again fearing she would upset her hosts.

"I couldn't think of a reason to go because I didn't want to insult his mother," she said. "I was brought up with extremely good manners. You do not go into someone's house and then insult them. I thought, if I leave abruptly without any reason, she's gonna think I didn't like her house, that they were not hospitable enough."

Norbert fabricated an excuse after calling home and learning from her daughter that there had been a minor fire in her basement. Though the blaze had caused no real damage, she played the story up while on the phone, giving the impression that almost her entire neighborhood had gone up in flames.

"I told Mrs. Jablonski that I was very sorry but I was gonna have to go that day because I was very worried about the kids and the house," she said.

Jablonski came into the bedroom while Norbert packed her clothes and explained his latest desire.

"He told me he had dug a grave for me and that he was going to kill me on the way to the airport. He said that the pain he feels losing a woman is more than he can handle," Norbert recalled. "I said, 'If you kill somebody, you've lost them right?' He said that [his way] nobody else can have them. He knows then that they're in that grave and they belong to him."

Jablonski said he planned to strangle Norbert with her own hair so the police could never find a weapon. Before leaving the house, Norbert cornered Mrs. Jablonski and warned that she'd call the sheriff if the family let their son take her to the airport alone.

The nightmare in Joshua Tree had come to an end and Norbert flew back to Indiana without breathing a word of her brush with rape and death. Before leaving Jablonski, Norbert promised to keep silent and not tell her story to the police. She even vowed to return to him in a few weeks after taking care of the fire back home.

"I was definitely putting an act on that I thought he was a nice guy, that I liked him, and [saying] he could have a good future if he'd get himself straightened out," Norbert said. "I was talking real heart to the guy. I did not at any time let him know how I felt about him."

Jablonski left his parents' home four months later and moved to Palm Springs, where he took up with yet another woman.

ELEVEN

Linda

"Phil needs help. I can't tell you anymore."

While Jablonski wooed Norbert with letters and promises, he also was ensnaring another lady he had encountered following his release from state prison. Like other women in Jablonski's past, Linda Kimball had seen the rough side of life by the time she crossed his path in the spring of 1977. When she met Jablonski at a Junior Chamber of Commerce gathering in Yucca Valley, Kimball had been near the end of a bad marriage.

Jablonski would later say that he fell in lust with Linda from the moment they first met. He would also claim she had a thing for him. They got close during a Chamber dance, where Jablonski said he won her with sweet talk. He told her that his kisses were sweeter than wine and that he knew how to treat a lady right.

"I walked her off the dance floor and whispered, 'If I had the chance, you wouldn't be in that dress long'," Jablonski recalled.

Their affair started days later when Jablonski stopped by Linda's home and swept her in his arms. Kimball left her husband after becoming pregnant with Jablonski's child and in August 1977, the pair moved into a nice two-bedroom apartment in Palm Springs, less than one mile from the city's police department. They occupied a corner apartment well off the street and filled their nest with secondhand furniture and throw rugs.

On the outside, they looked like a struggling young couple full of promise and hope with a new child due before the end of the year.

"He seemed to have no trouble getting himself involved with women who let him do the things he wanted to do," Murray, the deputy district attorney, said. "Rose Ludwig escaped from him, but not until a doctor told her to get away. Ann Riordan busted out after a few years. Linda Kimball chose to stay, and while we don't know what went on between them, we can only assume what it was like since we know he tried to hurt every woman he met."

During the early part of his life with Kimball, Jablonski appeared to be on good behavior. He held down a job, went to school and appeared to be leading a normal life.

"He seemed to be doing OK," Murray said. "Maybe his joining the Junior Chamber of Commerce was an attempt at normalcy."

Jablonski added to the image of normalcy by taking welding classes at the College of the Desert, but his skills were poor and his body was soon covered with burns. He also served as a maintenance man for the city of Desert Hot Springs while Kimball worked for a jewelry store.

Her co-workers recall her as a slightly plump 29-year-old who was outgoing and loving to her daughter. She had gained weight after the birth of her child and seemed determined to slim down for an upcoming high school reunion. The birth of this Jablonski baby, a girl born on Dec. 9, 1977, had no affect on his deviant behavior toward women. It may have heightened his anger and brought on worse acts. Court documents suggest Jablonski felt neglected by his wife who diverted attention to the newborn. His bad feelings evolved into jealousy and resentment.

Neighbors inside the apartment complex grew suspicious of the young couple. Most remembered Jablonski not because he towered over the rest of the tenants, but because he lurked about the area and paid unusual attention to the other women living there.

One neighbor, Meagan Sheehan, told police that Jablonski often walked into her apartment uninvited and warned her how dangerous it was to leave her doors unlocked. He told her that a "mad killer" was in the area and that the criminal often attacked mothers and their children.

At age 32, Jablonski was firmly set in his ways. Though he might blame his violent proclivities on war scenes that had never really occurred, or on indignation toward the government for failing to treat his damaged mind, he was still a man determined to cause destruction.

The warning signs surfaced following the birth of his daughter. Money ran low, stress levels ran high, and Jablonski began acting strange while in the presence of Kimball's mother, Norma Fane, who recalled that he liked to brush up against her and rub his hands against her body.

Two other neighbors, Mr. and Mrs. Daniel Fleming, recalled Jablonski had his daughter christened and that at first, he seemed like a quiet, shy man. During gab sessions over coffee with Kimball, Mrs. Fleming said her neighbor complained about Jablonski, saying his erratic work life strained the family's finances. To Mr. Fleming, Kimball seemed like a pushy woman making overbearing demands of her man. But other neighbors in the small complex saw a different side of Jablonski and kept far away whenever he came near.

Claire Morton, a 28-year-old cocktail waitress living across the courtyard from Jablonski, always felt nervous around him. She said he came into her apartment one day, grabbed her and pulled her close for a passionate kiss. She was repulsed by his behavior, but brushed it off as a rude pass, not uncommon to the ones that came as an occupational hazard with her job at a local hotel.

Gail Fletcher, who lived right next door to the couple, became friends with Kimball. She said Jablonski had no respect for his common-law wife. He tended to pay more attention to other women than he did to the mother of his child, frequently by complimenting strangers, while ignoring the woman he lived with.

Ronald Fletcher had a special dislike for Jablonski. He told police that he saw his neighbor traveling in and out of all the apartments in the complex as he visited with the single women who had moved in. He said Jablonski even pestered Mrs. Fletcher while he was away from the apartment.

In the summer of 1978, someone placed two obscene phone calls to Mrs. Fletcher and warned the 26-year-old housewife, "I'm going to make you suck my dick, and I'm going to rape you and your children."

The Fletchers never found out who made the calls.

Norma Fane had also received crank calls in the spring of that year. At first, the caller breathed into the phone before disconnecting. Fane recalled that it sounded as if the caller had something stuffed in his mouth. From March to April she received between 10 and 12 obscene messages from the mystery caller before having her number changed and removed from the public listings. The calls began anew in early April and this time the voice made threats.

"I am going to rape you," the voice mumbled during a 6:30 a.m. call.

Fane described the voice as one that, in her opinion, belonged to a 30-year-old man. She said that she could not recognize the voice, but told police that only a few people had her new telephone number. Kimball was one of those people, which meant Jablonski knew it as well. By mid-April, Fane suspected that Jablonski was behind the harassment, but she told police that she did not want any protection.

July 6, 1978 had been hot enough in Palm Springs for Fane to leave the air conditioner on all day. To ventilate her home that night, she left a sliding screen door open before going to bed. Her slumber was interrupted at about 1 a.m. when Jablonski entered through the open door and silently stepped into her bedroom. His presence disturbed her sleep and when she awoke she found a large form standing above her bed. Before she could cry out, Jablonski placed a hand over her face and moved an ice pick to her throat. "Be quiet or I'll kill you," he said.

Fane recognized the voice and tried to put an end to the frightening scene.

"What do you want, Phil?" she asked.

"I want you. All I want to do is hug you," he replied.

Fane talked to her daughter's lover to calm him down. Her soothing words convinced him to get off her bed and move away from her toward the bedroom's window.

"Do you want to call the cops?" he asked. "Do you want to call Linda?"

Fane was not sure what to do, so she told Jablonski she would do nothing as long as he left. Instead, he grabbed her and started to drag her off, but Fane escaped his grasp, ran out the door and drove off to safety. Fane later called her daughter, telling her that a stranger had tried to rape her. By the time the call came to Kimball's home, Jablonski had returned to his girlfriend's side. He was shocked by the news and quickly returned to Fane's home with Kimball to search for the mystery rapist.

"She does not know why she did this charade," Murray said of Fane. "She was not sure that she wanted the police involved since this guy was the father of her grandchild."

According to Murray, Fane and Kimball's relationship had been stormy in the past. Of late, mother and daughter had moved closer together and Fane did not want to do anything to ruin that reconciliation. Still, she could not keep silent about what had occurred that night, and while Jablonski and a neighbor went off to search for the unknown attacker, Fane told Kimball the truth. But again, she took a conservative step and instead of having Jablonski arrested, arranged for him to meet with a psychiatrist.

Jablonski was interviewed at the Pettis Memorial Veteran's Hospital in Loma Linda the next day. A staff psychiatrist, who was told of the previous rape attempt on Fane, advised against filing criminal charges. It was the doctor's opinion that Jablonski could be treated as an out-patient with medication. Nevertheless, Kimball packed up, left their apartment with her daughter and moved in with Fane, considering it the best way to solve this family crisis.

On July 11, Kimball looked tired and depressed according to Ian Jeffries, who lived in the apartment complex. She told him that she was splitting up with Jablonski.

"Phil needs help and I can't tell you anymore," she told Jeffries. "I will tell you later on."

By morning on July 12, Jablonski was flooding Fane's home with frantic phone calls. He pleaded for a second chance, begged for Kimball's return to his life and threatened suicide if she deserted him. Kimball consulted a priest who told her to leave immediately and never return to the apartment she shared with Jablonski. That night, Jablonski invited Ken Grady, a co-worker for the city of Palm Springs, to share a spaghetti dinner. Grady was surprised to find Kimball away from their home and recalled that Jablonski seemed extremely upset about her absence. He said Jablonski made several telephone calls that night to Kimball and appeared on the verge of hysteria.

Despite Jablonski's frantic cries for attention, Kimball held firm and seemed determined to follow in the footsteps of past Jablonski women and not return to her abusive lover.

The final warning and perhaps the last chance to avert tragedy came on July 14, when Kimball took Jablonski back to the Loma Linda hospital for a second opinion. This time she met with a different doctor, who strongly advised bringing assault charges against Jablonski. The psychiatrist felt his colleague had been wrong to recommend medication for the man and told Kimball that, in his opinion, her lover was a dangerous man. Kimball drove Jablonski to his parents' home in Joshua Tree, but this time she stayed inside the car, while he walked to the house. Mrs. Jablonski glanced toward the car and thought it was odd that Kimball chose not to come inside and socialize as usual. She later told investigators that Kimball seemed upset.

After departing the Jablonski home for the final time, Kimball drove to her mother's in Palm Springs and told her about the doctor's latest warning. Fane was reluctant to act, fearing Jablonski would not be jailed, and would become angered by her efforts to have him arrested.

On Sunday morning, July 16, Jablonski called Kimball to say he loved her and their little daughter. He said he was staying at his brother's home in Palm Springs and that he had planned to go fishing. Though Kimball had no desire to see Jablonski again, she needed to retrieve diapers from their apartment. Believing that he was away, she went to the apartment at about 11:30 a.m. He was there when she arrived.

"Linda didn't know she would only live another 10 minutes," Jablonski recalled. "She would never enjoy motherhood."

With cool efficiency, Jablonski placed a cord around Linda's neck and went to work. "I had already made up my mind," Jablonski recalled. "Linda was not going to leave alive. We talked for a while and she gathered [our daughter's] stuff. She screamed for a few seconds. Linda knew the screams would not help. I applied more pressure and said, 'Linda, die, damn it, die.'"

Jablonski's neighbors, the Fletchers, heard what they later described as three or four rhythmic bumps against their wall, followed by a sudden thud. A few minutes later they saw Jablonski, dressed in a white shirt and tan slacks, walk away from the complex and drive off in his wife's 1972 Ford LTD.

By noon, Fane had grown worried about her daughter and began calling the Jablonski place to find out what was keeping her so long. When she got no answer, she drove toward the apartment.

Jablonski's father was on his way there as well, to take his son to the hills on a fishing trip. It was just after 1 p.m. when Mr. Jablonski walked into the courtyard of his son's complex. He knocked on the door and got no response. After noticing that the door was unlocked, Mr. Jablonski pushed it open and called for his son. He stepped inside the living room and moved through the home. He discovered the body resting face up on the floor at the foot of Jablonski's queen-size bed. Its face was coated in blood, leading the old man to fear that his son had been killed or had committed suicide.

After screaming his son's name, Mr. Jablonski ran from the bedroom and alerted Jeffries in the next apartment, who called police.

Bobbie Sheehan, the neighbor who lived across the courtyard, heard nothing that day until Fane arrived just after 1 p.m. and screamed hysterically upon finding her daughter's remains.

Gail Fletcher remembered the scene as well.

"She [Fane] was just screaming, just plain freaking out," Fletcher told police. "She was distraught and she kept saying, 'That maniac,' and saying how she should have called the police. She just kept saying it over and over. She said Phil had called her and said he was going to kill Linda and himself."

Palm Springs Police detectives Thomas Barton and James Heazlett arrived and were taken aback at the scene. They found Kimball face up on the floor of the bedroom with a trail of dried blood smeared across both sides of her face, collecting in a reddish pool behind her head.

Kimball's pants had been partly removed and her blouse had been pulled up above her waist. Her right arm rested on her stomach. Her left hand, with a yellow metal and white pearl wedding ring, remained trapped beneath her back, as if she were hiding something. Between her arms ran a cloth woman's belt that Jablonski had used to tie her up. A leather belt was looped and cinched around the left side of her neck.

Kimball's eyes were shut and part of her tongue peeked through her clenched teeth. There was a large purple bruise on her chin and other marks near her eyes, leaving no doubt that her attacker had beaten her before pulling the leather strap tightly around her neck. Similar wounds were found near her thighs and hips, and a dirty, white pair of men's jockey briefs rested on her privates.

"It was pretty bloody—a very messy crime scene," Heazlett said.

Kimball had been stabbed twice in the back with an eight-inch serrated Town & Country knife that had been removed from the kitchen. The blood-stained weapon was found at the base of a closet door three feet from her body. Puddles of water mixed with blood were found in the bathroom shower near a frothy bar of soap, indicating the killer had cleaned up afterwards.

It was obvious who had done the crime, but unclear where Jablonski had run. He knew the area well and liked to hike, camp and fish in the mountains. He had cash, relatives and a car, which meant he could be just about anywhere, doing just about anything.

After researching Jablonski's history, starting with his bizarre behavior in the military, Barton feared the Kimball murder might be just the start for a man who clearly hated women and would not hesitate to attack without provocation.

"We knew we had a real time bomb on our hands," he said.

Sometime after the murder, Jablonski went to his parents' home in Joshua Tree and stole a .22 caliber rifle. He next cashed a $20 check at an Apple Valley grocery store and called his sister, Nettie, on July 17.

"I'm sorry for what I did," he told her. "I'm going to join Linda and kill myself. I have a .22 rifle and I can't stand the thought of going back to prison."

The investigators advised Jablonski's neighbors to leave, fearing that he might return to the scene and slaughter them for revenge. Fane also went into hiding and Jablonski's entire family was put on alert. Similar warnings were sent to Ann Riordan in Michigan and Sandra Norbert in Indiana.

An all-points-bulletin alert went out and citizens were told to watch for the suspect and his brown LTD. They were also cautioned to be very careful and not to tangle with the suspect who was armed and dangerous.

The cops used everything they had to track him down. Their efforts included the use of an airplane to scan vast areas of desert and mountain sites and they reviewed tips from Jablonski's sister, Patsy, who claimed to have had visions about her brother's whereabouts.

Nettie Jablonski told detectives that she had seen a car parked on a hillside above her parents' Joshua Tree property late one night after the murder. She said the car had driven slowly up and down a road along the ridge, which gave the unknown occupant a good view of the family's home and barn below. The car moved off into the darkness before investigators arrived, leading Barton and Heazlett to believe that Jablonski was getting ready to come home.

Leaving nothing to chance, Heazlett spent a nail-biting evening hidden inside the Jablonskis' horse corral and watched the property with a shotgun at the ready.

"It was real spooky," Heazlett recalled, thinking back to the lonely night he spent peering into the darkness with nothing for company except an excited horse, whose restless hoof stomping added to the unease.

"At about 3 a.m. the horse started kicking rocks at me and I kept hearing them bounce on the dirt all around me," Heazlett said.

Jablonski never returned to the family compound. Instead, he spent days traveling in the LTD, driving to grocery stores in Riverside, Highland, and Benson, Arizona. He needed time to think and used the empty highways that lay before him to relax his mind so he could ponder what had occurred.

"The Kimball murder is the first time he completed his full fantasy," Murray said, referring to Jablonski's building sadomasochistic lust. "His past sex acts [with Ludwig and Riordan] extended his fantasies beyond mental imagery."

But with Kimball he had broken through to a new level. What was once a dream had become very real. He needed time to savor the accomplishment of his goal, and on the open road he was alone to enjoy all that he had achieved.

"This may have been a very exciting time for him," Murray said. "But the reality can never match the fantasy, which is why these kinds of people become serial killers. The fantasy [of the violent acts] is always exciting. They want to test it out in reality and when they do, the reality never measures up to the dream. Something always goes wrong, like the victim does not scream loud enough, or she is too old, or too young, or maybe she fought too much."

According to Murray, the killer's mind was probably reeling inside the LTD, and in time Jablonski grew disappointed in the crime. Indeed, the attack had not lived up to his level of expectation.

"If you want to get away from it all and not be interrupted, what is better than an isolated interstate?" Murray said. "Your mind can run wild and I think that is what was going on with

Jablonski. He was reliving the murder and comparing it to his fantasy and planning the next one.''

The planning ended on July 19, when he spotted an advertisement in a pennysaver newspaper placed by Penny Carey, whose husband had been interested in selling a gas stove and oven.

Jablonski called the young woman from the road and asked for detailed directions to her home. He arrived at about 1:45 p.m. She ushered him into her home and walked into her one-year-old daughter's bedroom where the gas range was kept on the floor. When he asked about the oven, she took him into the garage, where Jablonski examined the appliance and appeared to be deep in thought. After returning to the main house, he expressed some interest in the items and told Carey he wanted them for a camping trailer.

Seeing the woman was alone, Jablonski said he needed to visit his wife at work and discuss the sale with her. He said his wife was on a lunch break and that he'd be back with a firm answer in a few minutes.

The young mother thought it was a bit late for a lunch break, but was content to wait for the man in the brown LTD to come back. While Jablonski was away, Carey prepared a meal for her daughter and her three-year-old son.

Jablonski returned 15 minutes later, parked in front of the gate before the Carey home and walked to the front door. He wanted to see the items once more and measure them to see if they would fit inside his camper. Carey walked into her bedroom to fetch a ruler. Jablonski was right behind her. He followed her back into the baby's room to measure the range before heading into the garage to re-examine the oven. Carey's curious three-year-old son followed his mother and the tall stranger.

Jablonski offered Carey $150 for the stove and oven. The price seemed fair to her and the two moved into the house to settle the agreement.

Carey walked ahead of the stranger and bent down to place her daughter into a walker. Out of the corner of her eye she saw the stranger scoop her son into his burly arms. When the mother spun around, Jablonski had a six-inch fillet knife to the child's throat.

With the boy in his grasp, Jablonski said he'd kill the child unless Carey did as he demanded. He ordered her into a bedroom and told her to get undressed and lay down. She tried to talk him out of the assault by fabricating a story that she had venereal disease. Jablonski told her to shut up and again warned that her son's life was on the line.

"You don't want to kill a cute little boy," she implored.

"No," Jablonski replied. "I just want your clothes off. I'm not going to hurt you. I'm just going to screw you and you've been screwed before."

Carey did as he had ordered. She took off her clothes, sat on the bed, waited for the inevitable, and asked the big man to let her kids leave the room. But Jablonski was not in a charitable mood. "They're my insurance," he told her as the little girl—still seated in her walker—pushed her way into the bedroom.

Jablonski set the boy down and kept the knife poised toward his neck. He dropped several coins from his pockets onto a dresser, disrobed and placed the weapon atop his pile of clothing.

As he crept toward his naked prey, the young woman leaned back and lashed out with the heel of her foot, striking the big man in the groin. The pain shot through Jablonski's body and put an end to whatever fantasy was working its way through his mind. But the blow hardly slowed him down. He fell on top of Carey before she could get off the bed.

Jablonski moved his large hands to her neck and squeezed while the young mother pried at his vise-like fingers and tried to scratch at his eyes. Her efforts proved useless.

The last thing Carey saw was the vision of her arm suspended in the air as she made a last-ditch effort to reach her attacker's eyes.

She awoke 30 minutes later to the cries of her daughter and the sight of her son seated inside her bedroom. Carey's nose was bleeding and her body ached. She did not have the strength to rise from the bed, so she rolled off the mattress and crawled toward the sound of her baby, who was locked inside the baby's bedroom.

Still weakened, Carey crawled through the house making sure the intruder had left. Using her arms to hoist herself up, she glanced out the front window to make sure his car had gone, then called her husband for help.

It was only after she was treated at the hospital for her injuries that investigators discovered how close Carey had been to death. Upon examination, her physicians noticed a series of red blotches around her cheeks and eyes. To the untrained eye, the marks looked like an unusual rash, but homicide detectives know these signs all too well. According to Murray, this condition, known as "petechial hemorrhaging," is often found on strangulation victims whose facial capillaries have burst beneath the skin when the flow of blood to the head is violently constricted.

"That shows she was real close to death," Murray said. "We don't often see that in living people. When you see it on a corpse you don't need much more evidence to indicate death by strangulation. She was very, very close to death and this [again] is typical of Jablonski's fantasy."

Carey described her attacker to sheriff's deputies as being a man of about 45 years of age. She said he had brown hair and a pot belly. She estimated his weight at between 250 and 280 pounds and said he stood over six feet tall. She said he was clean-shaven, but his clothes were dirty. Carey added that her attacker had large hands but a small sex organ.

Word of the assault spread through the ranks, and by the next day Barton and Heazlett were interested in hearing more about the fat intruder. Carey was taken to the county courthouse to examine a series of seven black-and-white photographs of different men.

"That's him, I'm positive," she said after peering into the face of Phillip Jablonski.

During the next week, Jablonski sightings came at random. One person claimed to have seen his car pass the Palm Springs apartment complex he had shared with Kimball. He was seen again in Palm Springs on July 24. Two days later he bought gas in Benson, Arizona.

"It was very intense," Barton recalled of the search. "He

was in and out of our area. We knew he was going to go off. It was scary because you never knew where the guy would be next. He was up and down the area like a yo-yo. He ran everywhere he could, and finally ran out of money.''

The search came to a quiet end on July 27, when Jablonski called his parents and announced he was prepared to give up.

The 11-day manhunt ended outside a self-service gas station in Desert Hot Springs after Jablonski's mother told investigators her son was waiting there to be arrested. Jablonski was unarmed and offered no resistance when officers arrived.

''There was a real sense of relief that he was in custody before he killed someone else, be it another woman or a police officer or a member of his family,'' Heazlett recalled.

They booked Jablonski for murder and for the attack on Carey, then located his car and searched it for evidence. In addition to finding a credit card inside the car that belonged to Carey's husband, the investigators spotted a note Jablonski had left behind.

''Killed to date: Linda Kimball common-law wife,'' it began. ''I told her she would never raise [our daughter] alone or leave me alive. She begged me not to kill her. You screamed, but it was cut short.''

Jablonski was behind bars once more and again facing powerful evidence of a terrible crime. As usual, Jablonski seemed at ease speaking freely with the investigators. The conversation yielded very little, except to convince the detectives that this man was even stranger than they had imagined.

''He had a set of eyeballs that were different,'' Barton recalled.

''[It was] a thousand-yard stare that looked through you, not at you,'' Heazlett added.

That look did not vary during Jablonski's interrogation inside a Palm Springs Police Department conference room on the night of his arrest.

Jablonski started things off in a light mood by ribbing Heazlett about being a lieutenant in the National Guard, before relating his tales of Vietnam. He told the investigators that he had been shot in the side during the war, but that the wound did not leave any scar. Next came a story about an ambush Jablonski said he witnessed.

"They had us on a search-and-destroy mission. And we were searching for survivors of another ambush and when we went through a village we chased out some Viet Cong, and as we were leaving to another area that's when they hit us. And half the platoon was [lost]."

He continued with standard gripes about the war, blaming the government for the war's failure.

Jablonski mentioned that he had tried to become a police officer in the city of Fontana after the war, and was one of the force's top candidates. He claimed the job had been his for the taking, adding that he had declined the offer after another cop was shot on duty.

When it finally came time to discuss the Kimball case, Jablonski's affable manner changed and he chose to remain silent until speaking with an attorney.

"Well, OK," Heazlett said as the interrogation ended. "There's no sense in keeping you up any longer. I'm sure you're tired. So we'll take you back to the jail and you can get yourself a good night's sleep. It will probably be the best sleep you've had in a little while."

Heazlett and Barton figured they had a strong murder case against him and, when coupled with the assault on Carey, they thought Jablonski would be in prison for the rest of his days. But the facts surrounding the Kimball murder suggested a crime of passion, according to Ron Soda, the San Bernardino County Deputy District Attorney in charge of the prosecution.

"The investigators and I looked at all the facts and we tried to figure out how to make a first-degree murder conviction stick, but we could not, so we went for second-degree," he said.

The difference in degrees was significant. Had Jablonski been convicted of first-degree murder, he could have received a life sentence. Under a second-degree sentence, he would get a much lighter term, making him eligible for parole in about five years.

"The circumstances and the facts were more consistent with

a crime of passion,'' Soda recalled, adding that without the ability to prove Jablonski planned the murder, a first-degree prosecution was all but lost.

Jablonski added some difficulty to the prosecution by seeking an insanity defense, which led to a number of jail examinations by court psychiatrists who found him legally sane, but socially and morally corrupt.

Robert L. Flanagan, a Highland, California psychiatrist, probed deeply. He examined past interviews done with members of Jablonski's family and his past girlfriends. He spoke with Fane and Jablonski himself to try to gauge the defendant's mind.

Jablonski was candid with the doctor. He said that he had been raped at age 12 by two men and had committed incest with his sister, Patsy. He admitted taking nude pictures of his first wife, Rose Ludwig, and of pushing her underwater while she bathed. Jablonski claimed he needed to be rough with women.

"Instead of using manhood, I use brute force," Jablonski admitted. "I just feel I can't satisfy any woman in bed unless I use brute force. I don't know how to stimulate a woman to the point of satisfaction."

While saying he had the physical good looks to attract women, Jablonski confessed to an inability to satisfy them sexually without the use of muscle. He acknowledged having knocked out Ann Riordan on their first date and raping her.

"He said that his sexual practices with this woman included tying her up and subjecting her to painful intercourse," Flanagan wrote in a Jan. 24, 1979 report.

Jablonski also confessed to having forced one of Riordan's female friends into having sex. According to Flanagan's report, Jablonski coerced her into oral sex. He took pictures of the sex acts and whipped his partner with a fly swatter. When the woman threatened to tell about his strange behavior, Jablonski held her at bay by saying he'd distribute the pictures and tell her estranged husband all about their sex games.

Jablonski told Flanagan that he enjoyed having power over this woman. He said it excited him. He also admitted to being crushed when Riordan deserted him, saying he raped Robbins in 1972 out of revenge.

"A woman hurt me and I thought I'll just strike back at her," Jablonski said, and added that he chose her as a victim because Robbins had told him that her greatest fear was being raped.

He admitted trying to rape Fane and said that Kimball had "torn his heart out" by leaving him. The pain of another abandonment was too much for him, Jablonski said. As usual, he reacted with brute force.

"He said that he strangled her with his hands, removed her clothes, had anal sex with her," Flanagan wrote. "He said she was semi-conscious and she was still breathing."

Jablonski said he stabbed Kimball in the back to silence her for good. When that did not work, he put the leather belt around her neck and pulled tight.

"We had a beautiful relationship going," he told Flanagan. "I didn't want to lose her."

It is hard to determine why Jablonski admitted to so many deviant acts during this interview. It may have been his way of ingratiating himself with the doctor, or a calculated move to get assigned to a mental hospital instead of a prison. Whatever the case, Flanagan seemed to understand him well.

"By his own account, the defendant has succeeded in bringing harm to practically every woman he has encountered in any meaningful way," the doctor concluded. "He poses a most serious threat to the lives of others and particularly toward women. Sadism is a prominent personality characteristic. The defendant is a calculating individual who utilizes threats and other techniques of extortion for self-serving purposes.

"This individual has been offered the advantage of psychiatric treatment in a whole host of settings and situations since 1968. He has avoided, evaded or otherwise proved himself absolutely refractory to such programs of treatment whether he had been exposed to them voluntarily or involuntarily. . . . He is considered most clearly a serious danger to the health and safety of others."

The opinion was shared by other doctors who examined Jablonski as well.

"He suffered a significant amount of physical and sexual abuse as a child and was very dependent on his mother, but at the same time has identified with his sadistic father," wrote Dr. Robert B. Summerour in February 1979. "He has major distortions regarding sexual feelings, believing that he is unable to satisfy a woman sexually unless he inflicts pain on her. In fact, this is a projection, in that it's doubtful that Mr. Jablonski himself is satisfied unless it is associated with sadistic behavior."

Dr. R. Rose, a court staff psychiatrist had a similar view, finding that Jablonski was "locked into a triangle of intense hate and perverse sexuality involving a mother figure, a feminine whipping post and himself."

"It seems to him that he is continually subjected to domination, overprotection, overcontrol, belittlement and denigration by a castrating maternal figure," Rose stated in a March 1979 report to the court. "As a result, he has ongoing feelings of extreme insecurity, inferiority and dependency combined with intense rage and frustration. Consciously or unconsciously the inmate repeatedly involves himself in a triangular relationship wherein he is typically babied, pampered and overprotected by one female party, while he vents anger and self-hate in a sexually perverse manner on another passive and more or less consenting female party.

"The more he feels himself to be psychologically whipped and abused by one party, the more he feels justified in gleefully and passionately physically whipping and abusing the other party.

"The inmate stated he was quite desirous of treatment in one breath, and in the next breath he described all of his past therapists as incompetents, who did him no good whatsoever. In reality, the inmate deftly looks for someone to blame all of his aberrant behavior on as a means of avoiding any responsibility for his actions and as a rationalization for not changing his behavior one iota in the future."

The experts had spoken and in plain English had determined

Jablonski was a sexual monster likely to repeat the same violent pattern over and over again.

On March 2, 1979, Jablonski received a sentence of seven years in prison after pleading no contest to second-degree murder. At the time, it was the maximum term allowed. The decision was reached after Indio Superior Court Judge Richard Marsh reviewed reports and testimony from the psychiatrists and determined that Jablonski had not committed the crimes for sexual gratification.

In closing the case, Marsh said he would submit a formal recommendation to prison authorities in the hope that Jablonski would receive the best therapy available within the prison system. The defendant's attorney, County Public Defender Malcolm MacMillan, predicted that his client's mental condition would deteriorate in prison, all but guaranteeing that when Jablonski walked free, he might resort to violence.

"I thought he was scary," Soda, the prosecutor, recalled of Jablonski. "He just did not seem right. He was frightening. The way he looked gave you the feeling that he was capable of anything."

Norma Fane believed that the system had failed her daughter and after Jablonski's conviction she filed a civil lawsuit on behalf of her granddaughter against the Veterans Administration, and alleged that doctors at Loma Linda hospital were to blame for her daughter's murder. She said that the doctors who had originally examined Jablonski days before he strangled Kimball were responsible because they determined he could be medicated and treated as an out-patient.

Fane was awarded $282,000 in damages and the case changed the way psychiatrists were expected to view dangerous patients. The court's ruling obligated doctors at federal institutions to warn third parties about violent patients.

Though a doctor at the Jerry L. Pettis Veterans Administration Hospital had concluded that Jablonski was "potentially dangerous," the staff found insufficient reason to involuntarily admit him, according to press accounts of the civil case.

In upholding the civil award in September 1983, the U.S.

Ninth Circuit Court of Appeals determined that staff doctors did not do enough to protect Kimball's safety.

By then Fane had left Palm Springs to raise Jablonski's daughter on her own and Jablonski was more than halfway through his prison sentence for murdering Kimball.

TWELVE

Mother

"All I know is I screwed up my life and her life and everybody else's life."

By 1985, Jablonski and Carol Spadoni had been married for three years, but in all that time they never shared a truly intimate moment. Despite his constant attempts to lure her to his bed during weekend visits that married inmates inside the Men's Colony in San Luis Obispo were entitled to, Spadoni refused to be alone with her over-eager husband.

Jablonski's intense sexual appetite had been well demonstrated throughout his life. The years in prison were extra hard for a man whose actions were directed by the most primal of urges. For a time, Jablonski tried to keep his demons in check by occupying his time as an aide to the prison chaplain, or crafting wooden toys in prison shops. These endeavors diverted his mind, but did little to diminish the tension that continued to build as the years of confinement dragged on.

Although Jablonski could present a relaxed front on demand, a different animal—one with an insatiable sexual need—thrived just beneath his seemingly calm exterior.

Evidence of this shadow-dance between good and evil lingered in the letters he sent to the women in Burlingame. In these notes, Jablonski often showed his other side to Spadoni and Peterson by describing his sex-filled fantasies.

"I love to perform oral sex on a woman," he wrote in one note to Spadoni. "Maybe it's the look she has on her face when I finish doing the act. I love to see my lady with my manhood in her mouth. It shows me she is completely mine."

But juxtaposed to the crudeness were missives of a tender nature.

"It is sure great being married to the same woman for almost three years," he wrote Spadoni in 1985. "I am so glad I met you. I am so madly in love with you. . . . You are so beautiful. You drive all the men crazy. There is nothing in the world I would not do for you. I feel lost without you. I am in heaven when I am in your arms. I am completely lost when I am around you. You are my world, my stars, my moon. There is nothing in this world without you. I fall deeper and deeper in love with you each day. I can't do a day without you. I fall deeper and deeper in love with you each day."

Amid the affectionate composition of the love letters, Jablonski usually included a touch of evil. The tone of the letters rose and fell at random. Jablonski would gush over "his ladies" and fill the page with dewy language more suited to a teenager under the romantic spell of a young girl. A radical shift could occur in the next sentence and change the prose from puppy love to hard sex. It mattered not if the letter was meant for Spadoni or for Peterson, a woman more than 20 years Jablonski's senior.

In a 1982 note to Peterson, whom he often referred to as "Rebel," Jablonski expressed sorrow over the death of one of the women's pets before he lavished thanks upon his new mother-in-law.

"God takes dogs and animals into heaven," the letter began. "Carol needs us both dearly now. It is great that Carol has a mother like you."

The letter soon took a shift, revealing clues to Jablonski's true purpose and his dreams of what might one day become reality.

"You better not start gaining weight, or I'll have to take you over my knee. You got that sexy?" he wrote to Peterson. "It will be great to see both of you when you come to visit. I just wish we could visit more often. I love to hold you both in my arms and squeeze. I know I get out of line once in a while, but I don't think you mind as long as I don't do it in front of a lot of people."

In past visits with Peterson and Spadoni, Jablonski did more than ponder the acts he wanted to perform. Once in 1982, he bit his wife on the neck and made a grab for Peterson.

"I broke my word," he wrote Peterson after making the crude move on both women. "No more for a long time. I am sorry about the pinch on the butt. You better start working out and that's an order, or your skin will fall off, then you won't look so sexy."

Murray, the San Mateo County prosecutor, said Jablonski's writings provided investigators with a road map into the depths of a depraved soul.

"The letters were instructive to understand how his mind works," Murray said. "The goal was always the same. It is like a typical seduction except he will take it to the extreme. The letters show his method of seduction."

The method had worked before on Sandra Norbert. Now it proved useful on Peterson and Spadoni, who were apparently not put off by his strange letters and aggressive behavior. In spite of all the warnings, they responded to his notes and continued to visit. They seemed to care about him and showed their concern by sending him money to buy simple items like toothpaste and soap inside the prison facility.

For a man bent on dominating every woman that came within range, the sight of these two ladies, seemingly at his disposal, must have filled Jablonski with a sense of great power. If, as Murray believes, Jablonski considered the women mere chattel, then Spadoni's refusals to participate in Jablonski's bizarre and violent sex games must have only made things worse.

Jablonski was not one to take rejection with good grace. Just as he had done with the other women who came into his life, Jablonski spent hours dreaming about having the bodies of Peterson and Spadoni all to himself. In those fantasies, Jablonski imagined wrapping Spadoni's long brown hair around her slender neck and pulling the strands even tighter.

The hair strangulation fantasy was a dream he had once held for Norbert, but now he had new faces to substitute into his dangerous game. In this current fantasy, Jablonski saw Spadoni gasping for air as he twisted the brown locks around her throat. The choking would leave her body limp and helpless, just as had occurred with Ludwig, Riordan and Kimball. In his dream world, Jablonski mounted this rag doll from behind and enjoyed the anal sex he so craved while the skinny, lifeless toy shook beneath his powerful body.

Sick dreams are all some inmates have within the dull and lonely world of state prison. Jablonski's active mind could take him far away and put him in a utopia where he was in control.

Murray supported that notion while recalling a lecture he once attended given by a member of the FBI's behavioral science unit, the team that researches serial killers.

"They told us about this one fellow who they spoke with after he was caught, and they asked him how he would spend the rest of his life in prison," Murray said. "They asked him if all his crimes were worth it . . . The killer said he'd have no problem because he would always have his memories."

Like the subject of that FBI story, Jablonski was also at home with his visions. As a young man, he liked to wander into the mountains around San Bernardino and dream about accomplishing heroic deeds in the military. In later years, his imagination ran wild with thoughts of carnal conquests. After Kimball's murder, he spent more than 10 days traveling the roads between San Bernardino and Yuma, Arizona, reflecting on the exciting memories of her savage death.

Perhaps that killing, and all the other vile acts Jablonski had committed on women since his teen years, kept him occupied inside prison. Like the serial killer studied by FBI experts, Jablonski had his memories and could relive scenes of past "glory" inside his mind.

Now Spadoni and Peterson were the stars of his perverse memories.

For a time, Jablonski kept his sick pleasures alive by daydreaming of what he might be able to do with his bride if he ever got her alone. The seductive thoughts sustained him through the first few years of prison life. The deviant musings were taken one step closer to reality for Jablonski by carefully describing them on paper. The notes created added pleasures as well, since he knew his words would be read by others and would produce a reaction.

But merely fantasizing was not enough after awhile. The need to act out these ideas grew inside him as the months rolled by.

The opportunity came in July 1985 when Jablonski set up a family meeting with Spadoni and his parents. The group was supposed to gather inside a two-bedroom trailer within the Men's Colony in San Luis Obispo. For inmates awaiting conjugal visits, the tiny honeymoon trailer seemed like an oasis of passion amid the guard towers and barbed wire.

Jablonski had it all figured; he and Spadoni would bed down in one room and his parents could have the other. It looked like one of his long-held dreams might be realized.

But just as she had done the 13 times before when Jablonski secured private quarters to consummate their marriage vows, Spadoni backed out and told Jablonski's parents that she was sick with the flu. Once again, the eager husband would spend a night alone with only his fantasies for company.

In Jablonski's mind, Spadoni belonged to him, and her latest refusal was only the most recent in a chain of snubs he had known since Ludwig stranded him in El Paso more than 10 years earlier. And just as it had always been whenever a woman turned her back on Jablonski's needs, the time had come for some female to pay the price.

In this case, the only woman within reach was Jablonski's 73-year-old mother. Before that weekend was done, the very lady he had once tried to protect from an abusive husband would learn that the acorn truly does not fall far from the tree.

The family visit had been arranged weeks before and took place during the weekend of July 13 to July 15. Coincidentally, the fateful visit occurred nearly five years to the day of Kimball's murder.

The family gathered inside Trailer D, a small unit that had a master bedroom, hall bedroom, living room with a television, kitchen and bathroom. It was a comfortable setting and a vast improvement over the prison cell where Jablonski spent most of his time. The first two nights passed with relative ease. Mrs. Jablonski recalled that her son seemed a bit distant after learning that Spadoni had not made the trip.

"His mind seemed to be way off somewhere," she later recalled.

Jablonski's parents also found it odd that their son spent part of the weekend playing with a two-foot-long white shoelace. They remembered that he kept running the string through his hands.

"My guess is he brought shoelaces so he could play his S & M strangulation games with Spadoni," Murray said. "That was the fantasy he had had for years."

"His crimes are all about fantasies," said Morse, the San Mateo D.A. investigator. "And if he is in prison, they get worse. He sits in his cell, jacking off, thinking about what he's going to do next. If one fantasy makes him hotter than the next, then that's what he's going to do when he gets the chance. It grows and it grows until you can live out the fantasy."

On the morning of July 15, Jablonski's mood turned violent. He erupted when his mother emerged from the master bedroom and spoke to her son. "I see you're up," she said to her 39-year-old son who was standing in front of the television set in the trailer's living room. He responded with a dull, "Yeah." She turned her back and moved in the direction of the hall bedroom.

Jablonski grabbed the elderly woman from behind, placed his left arm around her neck and covered her mouth and nose with his right hand. As she struggled, he used his large body to muscle her toward the hall bedroom. The two fell to the floor inside the bedroom. Mrs. Jablonski's head landed on the edge of the mattress. Her son was on top and his head and shoulders pressed her down against the bed.

With his hands still encircled around his mother's face and neck, Jablonski applied pressure. Mrs. Jablonski could feel her strength giving way as she struggled for air. With her last ounce of energy, she forced her face away from her son's hand.

"Help me," she yelled. "I don't want to die."

Phillip Jablonski Sr., the 80-year-old family patriarch, was resting inside the master bedroom at about 6:30 a.m. when he heard the sounds of a scuffle just beyond his door. Recognizing what he thought were the sounds of someone gagging, he jumped from the bed to investigate.

The elder Jablonski spotted his son's feet sticking halfway out the hall bedroom. "What the hell's going on?" he yelled, then yanked his son's hair and dragged the inmate off his terrified wife.

As Mr. Jablonski pulled, his son began to sob. "Don't leave me," he whimpered as tears welled in his eyes. Mrs. Jablonski pleaded with her husband to call the guards and the attacker begged for mercy and forgiveness.

"No, don't," Jablonski implored them, before weeping on the bedroom floor like a child.

The parents did as their son asked and kept silent about the attack. The three remained inside the trailer for nearly four more hours, barely speaking a word. Mr. and Mrs. Jablonski would later recall that their son reverted to a cool mood after the attack, and acted as if nothing strange had taken place.

Shortly after the traumatic visit with their son, Mr. and Mrs. Jablonski spent the night in Pollock Pines, California, with their daughter, Phyllis Farris. At first, Phyllis paid little attention to the light blotches on her mother's face. She would later tell investigators that she overlooked the bruises because she was so happy to visit with her mother.

Later that night, Phyllis noticed that the blotches had become darker. "What happened to your face?" the concerned daughter asked. "We'll discuss it later," Mrs. Jablonski replied. The truth emerged that same night when Phyllis grew worried upon hearing her mother sob inside a bedroom.

"Phillip tried to kill me," Mrs. Jablonski admitted.

Phyllis took pictures of her mother's bruises to preserve the evidence. Days later, Mr. and Mrs. Jablonski met with an attorney, then set their thoughts down on paper.

"We are the parents of Phillip Carl Jablonski," the couple stated in a hand-written note sent to prison officials nine days after the assault. "We had a family visit. At this time, I, his mother, was strangled by our son. If I wasn't helped by my husband, I would have been gone. Due to the shock we were in, we just wanted to get away as we didn't know what to do.

"Now we expect him to be paroled in May of next year and sent here. We are afraid of him and do not want him here.

"There is more to this accident which should be looked into. I hope there is some action taken."

Jablonski's hope of early parole was eliminated and new criminal charges were brought against him. State prison investigators R.E. Bellman and T.W. Knight became the latest detectives to look through Jablonski's hefty criminal file to prepare for an interrogation with the notorious inmate.

Mr. and Mrs. Jablonski told the detectives that they were troubled not only by the attack, but also about the shoelace their son seemed fascinated with during the fateful weekend visit. The parents felt their son had brought the string into the trailer and that he had intended to kill his wife had she appeared for the scheduled visit.

On September 4, 1985, Bellman and Knight met with Jablonski inside a Men's Colony conference room. In a pattern that had been seen before by other detectives, Jablonski spun lies at first, but eventually gave up enough honest information to reinforce the long-held belief that he was a sick and dangerous fellow.

He admitted to being mad and frustrated over Spadoni's reluctance to visit him that weekend.

"She's one of these women that are real skinny," he told the detectives. "They gain a lot of weight and go back down again."

Jablonski seemed unwilling to accept Spadoni's excuses, especially when she claimed she was too embarrassed about her slender appearance to allow him to see her alone.

"It's getting ridiculous," Jablonski said. "She keeps coming up with this. I see her on visits all the time. I know how skinny she is. She is married to me and I accept her the way she is. I told her that before we were married."

When the detectives focused their questions on the attack made on his mother, the inmate grew very defensive. First he played the event down, saying that all he did was slap his mother out of frustration.

"She came out and started talking and she walked away and I hit her," he said. "We had been arguing that day and I just boiled over."

During the two-and-a-half-hour interview, Jablonski talked about his dog patrol work in Vietnam, his father's drinking problem and his nice relationship with Spadoni. Knight and Bellman concentrated on the attack and why Jablonski had brought shoelaces into the trailer in the first place. Through most of the interview he denied handling any shoelaces. But over time he revealed more details and eventually admitted jumping his mother from behind.

"Why do I get the feeling that you're not telling me the truth?" Bellman asked when Jablonski denied sneaking the shoelaces into the trailer. "You're not even looking at me. You can't even look me in the eye when we're talking about this. . . . I can't figure out what was going on in your mind or what you intended to do with your mother."

Neither could Jablonski.

"All I know is I screwed up my life, her life and everybody else's life," he said.

After he admitted that he had, in fact, forced his mother into a bedroom, Jablonski tried to explain it all away, saying the whole episode was done on impulse.

"I realized what I was doing and stopped," he said, denying that his father had pulled him off the bed and probably saved Mrs. Jablonski's life.

"She was on the floor and my hand was off her mouth and she screamed," Jablonski told the investigators. "I stopped and that was when my dad come in. She was sitting on the floor and I sat on the bed and we was talking."

When sternly confronted with his parents' version of the assault, Jablonski remained in denial.

"My mother has always had long, dark spots on her face," he said when asked about the bruises that his sister had seen and photographed on Mrs. Jablonski.

Jablonski tried to snow the detectives by claiming no shoelaces had been inside the trailer. After being bombarded with questions by the detectives, Jablonski admitted finding ''a piece of sheet'' inside the trailer. It would take nearly the entire interview session for him to admit that the sheet was really a shoelace. But even then, Jablonski never explained how the object got into the trailer, or what he needed it for in the first place.

He also never came clean about his plans for his mother. To the very end, Jablonski blamed the episode on a strange impulse, even though Bellman and Knight had other views.

''You knew exactly what the hell you were going to do when you grabbed your mother,'' Bellman said. You can't stand or sit there and tell me you don't. I know what you were going to do. There is absolutely no reason for you to come up behind your mother, grab her, take her in your bedroom and try to keep her from screaming. Now that's pretty damned obvious.''

''It might be obvious to you but it wasn't obvious to me. I don't know what I was going to do,'' he said.

''If she hadn't gotten away and you'd have choked her, you still don't know what you'd have done to her,'' Bellman responded. ''You have no idea what you would have done. She may have been another victim. Boy, that's real comforting. . . . I frankly believe that if you were honest with yourself, you'd realize that if your father hadn't been there, we might have another victim.''

Near the end of the interview, Jablonski claimed that he had been reluctant to admit the attack because he feared Spadoni would learn about the incident and leave him for good.

''I don't think she'd understand,'' he told the detectives. ''She means a lot to me.''

What Jablonski meant to Spadoni was hard to fathom. When Knight interviewed her about the July attack on Mrs. Jablonski, Spadoni said she would consider divorce as a means of keeping her husband away.

''I'm worried [about] what he would be like when he gets out,'' she told the detective during a March 1986 conversation. ''That could have been me that was attacked. I really don't know him. Phillip and I were pen pals for a year before I started visiting him in San Quentin. When he asked me to marry him, I finally agreed. Even on our wedding day I was uneasy about the marriage, but thought I was just the nervous bride.''

Spadoni's faith in her husband had been shattered and now she had reason to fear for her own safety.

"I can't trust him anymore," she told Knight. "He could have been paroled here if he had not attacked his mother. I don't want him around me. I want to know him better. I would be very concerned if he showed up. Even being in the area would make me uneasy. He was so close to parole. I am so terrified. It could have been me."

News of the attack found its way to Norma Fane, the mother of murder victim Linda Kimball. On March 25, 1986, she wrote letters to Daniel J. McCarthy, then director of the state's Department of Corrections, and Senator Robert Presley. She urged them to get involved in the case and take steps to ensure that Jablonski would not be paroled. Under the terms of his 1978 conviction for second-degree murder, Jablonski had expected to be freed in May 1986.

"I believe with all my heart that Mr. Jablonski will again find a victim," Fane wrote. "I do not wish any other family the pain and grief which I have suffered."

Jablonski was prosecuted for attempted murder and assault on a non-prisoner by the San Luis Obispo County District Attorney's Office. The crimes prevented his early parole and kept him behind bars for an additional five years.

Both his parents died about six months after the 1985 attack. Spadoni and Peterson continued to write him letters despite their new concerns. Jablonski, meanwhile, concentrated on his letter writing, adding two new females to his circle.

THIRTEEN

Helen and Shirley

*"I figured if I had a friendship like that, my life could
go on, not down."*

Just weeks after the assault on his mother, Jablonski began
writing to a highly religious woman from Louisville, Kentucky
named Helen Blair, who had written to the inmate at random
with hopes of bringing Christ into his life.

"I did it for God," Blair recalled of the motivation behind
her letters. "I really thought it was something I could do from
my home. I was taking care of my aunt and mother at the time,
so that took the place of working outside the home."

Blair first learned about the prison pen pal association through
her ties to the PTL Ministry, a religious organization founded
by Jim and Tammy Bakker in 1973. During the mid-80s, the
PTL network encouraged its members to reach out to prisoners.
Blair was happy to help the cause and, like Norbert, she chose
Jablonski's name at random. He would be the only inmate she
ever wrote to.

"I felt I could help him and maybe act like a family member,
like a member of the Family of God," Blair recalled. "He
wrote back that he was in there for murder, but that went right
past me. It did not make an impression on me. It did not matter,
because I was going to be a Christian sister to him."

Jablonski avoided lurid fantasies in the letters sent to Kentucky. Of all the pen pals Jablonski wrote letters to, the ones
to Blair were the most honest. Though his notes did include

some nonsense, like his stories about Vietnam, Jablonski opened up a bit with his Southern friend.

His fairly honest replies to her might have been an early ploy to bring Blair under his influence, as he had done with Norbert. Then again, he might have found her letters so caring that he actually wanted to keep things straightforward with this particular woman.

"I like being addressed as Phil," Jablonski wrote in a July 31, 1985, letter to Blair. "I am 39-years-old and I've been in prison close to 10 years on a charge of murder. I have a big family, it's like a gang when we all get together."

Blair came from a good-sized clan as well and, unlike many of the other women Jablonski came across, she had a solid head on her shoulders. Blair kept the letters on a respectable level and wrote about his need for religion. She avoided Jablonski's efforts to get her to tell him anything personal.

"I was not looking for a boyfriend," Blair said. "He would always ask me to tell him about my problems, but I was not going to do that because it did not feel right to me. I did not think that was any of his business. I like to think that my guardian angel was watching out for me."

Besides that unseen force, Blair's connection to her faith and family kept her well-centered. Though other Jablonski women had been through horrible marriages or suffered abuse as children, Blair was surrounded by friends and family in her hometown.

"I am very family-oriented," said the mother of eight. "I would not miss church on Sunday if my life depended on it. I had no interest in anything other than helping him find God. I felt blessed and wanted to hand it back around."

In succeeding letters sent to Kentucky, Jablonski opened up to Blair. He also made sure to include a touch of the Almighty for good measure.

"All things are possible through prayer," he wrote in an October 14, 1985, letter. "I called my folks last week and they sounded cold toward me. I don't blame them 'cause of what I done to my mother. . . . The Lord has lifted my spirits, but I still feel worried."

In a March 5, 1986, letter, Jablonski gave Blair his version of his world before crime. "Well, my life before prison was not much. After getting out of prison the last time, I joined the Jaycees, had an affair with another man's wife. She moved in with me and my folks. We lived there until she moved in with her mother. I was attending college to get my degree in welding. We finally got our own place. Her mother got me a job with the city and I obtained a position as assistant road foreman. We had a fairly good life going for us. A nice house and two cars. Then I started an affair with my mother-in-law. She looked young for her age. There wasn't anything she would not do for me or her daughter."

Soon, Jablonski had convinced Blair to give him her phone number, just as he had done with Norbert.

"He talked like a college professor," Blair recalled. "Very erudite. He had a tone of voice that was wonderful. He did not use any slang expressions. He had a wonderful phone personality. I can't say enough about that. He sounded very intelligent."

As the months passed, Blair continued to keep her distance from the inmate. She sent him books by G. Gordon Liddy and James Michener and wrote about the doings of her family, but never said anything about herself.

Jablonski, in turn, was thankful for the notes and the books. His letters spoke about the doings inside prison, which included the attempted suicides of other inmates, the closure of a prison hobby shop and the ups and downs of his criminal prosecution for the attack on Mrs. Jablonski.

Though Jablonski tried to have that case dismissed, alleging he had been insane at the time he attacked his mother, his letters to Blair showed that he was very much aware of the criminal court process, hardly the behavior of a mentally ill person.

"I have two weeks until my trial," he wrote her in August 1986. "I have not seen my court-appointed doctors. There are reports due in court and it is not looking good. If I don't see them by then, I am going to withdraw my plea of insanity and just go to trial and leave my fate in God's hands. So keep me in deep prayer."

He explained his feelings about therapy to Blair, sharing with her the prison doctor's theories about the women he had been attracted to.

"[In] my last session with my doctor we found a pattern in the type of women I marry," he wrote. "Rose was dependent on me 'cause she married me to get out on her own. Ann was 17, and was the first time away from home. I was older, so she was completely dependent on me. Linda was independent. She had goals in her life and a job. But dependent on me to protect her."

Through the five years of their pen pal friendship, Blair never questioned Jablonski's motives. She had no reason to believe he posed a threat to her. She last heard from him around Christmas of 1990 after he had been released from prison and sent to live in Indio.

"The last thing I sent to him was a small decorated Christmas tree," Blair recalled. "It was about a foot high and it came with decorations."

She included little gifts of soap and other toilet items so Jablonski could have something under his little tree. She figured the present would brighten his small room inside the halfway house and remind him that someone cared about him.

"He called to thank me and said things were looking up for him," Blair said, recalling the last conversation she had with Jablonski in late 1990. "He sounded real upbeat. I never heard from him again. I thought he was doing super good."

She had no idea that Jablonski had already written her name on the backside of his sinister snake belt, placing her on his personal hit list. The horrid truth remained a secret until after Jablonski's arrest in Kansas, where investigators discovered the belt and her name.

Blair was at home when investigators from Burlingame called, telling her for the first time how close she had come to death at the hands of a man she had sought to heal through faith.

"They called and said I was no longer in danger," Blair recalled. "I sat on the floor of my living room and said, 'Excuse me?' They said he was apprehended in Kansas and asked if I knew about the belt. Of course, I had no idea what they were talking about.''

Fortunately, Blair had kept the letters Jablonski sent her during their five-year correspondence. She turned them over to the California detectives so they could pore over them for insight.

"I kept the letters, because my daughter-in-law said they might make a good book," said Blair, who has since given up writing letters to prison inmates. "It was a strange experience. I will never do anything like that as long as I live ... Of the millions of people in the world, I had to be a pen pal with a crazy killer.''

In Blair's mind, Jablonski was a fallen soul, caught in hell's grip. "Satan had a hold of him, there is no doubt about that," she said. "I feel dreadfully sorry for the people whose lives he touched.''

Even today, Blair believes her guardian angel would have kept Jablonski away from her had he not been stopped in Kansas.

"After they arrested him, one of my kids said that God would not have allowed him to kill me," Blair said. "Something would have happened.''

Jablonski had placed another pen pal's name upon his death belt. Like Blair, Shirley Thorp was a Southerner who lived in Knoxville, Tennessee. It is very likely that he was headed toward both women's homes in the spring of 1991, to extend the trail of mayhem he had begun in California.

Jablonski and Thorp became acquainted in 1989 when he spotted her picture in a pen pal magazine called *Latin International*. Unlike Blair, Thorp was interested in romance, which gave Jablonski the incentive to begin his familiar style of seduction. Thorp was unmarried, aging and in weakened health at the time, so she figured writing to pen pals might be a good way to meet men. She remembered signing up with a friendship club in Sacramento, but had no idea how her name, address and picture found their way into a state prison yard.

"I was not married and I decided that I would pick someone and write to them," Thorp recalled. "I don't know why I started the writing. I worked seven days a week as a nurse and a lot of the people I took care of died on me and there are times when you are glad to be in touch with someone.''

Jablonski responded to her with great interest. "He kept writing and writing," she recalled. ". . . It would tickle me to get a letter. I would run to the mailbox to get his letters. I needed to enjoy myself a bit because all I did was work.''

In his initial letters, Jablonski lied, promising his Southern belle the world, and claiming he was in jail for a white-collar crime. He pledged his friendship and hinted at marriage.

"I believe a woman is a special gift sent from heaven. For a man to treat like a lady, to be loved and cared for in a special way,'' he wrote in his first letter to Thorp. "I am seeking an older woman who is not scared to be a woman and be spoiled by love and loving care. That loves to be hugged, kissed and walked hand-and-hand in public. If you would like to be spoiled with love for the rest of your life, I am your man.''

For a woman then in her 60s, Jablonski's romantic notions sounded pretty appealing. Thorp became more intrigued when Jablonski explained that he had enough energy and money to take care of her should she let him into her heart and life.

"I told him that my legs were bad and he said he was going to pick me up and carry me," Thorp said. "I think he was putting his feelings in his letters. . . . I really thought a lot of him at first, because I figured if I had a friendship like that, my life could go on, not go down.''

Thorp had never known a truly good man. Born in North Carolina in the mid-1920s and raised on a farm operated by her sharecropper parents, Thorp's life was destined to be hard and troubled. As a child she picked cotton on the farm and stripped sugar cane for molasses. It was an isolated life of toil and not much cheer that she shared with her parents and her three older siblings. By age 14, Thorp dropped out of school to help support the family, working in a cotton mill during a shift that started at midnight and ended at 8 a.m.

She married a childhood friend right after World War II. She was 17 and made an impulsive decision she would regret for the rest of her life.

"He treated me awful. He did not know what love was."

They spent most of their 12 unhappy years together living in the rural community of Tryon, North Carolina. Thorp said her husband was an odd character who'd work for about a week and then abruptly quit his job for no reason at all. He had a hard time in the army, as well.

"He was a psychomaniac," she said. "Every time they would put him in the army camp, he would run away and end up sitting on our porch."

Thorp collected her two daughters and fled after catching her husband in one of their children's beds. She resettled in Knoxville and hooked up with a construction worker whom she had met while working at a family-style restaurant. The two married and had two daughters. The family moved to Orlando, Florida. Thorp recalled that her home life was hellish; not only was her husband a heavy drinker, but he beat her as well.

The final straw occurred in 1972 when he came home "dog drunk" and reached for a shotgun.

"He looked at our little daughter and said, 'I'm going to get drunker and come and kill your mother.'" Thorp said.

She left him the next day and returned to Tennessee, where she worked as a nurse until her health started to fail her after years of hard physical labor. In short, Thorp was a perfect target for Jablonski, who had always thrived on lonely, unsophisticated women.

By the summer of 1989, Jablonski knew he'd soon be free from prison and placed on parole. His future with Spadoni and Peterson was uncertain. He feared the two wanted him to stay far away. Thorp would serve as a back-up plan should the Burlingame women prove unwilling to accept him.

With only months to win over his latest pen pal, Jablonski fashioned a new personality and portrayed himself as a wealthy man interested in a peaceful life with a matronly woman. Relying on the tricks he had used to influence Spadoni, Jablonski filled the Thorp letters with sappy affection.

"Beautiful Shirley, I can take away all the abuse you have suffered at the hands of men or whatever way you have been abused in your life," he wrote in July 1989. ". . . Maybe we can start this new chapter in our lives as special friends and something real special that calls for a ring."

In response to questions she had about his criminal past, Jablonski created a new fantasy. He said that he had inherited a great deal of money from his parents' estate and had the means to buy Thorp a house, should they marry. He also described himself as the victim of a government investigation into white-collar crime. He claimed that he had been prosecuted for selling shares in a business he had started, without acquiring the proper paperwork or approval.

"They sentenced me to a year," he wrote. "They say the best is worth waiting for. I sure hate to lose the best but I feel there is a strong attraction between us. Honey, I hope you don't mind me saying that I don't need anything material from you. I am interested in you as a person. . . . I am the special one you are looking for. You will always be the apple of my eye, the center of my life and the most important person in our relationship.

"You will be treated like a young lady in public, in the house and in the bed. I believe a lady should run the house in the way she sees fit. I believe the man is there to provide and protect his property and wife."

Thorp had sent Jablonski her phone number by the summer of 1989, and began accepting his collect calls. He, in turn, started to decorate the envelopes mailed to her with hand-drawn hearts, butterflies and flowers.

This fiction would have never worked on Blair, but Thorp was very intrigued by this apparently wealthy suitor, who took the time to write like an infatuated teen.

"I was thinking he would stay with me," Thorp recalled. "He said he had $150,000 saved up and had an inheritance from his mother and dad. He was building me up. He would say, 'Baby, I will be there and I will take care of you.' "

Though Blair's four daughters told her to rip up this man's letters, she took Jablonski at his word. "Look at all the money he has saved up," she told them. "He will build us a house."

By the end of July, Jablonski had Thorp hooked.

"You've done me the greatest honor of becoming my woman," he wrote her in a July 30, 1989, note. "With both our checks and me working, we can get our own place, plus allow you to take it easy for the rest of your life in my loving arms. Hope you don't get nervous when we are alone. I'll make it real easy for you to feel comfortable in the presence of a man. Spending a day with me will make you forget all the fear of men you have."

He claimed to have the ability to secure a good loan from the Veteran's Administration and hinted there would be plenty of money to build a place that could accommodate her kids and grandchildren. No Jablonski correspondence would be complete without a reference to his fighting days in Vietnam. In August, he told Thorp that he had received a shoulder wound in combat and been awarded a Purple Heart and a Silver Star. He also claimed to have earned a Bronze Star for holding a machine gun position that was almost overrun by the enemy.

"At the time I just did not have no one to talk to and I thought it would be good for him to be here," Thorp recalled. "I thought he would be a good guy."

As Jablonski's parole date edged closer, he began to shed his good-guy image in his letters. After receiving a new picture of Thorp and her family, he started referring to her as "Shirley Jablonski."

Inspired by the picture, Jablonski began to reveal some of his sexual desires.

"I was going to ask you if you are big or small-breasted," he wrote in August 1989. "I can see by your picture that you are a beautiful, big-breasted woman. I love big-breasted women, but I would love you even if you were small-breasted."

After Thorp injured her knee in August, Jablonski returned to a monetary theme, claiming he could not help her with any finances until he was out of custody. He said that all his money was tied up with an attorney, who prevented him from touching his wealth until he was free.

"If you are just looking for a man just for his money, you have the wrong man," he wrote. "If I find out that's what you are seeking, I'll drop you like a hot piece of metal."

The letter then took a bizarre twist, with Jablonski asking Thorp to send him nude pictures of herself. "Take a picture bra-less," he wrote. "Take your bra off, then put on a blouse and leave the front open a little so I can see part of them big beautiful breasts. If this offends you, I am sorry. I will never ask you to do it again."

In subsequent paragraphs, Jablonski boasted that he was "worth waiting for," and added that he was the best man for Thorp.

"Would you like to come to California for the wedding?" he asked her. "I know a nice peaceful chapel. It's located in the high desert and sits just below a mountain. When the sun is rising or setting, it is just a beautiful place to hold a wedding for a beautiful woman."

Suddenly, Thorp was not so excited with all the letters arriving to her home. Jablonski's abrupt shift in tone had given her cause for concern. She did not like his vulgar language and objected to being referred to as his wife.

"I once thought he would make life easier for me, but then he started writing nasty letters," Thorp recalled. "I snapped at him on the phone and told him I wanted him to stop writing that kind of stuff. I should have done something about it, but I did not really know what to do."

The evil genie was out of the bottle and Jablonski was not about to let anything halt his pursuit of a woman he now considered his soulmate.

"You can kid yourself, but you know that soon after we close the bedroom door, I am going to enjoy undressing you and spreading your beautiful legs . . . we will reach a beautiful height of love," he wrote her in September. "The only way you can stop me is to lock me out of the bedroom or refuse me the pleasure of your love. I am your man and you are my woman. You are more than that, you are my savior. Shirley, you brought love into my life."

He began addressing her as his "dearest wife," and closed his letters with, "your loving husband, Phillip."

He wrote of spending nights with her and her daughters,

watching television and enjoying the warmth of his new loved ones.

By the fall of 1989, his letters had shifted again. Though he continued to pepper the notes with demands that Thorp parade around the house without a bra, he hinted at his desire to dominate her. "If you try to get away from me, I am going to put you in the closet and lock the door and never let you out," he wrote.

Thorp's protests at his vile expressions didn't stem the tide; in fact he reached even deeper inside his depraved mind to shock her with more perverse desires. "I can't wait to walk up the stairs to your bedroom, then slowly undress you and ram my penis over your butt. . . . Your butt is mine to enjoy."

"Our wedding will be so special," he wrote in October. "Everything from that time will be really special. I am taking your life forever. I own your body and soul. It has to be that way 'cause that is the only way I can make our lives so special together. The minute you pick me up from the airport, your days of being an independent woman are over. You are mine, you will not have a word to say [about] what happens in your life from then on. If I say we are going somewhere, we go. If I say we make love, we do. Understand."

Surprisingly, Thorp replied to his letters and continued to accept his collect phone calls, even though she grew worried about what could happen when Jablonski was released from prison. In her mind, there was no engagement or any promise of marriage. Jablonski was working on a different level.

"I did not really think he meant these things," she said of the strange demands. "I started to think about it and decided I did not want to see him if he came out."

By late October, Jablonski appeared singleminded. The letters mentioned "special" sexual positions he had in mind. "The bedroom is my playground," he wrote. "And you are my toy. You have no say on how I use you."

Most of the letters still came with hand-drawn hearts on the envelopes and Jablonski affectionately referring to himself as a "loving husband." But he continued to try and control her by instructing Thorp on how to present herself when he appeared.

"I don't like my women to wear make-up of any kind," he wrote her. "No lipstick, eye shadow. You put it on, and you will wash it off, or I will. If you disobey, I will treat you like a child. Our wedding day is going to be beautiful and I don't want it ruined by you wearing make-up to take away from your beautiful face. None of my women have worn make-up and it is not starting with you.

"If your daughters don't like the idea of their mother not wearing make-up, that is their problem. I am taking charge of your life now.

"You said you wanted a man that is loving, gentle and able to help you heal your past. You have that man. I am going beyond that. There is no discussion on the matter. . . . Now for your hair, let it grow longer. I like it below your shoulders. I love you deeply and care more than I have for any woman. I want you for the rest of my life. I have to be honest with you even if it means I could lose you."

In late October, he addressed the letters not to Shirley Thorp, but to "Shirley Jablonski." At the same time, he continued to barrage her with instructions of how he would take control of her life. His sexual demands became bolder each week, giving true insight to Jablonski's sick wishes for the future.

"There is not an inch of your body I will not use sexually," he wrote her. "Please get that through your mind, nothing is off limits. I am serious when I say that our marriage is until death do us part."

The craziness had gone on long enough. She demanded he stop calling her "Mrs. Jablonski," and sent a letter to the prison warden to learn more about this white-collar criminal who claimed to have a wealth of money waiting for him on the outside.

On Oct. 26, 1989, she received a three-paragraph form letter from the warden of the California Medical Facility in Vacaville who informed her that Jablonski was presently incarcerated in a mental hospital.

Four days later, another Jablonski letter arrived at her Knoxville home. It came with the now familiar salutation of, "Good morning, beautiful,'' and quickly shifted into the area of rough sex.

"Once you close the door to the bedroom, you become a slave and your body is mine to enjoy any way I want,'' he wrote. "And that includes your mouth and your face.''

The message started sinking in for Thorp. Jablonski was due to be released in six months and seemed convinced that Thorp was to be his wife. To protect herself, she wrote critical letters to him, chastising him for thinking of her as a sex slave. This was not the kind of relationship she wanted and she hoped this might be enough to put him off.

Jablonski continued to write her until after he was paroled. In most of those letters he apologized for his crude remarks and tried to win back Thorp's confidence. At times he asked for a second chance and even told her to ignore the dozens of previous letters that focused on sexual dominance.

"Honey, if you keep looking back at the crazy letters I wrote, then you are more scared of men than I thought,'' he wrote her in December. "I want to turn you on, not off. But you have to forget the ugly things I said.''

The bloom was well off the rose by 1990, at least in Thorp's eyes. Still, she expected Jablonski would show up on her doorstep one day. She, like Helen Blair, never knew how close Jablonski had come to fulfilling his dangerous fantasies. She only learned about the death belt and Jablonski's horrible past after his arrest for the murders of Spadoni and Peterson.

"The criminal justice system really blew it on this guy,'' said Eric Haseleu, the Burlingame police sergeant who investigated the murders. "They let a guy out who should have never been free. He is in prison for killing one wife and he tries to rape and strangle his mother. He was just a serial killer waiting to happen. There is no doubt in my mind the officer in Kansas saved Blair and Thorp's lives. He absolutely saved lives because Jablonski was going their way.''

Thorp has no doubt that she came within days of learning that Jablonski was not joking when he said his style of marriage really did mean until death do us part.

"I was on a [nursing] job when the police in Burlingame

called and told me all about him," Thorp recalled. "I said, 'Lord, have mercy.' He would have killed my kids. He would have made it to my house. Had he come to my house, my daughters would have been there. I am just glad he is put away and won't hurt anyone else."

What remains unclear is why these women came under his spell. Jablonski was certainly not an attractive man and his mind was hardly stable. His pen pal letters were littered with spelling errors and poor grammar, and though the notes contained some romantic thoughts, they quickly degenerated into images of pure debauchery.

Jablonski's power over these women still puzzles the detectives who investigated his crimes. Robert Morse, the wiry and gruff-voiced San Mateo County District Attorney investigator, blames it on a combination of naivete and a motherly instinct.

"You've got this guy that is in there for murder, and this guy is the opposite of attractive. He's a big, hulking guy," Morse said. "He's somebody you don't want to meet in a dark alley. He's just got that look. I can't imagine what he'd be to a woman. But he's got all these women writing to him. I've read all through those letters. I've gone blind reading them.

"These are lonely women acting out a mother instinct. I've seen that before. I have seen it with battered women and even rape victims. They have this motherly instinct and they think they can change them."

Morse refers to these women as "do-gooders," because they live under the false belief that their goodness can change the evil in the men who will bring them only pain. It's a tragedy hardly limited to pen pal relationships with prisoners and the women who find them attractive.

"These women believe these guys are not all bad," Morse said. "They think they can rehabilitate them and that the inmates never had a chance in life. They look for a reason. They will say, 'This guy is a human being.' The women mean well, plus it gives them something to do."

With Jablonski finally captured and facing potential death penalty prosecutions in Riverside County, Utah and Burlingame, it was time for the lawmen to focus attention on the small details that lock up a criminal case. That Jablonski would be convicted of murder was a virtual certainty, but there was no telling if he would earn a place on death row. Death penalty cases require painstaking work because every aspect of the investigation and trial is automatically reviewed by courts of appeal.

The defendant was captured and securely stowed in jail, but the job of delivering a conviction would not be all that easy. It would take three years for Murray, Haseleu, Morse and the combined efforts of many other San Mateo County detectives and officers to put the case together before the ultimate decision could be put to a panel of jurors to determine whether Jablonski's life would one day end with him gasping for air inside a gas chamber, or whether he would be allowed to fantasize and script more letters while serving the rest of his life behind bars.

FOURTEEN
Prosecution

"This is gonna be serious stuff."

Since the State of California reinstituted the death penalty in 1977, only three men have met their ends inside San Quentin State Prison. The process of bringing condemned men to the death chamber is a slow one as California courts take a cautious view toward state executions. Judges and appellate courts allow extensive reviews of capital cases and these legal delays can keep an inmate on death row for more than 10 years.

William G. Bonin was the last man executed in the Golden State. Known as the "Freeway Killer" for his habit of raping and murdering young men then dumping their bodies on the California roadways, Bonin spent 13 years on death row before exhausting his appeals. He was put to death by lethal injection in February 1996.

Before being put to death, Bonin told those gathered to witness his execution that capital punishment "sends the wrong message," adding that anyone contemplating "anything serious against the law" should first "go to a quiet place and think about it seriously."

Murray and his team of investigators, led by Haseleu and Morse, had hoped to add Jablonski's name to the list of killers awaiting the prick of a deadly needle within San Quentin's infamous "Green Room," as the death chamber is known.

"When you ask 12 people to deliberately vote on taking the life of a fellow human being, you have to appeal to every part of them," Murray said. "Intellectually, you have to convince them that the law and the facts of the case support it. You also have to make an emotional appeal and show it is morally correct to do."

To achieve that, Murray would present the evidence in a clear and honest manner. He is not a flamboyant prosecutor, and does not rely on dramatics to beef up a case. Looking much like a college professor, with his slightly receding hairline and precise manner of speech, Murray understood that the evidence and the surviving Jablonski victims would be enough to sway the jury to his way of thinking.

In the spring of 1991, when Murray first came onto the case, he had no idea how horrendous the suspect truly was.

"We knew it was a double homicide," Murray recalled. "But when I first got the case, we did not know the extent of Jablonski's background. He had not yet been caught. It was not known that we were dealing with a serial murderer."

Upon Jablonski's capture in Kansas, and further examination of the evidence and the suspect's history of violence toward women, Murray steadied himself for a long prosecution.

"When I learned that he had been sent to prison as recently as 1978 for murdering his common-law wife, I realized that [it] was something different," Murray said. "That this was not a typical murderer. This isn't just a guy in a rage. This is a guy who has a history. This is gonna be serious stuff."

The job of organizing the serious stuff into a presentable case would require careful gathering of all the evidence, which ranged from the tiny bits of beard Jablonski left inside the Peterson-Spadoni bathroom sink to the items found in the killer's car. There would also be a need to seek out Jablonski's past victims, who could explain what it was like to feel the suspect's powerful hands gripped around their necks.

These women, some of whom had not seen Jablonski in 20 years, would have to be contacted, cajoled and brought back for trial. Their presence in court would show jurors how much damage Jablonski had done before embarking on the killing spree, and help Murray guide them to a morally correct verdict.

In addition to the live witnesses and tangible evidence collected from the crime scene, Murray knew he'd have to fight off defense challenges to Jablonski's mental state. Past doctors had labeled the killer a schizophrenic. It was likely that Jablonski's defense team would use that old information to portray their client as a man out of touch with reality.

If a San Mateo County jury agreed, and deemed Jablonski mentally incompetent to stand trial, or insane at the time he committed the crimes, the killer would avoid the death penalty. Though the evidence was powerful, there is no such thing as a guaranteed verdict, as Jablonski had proven in past prosecutions.

But this time the stakes would be higher. Since prosecutors intended to bring a death sentence, Jablonski would be assisted by three experienced, court-appointed attorneys and every aspect of the case would be scrutinized, not only by the defense, but by future courts of appeal.

There could have hardly been a more skilled team assembled to handle the job. Though Haseleu was not as experienced as Morse, at least in matters of homicide, he more than made up for that with his dedication and enthusiasm. Murray had been seasoned after nearly 13 years with the district attorney's office, and Morse was the most experienced homicide detective in the county.

"A trial is very much a team approach," Murray said. "The sooner you assemble the team and begin working toward that, the better product you get. If you wait for months, until the investigation is complete, oftentimes the evidence a prosecutor might want for impact at trial is hard to get."

Though police and prosecutors serve different functions, Murray said in his county the team approach is used to reduce barriers between departments. In the Jablonski case, Murray had been involved almost from the moment the bodies were found, as had Morse, his best detective.

Murray and Morse knew each other well and were used to being at the center of an explosive and sensational case. The pair had helped make legal history in 1990 by assisting in an investigation which led to the conviction of George Franklin Sr. The former San Mateo firefighter received a life sentence for killing an eight-year-old girl in 1969. The case became a sensation because much of the evidence against Franklin was based on the testimony of his daughter who had witnessed the slaying, but had repressed those memories for 20 years. She told authorities after a therapist helped her recall the hidden trauma during therapy. The case brought on a raging debate as to the validity of childhood memories and their use in criminal prosecutions.

Morse was in charge of the investigation, and his gut-level honesty helped convince the reluctant daughter to come forward with the truth. Though Franklin was convicted and sentenced to life, the case was overturned on appeal in April of 1994.

Morse, the son of a merchant sailor, is a scrappy fellow with green eyes. He wears his gray hair slicked back and favors white dress shirts and red ties. His face is lined with worry and age marks, a reminder of the hard cases and rough scenes that have played out before him during his years on various cop beats.

Morse is not interested in psychologists who probe a suspect's mind and come up with hypothetical excuses for their acts. He'd rather let the facts tell the story, believing most jurors can figure out the rest.

Morse was briefly a patrol officer with the Menlo Park Police Department, before joining the San Mateo County Sheriff's Department in 1972. His brutally honest demeanor helped him rise through the ranks and landed him in the detective bureau, where he established a stellar reputation for getting his man.

Morse had taken part in more than 300 homicide investigations by the time the Jablonski matter came to his desk, and it called for a seasoned hand to make sure everything went by the book.

Murray had his team in place from day one, and now it was time to let the game plan unfold.

"In some ways, the evidence was so strong it was like having the San Francisco 49ers play against a high school team," Murray said of his case. "Sure, the team should win, but there is always the dread that something could go wrong. The pressure of having a strong case is that if he were not given a death sentence, it would seem as if we did something wrong."

With Murray directing the action like a head coach, and Morse relaying the calls like a veteran quarterback, Haseleu and his teammates moved the case along at a steady clip.

The teamwork had begun when the bodies were first discovered inside the Burlingame bungalow. The game plan only grew stronger with the discovery of Jablonski's death belt, his tape and the gun inside his Ford. Still, the road ahead would be long and filled with legal obstacles at every turn.

First, the lawmen had to get Jablonski back from Kansas to California, a move made easier when the killer declined to fight his extradition. Next came the race to file the charges. Jablonski was wanted for crimes in Utah and Riverside County. Murray figured he had the strongest case. He also had two victims, which escalated the crime and virtually guaranteed a death penalty prosecution.

In order to seek a death sentence, California prosecutors must not only prove the defendant guilty of committing a premeditated murder, they must show what are known as "special circumstances." In Jablonski's case, Murray had to prove that the defendant not only killed both women, but that he did so with the intent to rape them.

Backed by the tape-recorded confession that gave a virtual blow-by-blow account of the crimes and the damning pen pal letters that outlined his bizarre sexual desires for both women, Murray felt he had a compelling case.

Jablonski seemed to sense that as well. Before he waived the right to fight extradition from Kansas, he predicted his future to Haseleu.

"I'm going back to prison for life or death row," he said.

Jablonski returned to California on May 12, 1991, and was housed in the California Institution for Men in Chino while awaiting a formal arraignment for the murders of Peterson and Spadoni.

Intent on keeping the grisly facts of the case hidden to avoid a media frenzy, Murray kept news of Jablonski's gruesome tape secret for as long as possible. He kept the press at arm's length by presenting evidence of the crimes to a criminal grand jury.

Grand juries meet in secret and the jurors are prevented from discussing the facts placed before them. This private venue allows prosecutors the opportunity to present evidence without being challenged by the defense or pestered by the media, which is forbidden to attend. Cloaked in that secrecy, Murray was free to play the tape, knowing full well that that evidence alone could almost guarantee an indictment.

On June 5, 1991, the county grand jury indicted Jablonski for the murders. The panel also found he committed the crimes while engaged in, or attempting to commit, rape and sodomy.

It would take more than two years to prepare for trial, as the detectives researched the killer's entire life and reviewed every step he took during his deadly cross-country road trip.

Should Murray be able to convince a county jury that Jablonski had committed the murders, he would still need to get a unanimous vote for a death sentence. California juries are required to not only weigh the evidence of a crime, but in death penalty matters they must also consider the good and evil aspects of a defendant's entire life. This part of a trial, called the penalty phase, is set up to determine if there is anything in the defendant's background that might warrant a reprieve from the death chamber.

This balancing act between mitigating and aggravating factors forces the defense and the prosecution to become experts on another man's life. At trial, the competing forces behave like rival biographers and present different aspects of the same man's existence. The defense and prosecution are expected to bring forth family members, old friends, past lovers, teachers, and almost anyone else who crossed paths with the defendant in order to paint different versions of the same human being.

As expected, Jablonski's defense team, led by Jeff Boyarsky, Gary Merritt and Richard Keyes, mounted a mental illness defense, taking a three-pronged attack. First they petitioned the court to deem their client mentally incompetent. If that legal step failed, they planned to enter pleas of not guilty by reason of insanity during the first stage of trial. Finally, as a last resort to save Jablonski from a death sentence, Keyes examined his client's childhood in an effort to show that the killer had been subjected to so much abuse as a child that he was not to blame for his acts. This aggressive defense would guarantee a long and expensive trial.

The first salvo of the legal war began in November 1993 when jurors took their seats inside a Redwood City courtroom and first set their eyes on the notorious killer. Though billed as a crazed menace to society, by then Jablonski's look had changed dramatically during the two years of incarceration.

The big killer sat slouched in his seat at the defense table and his eyes looked forward into emptiness. He shuffled in and out of court like a zombie and drooled inside his jail cell.

"He had lost about 60 pounds from the time I saw him in Kansas," Haseleu recalled. "His face was all withdrawn, his color was gone. He talked very slow and he walked very slow, that's what I really noticed. He had walked just fine after they caught him in Kansas, but when he walked into our court, he could barely move. I would not have been surprised if he was acting, but he was also under a lot of medication."

The change in his appearance was partly do to the heavy psychotic drugs Jablonski had received while in the jail. The defense attorneys said he needed the medications to calm his schizophrenic mind. The drugs and Jablonski's basic mental nature made it impossible for him to assist in his defense, Boyarsky argued in court.

Boyarsky told the eight-woman and four-man jury before him that his client heard voices and was not connected to reality. Murray, by contrast, said Jablonski's detached stares and occasional wide-eyed glances around the courtroom were part of a carefully planned act to manipulate the system and evade justice.

"I thought he was faking," Murray recalled. "He had a checkered history dating back to 1965 when the army found him to be schizophrenic. By that definition, he should have been very withdrawn, but he did not show that. He took college classes and wrote love letters to women."

Murray reasoned that in 1965, the army doctors had simply misdiagnosed Jablonski.

"This guy was a budding serial murderer back then and they

did not recognize him as a sadist," Murray said. "But once you get a label in the psychiatric community, it sticks."

Murray understood that the competency trial was a make-or-break moment in the case. If jurors agreed with Boyarsky, Jablonski would likely end up in a prison mental hospital until doctors deemed him fit to stand trial. That could delay justice for years or perhaps forever, because once one court finds a defendant incompetent, the term tends to stick, making it virtually impossible to get the subject released from a hospital and returned to court for trial.

Jablonski had already been examined by a battery of psychiatrists hired by the court. Their opinions varied. All agreed that Jablonski was a troubled man who suffered different levels of mental disease, but they disagreed as to whether his illness meant that he was unfit to stand trial.

In a July 30, 1993 report to the court, Alfred W. Fricke, a clinical psychologist from San Mateo, outlined Jablonski's unusual appearance and behavior in the months before his competency hearing. He reported that the defendant shuffled as he walked, drooled at times, shook from internal tremors and complained that he felt as if he were "floating out of my body."

During their sessions together, Jablonski struggled to answer questions for Fricke. The doctor noted that Jablonski had difficulty with intelligence exams and other psychological tests.

Fricke had consulted with Merritt, the defense attorney, before meeting the inmate, and according to his report, Jablonski's mental health had collapsed in the months following his arrest. The report indicated that Jablonski had been lucid when Merritt first met him in 1991 and had fallen into a stupor to the point where he did not know his own defense team and could not distinguish the front from the back of the courtroom.

A second court-appointed doctor, Jeffrey R. Weiner, found the defendant to be severely disturbed, but also warned that Jablonski could be malingering, or faking illness, in order to fool the experts. During his sessions with Weiner, Jablonski talked about nightmares and flashbacks from "Nam." He also mentioned the odd floating sensations, adding that he was hearing voices in his head.

He told Weiner that one of the voices was that of his sister Patsy, who "keeps bugging me, telling me I ought to die for what I did and she laughs," according to Weiner's report to the court. A male voice told Jablonski to commit suicide, while other voices gave a variety of opinions, he told the psychiatrist.

"The voices tell him that he is bad and that he ought to die, not only for the murders, but for not being a good brother and not being more attentive to his sister and his mother," Weiner wrote.

Jablonski went on to say that he had been hearing voices ever since Vietnam. During one interview session with Weiner, Jablonski noted that the voice was speaking to him at that very moment, advising that he work with the doctor, but remain cautious.

Though Weiner initially found Jablonski unfit for trial, he added that further examination was needed. "His responses to some of the formal questions on the mental status examination suggest either significant organic pathology, possibly due to medication, or conscious deliberate malingering," Weiner concluded. "Mr. Jablonski may, in fact, have a significant psychiatric illness which produces psychiatric symptoms, but the extent to which he might be emphasizing, exaggerating or distorting these symptoms in order to receive anti-psychotic medication is not clear."

Knowing that the expert witnesses can neutralize each other, Murray went on the offensive, relying on his most damning evidence to show how clear-thinking Jablonski was at the time of the murders. He hoped the tactic would show that Jablonski was malingering during his sessions with the psychiatrists in an obvious attempt to avoid a potential death sentence.

For the first time in open court, the public heard the killer's own account of the four murders as his breathless voice spilled forth from the tape he had made while on the road.

Jurors sat slack-jawed and stared at the defendant seated less than 15 feet away, as they heard him coolly describe his crimes.

"This is the mind of the murderer, made for his own purposes," Murray told the jury. "You will hear nothing about hallucinations in this tape."

Murray bolstered his case by presenting testimony from Jablonski's one-time auto mechanics teacher, John Tamulonis, and others who knew the defendant in the weeks before the killing, to explain that Jablonski had shown no signs of psychotic behavior before his crime spree.

The bank tellers who had cashed the checks Jablonski had stolen from Peterson after the murders testified as well, to show that the defendant seemed normal after the homicides.

Murray had lain the ground work for his argument in an attempt to fight off the testimony of Harry R. Kormos, a Berkeley psychiatrist who had practiced at Yale and in the United States Navy during the Vietnam War. Kormos had done a lot of work with war vets and was convinced that Jablonski was suffering schizophrenia, an illness that in his opinion could appear and disappear at whim.

Kormos examined Jablonski five times before forming his opinion. He determined that the defendant suffered from hallucinations, among other difficulties that made him mentally incompetent. He told the jury that Jablonski experienced weird facial ticks, and feelings of paranoia.

"I was impressed by the degree of withdrawal and lethargy I saw in him," Kormos told the jury, referring to his past interviews with the defendant. "There was no spontaneity there. He didn't ask me questions. He didn't tell me anything. He was just there, like almost at times as if he were an object rather than a human being. I would constantly be reduced to trying to find new ways of getting him to communicate with me and I frankly was not able to do it."

Kormos said Jablonski's inability to communicate was something typically found in schizophrenics. Though the prosecution suspected Jablonski was faking, Kormos said he was very familiar with the art of malingering and was convinced that the defendant was not acting. Kormos said he tested Jablonski's memory to prompt fakery, but found that the patient reacted in accordance with someone truly suffering mental illness. To support his position, Kormos pointed out that Jablonski had been receiving heavy amounts of anti-psychotic drugs like Haldol, Clonidine and Mellaril for months while in jail. The drugs were so strong that they would incapacitate anyone who was not actually suffering from schizophrenia.

"With that level of medication, I don't think that he would be conscious," Kormos told the jury. "I think that he would be asleep."

Kormos said that Jablonski was unable to say much of anything about the crimes he was being prosecuted for during their interview sessions.

"It is my feeling that his responsiveness is so impaired, either by the medication or by the schizophrenia, or by the combination, that he cannot function in the manner that I would feel he would have to [in order to] function in a trial," Kormos offered the jury. "Furthermore, with his hallucinatory experiences, he would be too distracted to be available to assist his attorney."

Murray saw it differently, and challenged Kormos' opinion on cross-examination.

"The fact that he is facing the death penalty and was facing the death penalty at the time you initially interviewed him, did that make you suspect malingering would be more likely than in the average case?" Murray began.

Kormos said the prosecutor's view was a valid concern, but stuck to his stated opinion.

Murray then relied on his own expert who had also spent time probing Jablonski's psyche. Dr. James R. Missett, a Menlo Park psychiatrist, had a different view. In addition to reviewing Jablonski's entire history, which included an examination of all his past mental evaluations and police reports of his prior crimes, Missett interviewed Jablonski twice before the competency trial.

"Jablonski has displayed over a period of one year an appreciation of the nature and possible consequences of the proceedings in which he is involved," Missett determined. "He has expressed the hope that, should he be found guilty, he will not be sentenced to death.

"Mr. Jablonski also shows, repeatedly, an awareness of the

possible consequences of various maneuvers he may undertake in the criminal justice system,'' he continued. ''For example, in his conversation with me he reported that he got the sentence he did with his earlier offenses on the basis of various deals. He was noted to report that the insanity defense is rather weak in this country. This certainly shows an awareness of some of the legal options available to him and how he might respond to them.''

Missett noted that Jablonski spent a great deal of time reading while inside the county jail. As for Jablonski's various stories of military achievement, Missett concluded his actions were ''more consistent with conscious lying than they are with being the product of an organic brain syndrome.''

Missett was further swayed by the fact that Jablonski quickly mentioned his alleged hallucinations when the psychiatrist first met him for an evaluation. The fact that Jablonski could not give any real details about his supposed flashbacks and nightmares from Vietnam only solidified Missett's opinion that the defendant had lied to him and was indeed mentally fit to stand trial for murder.

''The man knows what he is doing,'' Murray told the jury. ''He is playing a game. He is putting on for the doctors, and for you, literally the performance of his life.''

Despite the complexity of the mental-state evidence presented by the clinicians during the five-day hearing, jurors reached a verdict in less than three hours. They were certain Jablonski was faking it, which meant the matter could move to a full criminal trial and a second hearing to determine if the inmate deserved death.

FIFTEEN

The Evidence

"Brace yourselves. I'm about to lead you on a journey into the very depths of human depravity."

With the first legal hurdle cleared, Murray readied for a new jury that was due to consider Jablonski's guilt or innocence the following spring. The new trial would cover some of the same evidence discussed in the quest to decide Jablonski's mental competency. This time, however, Murray realized he would have to prove that Jablonski had not only committed the crimes, but had planned the killings as a way to sate his sexual desires and punish the women who had snubbed him. He realized the defense team would try to paint their client as a raving lunatic, who had slaughtered the Burlingame women during a frenzy of anger.

To show motivation, Murray relied on past letters the killer sent to Eva Peterson and Carol Spadoni focusing on the passages that dealt with Jablonski's strange attraction to his elderly mother-in-law. The jury was allowed to read through dozens of notes Jablonski sent to Burlingame during his many years in prison. Just a cursory review of the documents showed his desire for the older woman.

"Rapists don't rape for sex any more than alcoholics drink because they are thirsty," Murray noted, outlining his trial strategy. "It is all about power, control and anger. We knew he was upset with Eva and that he blamed her for Carol's reluctance to visit him or let him be with her in Burlingame. It made sense that he wanted to punish Eva."

Murray and the investigators never doubted for a moment that they could prove beyond a shadow of a doubt that Jablonski had done the killings. Among the important items of evidence that proved their case was the notebook found in Jablonski's car that listed the names and "death dates" of his victims. Murray also had the snake belt as well, which carried the names of female victims, and the dates of their executions.

"He is a serial killer," Murray recalled, reflecting on what drove Jablonski to leave such an obvious trail behind. "He needed to chronicle things, needed to memorialize things. It may be that by doing this, it filled a masturbatory fantasy and allowed him to relive the excitement of the moment by looking at the snake belt. Maybe it [the belt] is something that hooks him to the reality of what was done. The material is a reminder that his fantasy really happened. It isn't just something dreamed up. He has a memento to prove it."

Though armed with powerful evidence, Murray needed to remind the jury about the bizarre motives behind the sick crime in order to elevate the case into a higher level of punishment— one that could be worth a death sentence.

To counter the mountain of evidence Murray had gathered, the defense hoped to show that Jablonski never had sex with the two victims—a strange approach given what Jablonski had talked about on the tape. If the defense could disprove Murray's theory as to the sexual or vengeful motives behind the murders, or perhaps raise doubt in the minds of the jury by showing Jablonski killed the women during a spontaneous frenzy, they might manage to save his life.

At worst, if the jury felt Jablonski had indeed raped his victims, the defense team would argue that the acts had occurred *after* the women's deaths. If true, Jablonski could not be charged with any sex crime, because under California law it is not illegal to have intercourse with a dead body. If the rape allegations were eliminated, the defendant might again have an avenue to escape a possible death sentence.

"There was no doubt we would get some kind of guilty

verdict," Murray recalled of the case. "But if I got a second-degree murder conviction, I would lose and could not seek death. If the jury determined that he had driven to the house to see Carol and that during the visit something happened between them to upset him which caused him to shoot, we were out of court on the death penalty."

On April 6, 1994—nearly three years after Jablonski purchased a snub-nosed .22 to carry out his horrid desires—the arguments were put to the test. Murray was ready to retrace Jablonski's crime wave by explaining how two good-hearted women perished by his hands.

"Brace yourselves. I'm about to lead you on a journey into the very depths of human depravity," Murray told jurors as he opened his case. "This will involve murders, chilling in their brutality."

With a steady voice devoid of exaggerated passion, Murray laid out a map of what he intended to prove over the next several days. As always, his manner was calm and his language clear. He knew that his evidence was devastating and that there was no need to fill the room with overblown rhetoric. The prosecutor quickly outlined his view of the case by retracing the moves the dead women's friend, Ralph Galindau, had taken nearly three years before. He told the panel about Galindau's concerns over the women's failure to appear for their coffee shop gatherings, and of his terrible prediction as to what lay inside his friends' home. Murray also spoke in detail about the murders, keeping the jury transfixed by displaying police photographs taken of the crime scene.

"As you can see," Murray said, as a slide of Peterson's corpse was shown to the jury, "the body is located near the stairway into the kitchen. You can actually see in this area, there are bloody drag marks that lead from the kitchen into the area where her body was found.

"She had been shot just above the breast, in the left side," he continued, as the crime scene photographs advanced to keep pace with his commentary. "She had also been shot in the head, stabbed in the throat, and a towel had been wrapped around her mouth and she was shot in the mouth through the towel. As you can see, her clothing, from the waist down, had been removed and the clothing from the waist up pushed up above her breasts. There were marks on her nipple, and there were marks on her eyelids, as though a sharp instrument had been applied to the nipple and to the area above her eyes.''

Before the shock of the first violent images had settled in, Murray was on to the next ones. He kept a steady pace, again using crime photos to put the jurors inside the victims' home.

''The officers then proceeded into the dining area of the home and in this location they came upon a more chilling sight,'' he said, as the image of Carol Spadoni, her face covered in tape, flashed upon a screen before the jury. ''As you can see, her face had been wrapped with silver duct tape, completely, including her nose and mouth to the point that she could not breath. She had been shot in the right temple. A close range wound, what doctors call a 'near-contact wound.' The gun had not actually been placed tightly against her head, but very close to it, leaving powder residue, both there and on her fingers. Apparently her hand had been put up to her head to protect herself.''

In addition to showing the jury just how gruesome the crimes looked when police arrived, Murray wanted them to understand that Jablonski had planned the murder. He told the panel that he would prove Jablonski had bought a gun five days before the murders—a clear sign of the man's evil intentions.

Murray also knew how powerful Jablonski's tape-recorded message could be, and how the killer's own words had haunted everyone who had ever heard the recording.

At the end of his opening statement, he played the legal trump card that Jablonski had so carelessly left inside his old Ford. Directing the panel's attention to a tape recorder he had set up in the courtroom, the prosecutor shared with his captive audience the most damning piece of evidence of all.

''Mr. Jablonski had made a tape for his own purposes,'' Murray told jurors. ''It's somewhat difficult to hear. As I play the tape, I'll put up on the overhead [projector] a transcription of the tape as you listen to it.''

For 10 minutes, the killer's voice filled the courtroom. The jurors sat slack-jawed as the nightmarish account of the crimes washed over them. Their faces went white as they listened to the killer calmly describe the murder scene. They took no notes as his voice explained what it was like to "watch 'em fall dead."

Several members of the panel looked at Jablonski while the voice from his past spoke in stilted whispers, retelling the most foul of deeds. Jablonski himself remained still as the tape played on. There was no expression at all upon his face.

The visuals from the crime scene, coupled with Jablonski's ominous words, made a crippling impact. The room went silent after Murray shut off the tape recorder. Even the judge seemed stunned. For several seconds no one spoke a word. Finally, Judge John Schwartz broke the tension by calling a short recess.

Murray had practically won the case with his opening statement. But the prosecutor had other uses for the recording. To Murray, the tape proved Jablonski's intent, but it also gave the jury an additional reference point to follow the chain of evidence. Murray spent much of the trial proving that almost everything Jablonski spoke about on the tape had actually occurred. He relied on the testimony of crime scene specialists, who had gathered the evidence from the Burlingame bungalow to support his claim. Time and again, Murray showed corroboration between what had been said on the tape and clues found at the murder scene. The verification came in items big and small, ranging from the palm print Jablonski left on a bathroom sink, which backed up the his claim on tape that he had cleaned up after the murder, to the tiny bits of beard found in the sink.

The tape also lined up nicely with the evidence collected in Indio and Utah, proving to Murray that Jablonski had left investigators with a fairly accurate account of his travels and deeds.

Not everything on the tape proved correct. For example, Jablonski claimed to have stabbed Peterson in the "ass" after having sex with her. In truth, he had done that to Spadoni. There were no such knife wounds on the older woman's lower body. Still, the slight discrepancies were easy to overlook when compared to the number of items that fell precisely in line with Jablonski's narration.

"I knew he was being accurate on the tape," Murray recalled. "In terms of the number of gunshots used, the mutilations and things like that, I knew it was all true."

The tape proved useful for other reasons as well.

"The second striking thing about the tape is the tone of his voice," Murray recalled. "It is very matter of fact, combined with a breathless glee. The third important part of the tape is the part when he talks about stalking other victims and the glee he feels while anticipating the capture of other people. It is just chilling to think that here was a predator who was on the loose, on the interstate. Those are the roads we allow our wives and daughters to travel on. To think that there was a predator just waiting to capture his next victim and torture them to death, that just numbs me. I have been in this business a long time, and I have seen a lot of horrible things, but that tape blew me away."

It had the same impact on jurors and the defense, which was in no position to dispute much of the evidence that pointed toward their client's guilt. Defense attorney Gary Merritt offered no opening statement, choosing instead to cross-examine the prosecution's witnesses and save his best argument for the end of trial.

"The case was uncontested at the guilt phase," recalled defense attorney Richard Keyes. "His tape-recorded statement made it a foregone conclusion."

On April 21, 1994, Murray and Merritt tried to sway the jury with contrasting closing arguments. They reminded jurors that it was their duty to leave their emotions outside the court-room and to consider only the evidence at hand. They agreed that the three-week trial had been unpleasant for everyone involved, but that it was time for all parties to do their duty and see to it that the accused killer got a fair hearing before 12 honest and open minds.

"Sometime in the early morning hours of April 23, 1991, this man packed his equipment, got into his car and began the long ride from Riverside County near Palm Springs to

Burlingame,'' Murray said as he began his closing argument. ''And when he had finished his work, we had two defenseless women who had been shot, stabbed, sexually degraded, sexually mutilated and butchered.''

He spoke about the nuances of circumstantial evidence, which were the nuts and bolts of the case. No one had ever seen Jablonski carry out his crimes, but there were telltale traces of him all over the Burlingame home. From fingerprints left on a garage doorknob he used to enter the residence, to the razor blade he left in the bathroom sink, to a drop of saliva found on Peterson's nipple that matched Jablonski's blood type—all signs pointed toward one man.

''It's sort of like a puzzle,'' Murray told jurors, referring to the tiny strings of evidence that, when tied together, make a strong rope. ''If we have a puzzle of the Golden Gate Bridge and it's all in pieces and we pick up the pieces of blue and look at it, there may be many reasonable interpretations of what that piece of blue is. It could be the sky, or it could be the water, maybe it's a car on the bridge, but we don't know.

''But as we get more and more pieces of the puzzle, a little bit of orange, a little bit of black, we start putting the pieces together and we start to form a cohesive picture.''

The murder picture had come together to perfection, because Murray had so much evidence on his side. The physical material placed Jablonski in the home. His notebook of the murders listed the date of the women's deaths. The letters he had written from prison explained his sexual needs, and the testimony of a former cellmate named Richard Muniz, verified the prosecution's claim that Jablonski was angry with Peterson.

''There is a double motive here,'' Murray told the jury. ''One motive is the statement that Mr. Muniz made to you that Mr. Jablonski was complaining that Eva was interfering with his relationship. That Carol was starting to listen to Eva. That Eva was preventing him from being paroled into the Northern California area and he didn't like it down in Southern California. An interfering mother-in-law is one motive.''

As for the second motive, Murray referred to a letter Jablonski had written Peterson in June 1982 in which the defendant referred to himself as "boss," and instructed Peterson not to work too hard until he had a chance to "make a play" for her. The letter concluded with Jablonski musing about his desires to grab the elderly woman's breasts and suck her nipples— acts strikingly similar to what the evidence showed occurred inside the Burlingame bungalow nearly nine years later.

"Since 1982, when he was in prison, from all the evidence that you have in this case, this is apparently the first opportunity [that] he ever was alone with this woman—outside of a prison setting—in order to carry out his perverted desires for her," Murray told the jury.

Recounting Spadoni's violent end, Murray asked jurors to consider what she had gone through after first being shot.

"We can only hope to God that she was not conscious," he told the jury. "Can you imagine the terror and the horror of having been disabled with a gunshot to the head? Lying on the floor seeing your mother shot, and then having this man take tape and start wrapping it around your mouth. Cutting off your airway around the nose. And you're struggling against that feeling of suffocation?"

Murray's closing was a tough act to follow, but Merritt gave it his best shot. He did not beg for mercy or try to excuse his client's behavior. Instead, the defense attorney asked jurors to follow the letter of the law and avoid becoming caught up in emotions over the terrible crime. He pointed out that there was no proof Spadoni had been conscious during the attack in order to blunt Murray's touch of drama. As for the damning tape, Merritt said the recording was filled with "fantasy and hallucinations."

Merritt attacked the rape and sodomy allegations by reminding the jury that while police investigators had uncovered tons of evidence, some as small as razor stubble, they never found any semen. There were also no pubic hairs found on the women's bodies. "We don't know if there was an ejaculation because we don't have any evidence of any sexual misconduct," he said.

In Merritt's eyes, this case was not about power, sex or

revenge. For him and his reading of the evidence, the crime was about madness.

"The motive in this case, as supported by the evidence, is not to have sex, it was to destroy sex," Merritt said. "When you look at this case, and when you look at the circumstantial evidence here, what do you have? You have a madman. You have a lunatic. You have a maniac. You have one of these. You have all of these. And what's the circumstantial evidence to produce that? Well, part of the circumstantial evidence that you want to look and listen to is the tape. Listen to him! Listen to him! . . . This man was a lunatic. This man was nuts. This man was out of his mind. A normal person doesn't do this type of thing."

Merritt described the crime scene evidence as proof that Jablonski had not come to Burlingame with any detailed plan of revenge, but had flipped out after meeting the women and [then] savaged them in a wild rage.

"The stab wound to Carol was a frenzy," he argued to the jury. "They all happened at once. The ones that happened all at once, the anus, the vagina, the stomach. Mr. Jablonski was attacking sex, not having it."

Merritt knew the jury had come to despise his client, so he tried to sway them with logic, reminding them of their oath to remain free from prejudice or passion while deliberating his client's fate.

Because prosecutors carry the burden of proving their case beyond a reasonable doubt, they are allowed the final say before jurors are instructed on the law and asked to deliberate a defendant's fate. Murray was not about to let the opportunity slip by without making an effort to solidify his argument.

"I agree with part of what Mr. Merritt said about this crime being a crime to destroy sex," the prosecutor began. "All rapes are an intention to destroy sex. They are not loving acts. They are acts of hatred. They're acts of violence. They rape out of a desire to dominate, humiliate and destroy the object of their hatred, in this case Eva Peterson. That is what rape is and it fits exactly with what that man did."

He refuted Merritt's claim that no sex had taken place by

saying that not all rapists leave semen behind, since some are incapable of reaching a climax. He also pointed to the crime scene and reminded jurors to consider how the bodies were found.

"The saliva, that's clear evidence of sexual intent," Murray told them. "Suckling on a breast, unless you're less than three years old, that's sexual act. [And] what about a woman with her lower garments stripped off her body and her upper garments pushed up to her neck? That doesn't indicate sex?"

Murray was willing to concede that Jablonski had some mental difficulties, but said his behavior showed a consistent plan of attack, and his actions proved how effective he was at carrying it out. Taken together, Murray said it was impossible to view Jablonski as an out-of-control killer on an uncontrollable blood quest.

The prosecutor also shot down Merritt's theory that the stab wounds showed Jablonski was engaged in a frenzied fit of rage, by explaining that the injuries were carried out with almost surgical precision.

"The stab wound to the breast [of Carol] is a very clean incision. We don't have . . . 50 stab wounds and . . . all kinds of slashing," Murray said. "This is very deliberate. . . . A man who knew what he was doing for whatever perverted and sick reasons he has, but not a frenzied action of a madman."

Again, Murray referred to Jablonski's taped message as proof the killer not only knew what he was doing, but enjoyed thinking about it.

"Listen to the way it's described on the tape," Murray advised the jury. "He's not rushing ahead in his words. He's not describing it in a frenzied tone. He's describing it fairly matter-of-factly with a great deal of enjoyment. What I find interesting, and see if you agree, is the tone of voice and the amount of almost glee that he expresses with the sex. It is about equal to the killing. He describes the killings, watching them fall dead, and that kind of thing with almost the same degree of enjoyment that he describes the rape and sodomy.

". . . Truth is what this case is about. And the truth is this man went there with the dual purpose to kill and to sexually punish that woman whom he believed was interfering with his life. I trust you'll do the right thing here.''

It took the jury of seven women and five men just three hours to agree that Jablonski was guilty on all counts, which included special allegations of rape, sodomy and multiple murder. As he had throughout the trial, Jablonski had no reaction. He remained expressionless as the verdicts were read, looking straight ahead, seemingly unaware or uninterested in what was occurring around him.

''I don't even know if he knows where he is,'' Merritt said after the verdict was announced.

With the second hurdle of a four-phased trial now cleared, Murray could see the end in sight and readied for what he hoped would end in an execution date.

SIXTEEN

Insanity

*"Jablonski knew he was not killing little men from
Mars, or shooting cabbages."*

The guilty verdict left Jablonski's defense team with only
two opportunities to spare their client from a death sentence.
First, they planned to use the testimony of a psychiatrist to
prove that Jablonski was insane at the time of the crimes. If
that tack failed, and the case moved into a penalty phase to
determine Jablonski's ultimate fate, the lawyers could argue
for mercy and blame the savage acts on his horrible upbringing
and abusive father.

The insanity ploy would be an uphill climb, and Merritt
knew it. It had been years since any San Mateo County jury
had found a defendant legally insane. The last example of
sanctioned madness occurred in 1978 when a murderer was
found not guilty by reason of insanity for killing a showboat
restaurant owner with a shotgun blast. There had, however,
been other county cases in more recent times where prosecutors
and defense attorneys agreed that a defendant was out of his
mind. In a 1989 case, opposing lawyers found that a man who
had killed his three-month-old daughter as a "sacrifice to God,"
was indeed out of touch with the real world.

Still, an insanity defense is difficult to win. Jurors have
become skeptical and view the mental health maneuver as a
legal loophole that allows the guilty to avoid prison sentences.
Though those found legally insane usually end up spending

most of their lives in state mental hospitals, juries have tended to reject the argument out of fear that those found not guilty by reason of insanity could end up on the streets.

"It is an absolute misconception that a prisoner will get out of the hospital sooner than prison," Redwood City defense attorney Gordon Rockhill told the *San Mateo Times* newspaper during the Jablonski trial. Rockhill, who had successfully defended Giacomo Messina in the 1978 showboat restaurant murder, agreed that jurors had long since become more suspicious of insanity arguments. "Jurors will assume it's a matter of convenience," he told the newspaper. "But the sad fact is that most people who commit heinous crimes are seriously mentally ill."

There is a big difference between being medically insane and being legally out of touch with reality. The factors clinicians consider are not always in keeping with how courts weigh the evidence. While psychiatrists could declare Jablonski a psychotic who drooled, babbled and claimed to hear voices, the defense team would need much more evidence to win.

"You can be crazy and still be sane," San Mateo County Deputy District Attorney Steve Wagstaffe told the *San Mateo Times* in the midst of the Jablonski case. "It takes more than a diagnosed mental disease or defect."

The legal task in the Jablonski case fell into the realm of psychobabble, as opposing mental health experts took the witness stand to argue over the killer's state of mind during the last moments of Carol Spadoni and Eva Peterson's lives. Under the rules of law, this part of the trial favored the prosecution. Because Jablonski's defense team had said their client was not guilty by reason of insanity, the burden of proof rested with them. That meant Merritt and Keyes had to convince the same jury that had just heard all the crime scene evidence that the convicted murderer did not know right from wrong when he drove to his wife's home in 1991.

Murray planned to counter the testimony of the defense's star expert, Dr. Kormos, by presenting a series of witnesses who had confronted Jablonski in the weeks before the murders and the days after the killings. Murray wanted to do more than confuse jurors with the testimony of another psychiatrist. He reasoned that the recollections of average citizens could be more powerful than the arguments of psychiatrists. Murray had hoped that the testimony would prove to jurors that the pathetic-looking man they now saw seated at the defense table was not the same character who been so cool and collected during discussions with a cop in Wyoming.

Murray also relied on the testimony of those who had encountered Jablonski at his auto mechanic class on the very night he took Vann on that fatal ride. In addition, he took the testimony of bank tellers who cashed checks the killer had forged on Peterson's account after the crime to show that he was in full control of his emotions and actions in the period right after the murders. Murray even called Burlingame Police Department Patrol Officer Ickes to recount his traffic stop encounter with the defendant. Ickes' statements not only placed Jablonski near the crime scene within minutes of the murders, but also proved to the jury that the defendant was smart enough to stay calm when confronted by a lawman.

"The defense psychiatrist said this guy was drooling and talking gibberish," Murray recalled. "But he was the same guy who talked himself out of a weapons arrest in Wyoming days after the murders."

Murray understood that logic was not on the defense team's side. For the jury to believe the insanity claim, the panel would have to discard the fact that Jablonski seemed to have had no difficulty making his way across much of California.

"The description the defense psychiatrists gave was of a man who was so psychotic that he could not say his own name," Murray recalled. "But in 1991, he was able to drive all the way from Southern California to the victim's home in Burlingame. It takes a fair bit of abstract thinking to be able to put a plan like that into effect. You have to have gas for the car and make sure you don't get any traffic tickets along the way. Certainly a person who is in the condition that their psychiatrists described could not and would not be able to do it."

He also used court-appointed psychiatric experts to shoot down Kormos' opinion about the defendant. Dr. Vitali

Rozynko, a psychologist from Palo Alto, interviewed Jablonski five different times in February and March of 1994. Though Rozynko said Jablonski's behavior was well beyond the pale of social acceptability, he determined the defendant was sane at the time of his crime spree. Rozynko found that Jablonski was a schizophrenic and a sexual sadist, but concluded that the evidence showed he understood the nature and quality of his acts. Unlike people who are found to be criminally insane, Jablonski was not suffering from a false belief that the victims were a threat to him Rozynko said.

"If a schizophrenic is very disturbed, he may not know right from wrong," Rozynko told the jury. "If he has a certain delusion, for example, if he thinks that the person that he is going to kill or has just killed is an enemy of society and he thinks that he would be a hero if he killed that person, well, we might say that he does not know the nature of the act."

Jablonski, however, did not fall into that category of madness. Rozynko found that Jablonski was not suffering from any delusions during his sessions with the defendant. The doctor said Jablonski's responses during their sessions were logical and coherent, even on such touchy subjects as his alleged Vietnam combat experiences and the murder of Fanny Vann. Rozynko told the jury that Jablonski spoke openly about both matters. According to the psychiatrist, Jablonski said he had carved up Vann's body because he had seen soldiers do the same thing to the Viet Cong during his tour of duty.

"This doesn't necessarily mean he was actually there," Rozynko said of Jablonski's reported duty as a tunnel rat in Vietnam. "He was certainly in a position to hear stories. And if you were in a mental health program like he was [in Texas] you certainly would hear a lot of that," Rozynko said.

Jablonski was also willing to speak with Rozynko about the murders of Spadoni and Peterson, telling the psychiatrist that he killed the older woman because she did not want him having sex with Spadoni. He also said that he shot his anorexic wife to put her out of her misery. At no time during their sessions did the doctor consider Jablonski out of touch with reality. He also concluded that there was no evidence he fell into such a state during his crime spree.

"I don't think there was any question that he engaged in goal-directed behavior before he came to Burlingame and before he killed Fathyma," Rozynko said. "He went around and he looked at a gun and he bought a gun. Before he came to Burlingame, he got money out of the bank. After the killing he used either a credit card or a check to get money to escape with. That is a sign of planning and a sign that he is certainly in touch with reality."

The Burlingame murders themselves were carried out with precision, Rozynko concluded, not in a crazy fashion as might be expected if the killer's mind was tainted with insane images.

"He certainly didn't run around without any purpose," Rozynko said. "Immediately after Eva refused to take off her clothes, he took out his gun and shot her. It didn't sound to me, the way he described it, that there was any hesitation whatsoever. He said you do that or I will shoot you. She did not, [and] he shot her."

Had Jablonski been in a crazed state at the time of the killings, as the defense had suggested, Rozynko believed the killer would have given some hint of this lunacy on the infamous tape he made shortly after each crime. Instead, the tape corresponded with most of the evidence at hand.

"Let's say, if Jablonski had thought that Eva was some sort of demon or something of this sort, he would describe the situation. This obviously did not happen. He described it very, very much like the physical evidence indicated it happened," Rozynko said. "He shot her above the breast. He tried to gouge out her eyes and that's what the physical evidence showed."

A second prosecution psychiatrist, Dr. George L. Wilkinson, added a few twists to the story. Though he, too, considered Jablonski sane, his sessions with the killer turned up slightly different opinions. The doctor concluded that Jablonski was suffering from Post Traumatic Stress Disorder as a result of his childhood trauma. He also termed Jablonski a sexual sadist, who tended to exaggerate his stories in an effort to deceive.

"Mr. Jablonski suffers from a number of severe mental ill-nesses,'' Wilkinson found. ''I believe that at times he is psychotic and at other times not. It is also apparent that he will amplify his symptoms, feign other symptoms and malinger in an attempt to enhance his feelings of self-esteem. He hopes that others will see him as extremely dangerous and extremely ill, both of which he is. Yet he craves the status of someone intensely feared and idolized for his power and cruel behavior.''

Wilkinson said that feelings of inadequacy, sexual sadism and rage toward women were persistent character traits of this defendant. Jablonski had been candid with Wilkinson during their pretrial interviews. He spoke about his upbringing, his past loves and his horrible childhood experiences. He even talked about the murders, adding that in the case of Spadoni and Peterson that he had heard a voice tell him to commit the crimes.

According to Wilkinson, Jablonski said he began to feel bad at the end of the Persian Gulf War in 1991, when returning veterans were lauded as saviors. He claimed that the adulation those fighters received upset him and brought back memories from Vietnam. ''They were treated like heroes and we were treated like dirt,'' he told Wilkinson.

He told the psychiatrist that he drove to Burlingame after killing Vann and that once he got to their home, he decided to rape the women. He said he had become very upset with Peterson and felt that she had been running his and Spadoni's lives. According to Wilkinson, Jablonski said he entered the women's home, argued with Peterson over whether he could take Spadoni to a motel and in the midst of this, he claimed to have heard a voice urging him to ''kill her.''

''He denies ever having been able to have sex with either Eva or Carol before or after killing them,'' Wilkinson reported to the court. ''He steadfastly denied that he ever planned to kill Carol or Eva, but freely admitted to his plan to rape them both. The rape of Eva was to be for punishment. He was unclear in his explanation for why Carol also should be raped, except possibly that he was angry at her for not wanting to live with him in Indio.''

Jablonski said that after the murders, he showered and shaved and ate some chocolate chip cookies and potato chips before he searched for money so he could make a run for it. He added that he tape-recorded his thoughts soon after the killings, saying that the tape was made so he would come across as a"big shot," or someone others might idolize, according to Wilkinson.

Though Jablonski told the doctor that he wished the women were still alive, he never expressed any remorse for having taken their lives. Wilkinson also found that Jablonski's chaotic and abusive family, and the fact that he had been raped at an early age, led to his hatred for women.

"His intense feelings of inadequacy in comparison to other men is one reason he chose women as victims," Wilkinson reported. "He appears to be recreating his own victimization with the women that he victimizes. He may at times appear to be a passive, inadequate but somewhat charming individual. Yet his unresolved rage, as well as abnormally intense dependency wishes, have led him even to attack his own mother. He is profoundly desperate for the nurturing attention of women, yet he also harbors huge resentment toward any perceived intrusion or control by them. His intense dependency needs leave him feeling extremely lost, abandoned and despairing when he fears a woman wishes to end a relationship with him. At the same time, the rage he feels towards women for prior hurts leads him to degrade and punish any available woman. His rage may be displaced following a conflict with one woman, to be acted out in the rape of a different woman. He feels his masculinity is so inadequate that he made his audio tape, embellishing his sadistic behavior with his powerful sadistic fantasies. Another expression of his feeling of deficiency in relationship to men is that he needs to kill women that he desires, so that no other men could, as he fears, easily win them for themselves."

Wilkinson also found that Jablonski wanted others to see him as dangerous and crazed.

"He craves the status of someone intensely feared and idolized for his powerful and cruel behavior," the doctor reported. "The most plausible explanation [for the crime] was that he was feeling emotionally distraught, lonely and abandoned while in Indio. [He] sought to overcome these feelings with the sexualized murder of Vann, and then came to Burlingame in search of Carol and Eva. By his own account, he planned in a rational moment to rape both women. However, based on his history, the desire also to kill the women was probably present. . . . His behavior afterwards in taking a shower and eating revealed an intense disdain for both women and also an unrealistic appreciation of the risk of capture. Counterbalancing this unrealistic appreciation of risk was his very realistic planning to obtain funds in order to facilitate his escape. He clearly avoided detection and made good on his escape, only to be overtaken by his need to kill again.''

Despite his wide-ranging review, Wilkinson reasoned that the evidence suggested Jablonski was sane at the time of the crimes. He based part of that conclusion on the tape recording.

''If one uses his recollections and description of the crimes immediately following them, there's a lucid description on the tapes that is, for the most part, accurate,'' he told the jury. ''There was a plan. He was going to rape [them], tie them both up. Let one watch while he raped the other. This all seemed to have a good set of planning without an underlying delusion that would have helped me understand his being psychotic. With the absence of the delusion, I couldn't see that this was psychotic thinking.''

The damaging evidence mounted with each passing day of the five-day sanity hearing. As had been the case all through the trial, the death tape proved too much to overcome. ''It was powerful evidence,'' Murray recalled. ''Jablonski knew he was not killing little men from Mars, or shooting cabbages. He knew he was killing Eva and Carol. He described it in graphic detail. He knew the nature and quality of his act. The fact that he had been to prison before and had fled the area showed that he knew he had done wrong.''

Jablonski also tipped his hand during the trial by paying subtle attention to the female court clerks and court reporters who worked for Judge Schwartz. Although he stared off into space during the trial, Jablonski followed the women with his eyes as they moved about the courtroom.

"The court reporter and clerk were attractive women," Murray recalled. "Whenever either of them moved, Jablonski would keep his head forward, but his eyes darted about like a lizard. He could not keep his eyes off them. The women did not find this very endearing. They said that he looked at them like a butcher looks at the chart [of a cow] on the wall. Like a man looking at the parts he is going to cut up."

SEVENTEEN
Life or Death

"I did not have the courage to face Satan head on."

San Mateo County is not the best place to go on trial for a capital offense. The citizens in this largely upper-class and well-educated land of Bay Area commuters take a harsh view toward crime and those who commit it. While their counterparts in nearby San Francisco County tend to favor long prison sentences over the death penalty, recent surveys done in San Mateo County show residents there are strong supporters of capital punishment. Records show that since 1983, nearly 90 percent of those charged with murder in San Mateo were convicted.

"Since 1982, almost every death penalty case in the county that went to a jury ended in a death sentence," Jablonski's attorney Richard Keyes recalled. "The district attorney in this county carefully selects death penalty cases. They pick the ones they are pretty certain will go for death."

By May 1994, the jurors had found Jablonski sane and were assembled once again before Judge Schwartz to delve into a new aspect of the case. The panel now would get a chance to learn all about this vacant-looking man who had sat across from them in court. They would hear all about his childhood from witnesses that both the prosecution and defense had located from his past. They would see the faces of Jablonski's old girlfriends and his former victims, as each recounted what life was like under the big man's mood swings and sexual demands. They would also hear, for the first time, the full details about Vann's murder and the slaughter that had taken place inside a small convenience store in Utah just days after Spadoni and Peterson died. The time had come to put Jablonski's life work up for review, and see how the scales balanced.

Keyes and Missett had come to know Jablonski's past fairly well and were determined to focus their energies on his hellish childhood, in order to raise a glimmer of sympathy with the jury. In essence, they would put Jablonski's father on trial, portraying the family patriarch as a savage beast who tormented his entire brood. It was their task to try and convince at least one member of the panel that Jablonski was not fully to blame for his murderous acts. In Keyes' view, people like Jablonski deserved some level of sympathy because, unlike contract killers, crazed criminals have little control over their terrible actions.

"The people who raised him were not real sophisticated and the environment he was raised in made him the object of serious abuse," Keyes recalled. "Obviously, his severe cruelty toward others is manifested by his five homicides, but he had been so molded and warped that this would be an expected reaction. . . . You should be given some sympathy for the things that have happened to you in the past."

Murray would also look to the past to determine Jablonski's future. Instead of searching for pity amid the man's crippled life, the prosecutor would build a case upon the recollections of those whom Jablonski had ruined. Using the testimony of virtually every female who had ever crossed paths with Jablonski, Murray expected to construct a mosaic of evil, one that was begun in childhood and expanded for 40 years.

Murray, Morse and the rest of the prosecution team had traveled across the nation collecting eyewitness accounts from Jablonski's siblings, his past pen pals, and his long-forgotten victims. They located the woman he had raped in 1972, and Dennis Seton, the neighbor who had come to her rescue. They spoke with Sandra Norbert, the pen pal Jablonski had attacked in 1977 after luring her to his home with Bible letters. They met with the housewife he nearly choked to death in 1978 following the murder of Linda Kimball. They also readied Kimball's mother for testifying along with the Palm Springs detectives who had investigated that killing.

The witnesses spanned a generation of crime. When fitted together, Murray hoped the jury would come to understand Jablonski better than the killer knew himself.

"I wanted the jury to see how cool and cunning he was with the surviving victims," Murray recalled. "I wanted them to see how he used his dog-handling job as a ploy in the 1972 offense and how he used a newspaper advertisement for a stove and threats against that woman's children in the 1978 attack. These were very callous things and I wanted the jury to be affected by them. I wanted them to see the depravity and ruth-lessness of it all. To show them that he is a cold and calculating person, not someone who is totally crazy and sick."

One by one, the living ghosts from Jablonski's past came to the witness stand. Some of the prosecution witnesses wept during their testimony, recalling wounds they had spent years trying to forget.

Patsy Jablonski brought the jury back to the 1950s and placed them inside the hell house on Severance Street. Recalling her early years inside her father's house, Patsy told the jury how their father strangled their mother and his children. "He used to pin us down to the bed or up against the wall by putting his hand to the throat," she said. "And he would lift us off the floor so that our feet would be, five or six inches off the floor."

In addition to explaining her father's often tyrannical and drunken behavior, she revealed her brother's early interest in sex, his incestuous tendencies and his rape attempt against her when he was a teenager.

"I started fearing him, being alone with him after the attack on me," she told the jury. "It was like when my mom and dad left, he would take his aggressions out on us. . . . There was a fear. It was like there was a fear that he was gonna hurt us. After the attack on me, when he tried to rape me, then when he came home from the service . . . I really got the deep fear."

Rose Ludwig came forward to reminisce about the shy boy

she had once considered her high school sweetheart. She told stories of being abused at the hands of her husband and the need to flee his presence to save her life. Ann Riordan, the innocent teenaged army hospital assistant who had been raped on her first date, continued the ugly oral history by taking the jury back to the Texas "lover's lane" where he first savaged her.

Rape victim Agnes Robbins, who had long since left California and resettled in Florida to put time and distance between herself and the nightmare she had suffered when Jablonski used his dog handling training to trick his way into her home, came forward as well. Though it had been more than 20 years since he had threatened her son's life and forced himself upon her, the events had clearly altered her forever. She trembled on the stand and cried while Jablonski sat just steps away and stared into nothingness.

Jablonski was not kept in restraints during the trial. Bringing a shackled defendant to court on a murder charge was considered too prejudicial. The defendant had been instructed to remain still during the course of the trial and had been warned that he would be shot should he pose a threat to anyone. To further prevent any temptation, a special chair was designed for Jablonski to assure total security for the court. His seat looked like all the others, but it had been filled with lead. The chair weighed well over 100 pounds, making it very difficult to move. Strips of tape had been placed behind the chair as a demarcation line. The court bailiffs had been instructed to watch the chair just in case Jablonski tried to scoot it back in an effort to move away from the table.

"Jablonski was told if the chair moved past the tape, that he would be shot," Murray recalled.

Throughout the trial he sat still. The chair never inched past the line of tape. Jablonski's expression showed little variation as well, even as Robbins sobbed on the witness stand.

"It was amazing to hear the witnesses get up there and talk," recalled Spadoni's cousin, Kres Daphne, who attended most of the trial. "You could see how this woman [Robbins] was haunted by this."

Dennis Seton came to tell his story as well. Because Jablonski had taken a plea bargain following his attack on Robbins, Seton never had the opportunity to recount what he knew. He had spoken with Robbins before the trial by phone and had learned that she would not attend unless he were there as well. When the pair met for the first time in 20 years outside the courtroom, she greeted him with open arms.

"She looked wilted, but I recognized her right away," Seton said of the emotional moment when hero and victim reunited. "I recognized her right away because she always had a beautiful smile. But she looked tired. I saw her, and my heart got real heavy for her. She threw her arms around me. But in my mind, I don't believe I saved her life; I told her that God put me there that night."

Seton carried himself professionally on the witness stand, just as he had done years before on the night he set out with a gun in his hand, but no shoes on his feet, to face down a rapist. His words brought the jury back to Dec. 17, 1972 when he found a terrified and naked woman pleading for help at his front door.

"She was crying and real emotional," he told the jury. "Just stating that she had experienced an individual that entered her home and put a knife to her throat and had raped her."

The retired air force sergeant explained how he rushed into the street with a handgun and found Jablonski walking away from the scene of the crime with his clothing in his hand.

"I told him to stop," Seton told the jury. "I said, 'Halt. If you move, I'll kill you.' He just turned around and looked at me and said, 'I'm going to drop this stuff.' I said, 'If you drop it, I'm going to drop you.'"

Sandra Norbert did her part as well, telling the jury how she came to know Jablonski through pen pal letters and his apparent interest in finding religion under her guidance. Norbert spared few details on the witness stand. She explained how she had hoped to get prison inmates interested in religion and continued to write Jablonski letters after he expressed a real interest in God. She walked the jury through her terrifying experience and the fear she felt at the sight of her pen pal armed with a razor blade.

On cross-examination Norbert admitted that she had lied to Jablonski at the time by saying she would never report his actions to police. As a God-fearing woman, Norbert was a bit embarrassed to admit to lying, but she made up for that with the most honest assessment of the defendant.

"As I was telling the lies, I was thinking to myself that it was wrong to lie and that I was committing a sin," Norbert told the jury. "But I did not have the courage to face Satan head on."

"Truer words were never spoken," Murray recalled of Norbert's performance on the stand. "All the while, when she was writing letters to him, Norbert was imagining that he was converting, intent to follow the path of Jesus. Meanwhile, I am sure Jablonski was really imagining what it would be like to have a rope around her neck while he sodomized her."

The legacy continued day after day, with each victim adding an extra layer of human torment.

Norma Fane came to court on May 24 to share the story of her daughter, Linda Kimball. She told the jury that when she first met Jablonski years before, he had seemed "perfectly normal," and that he had no difficulty expressing himself. She brought the jury into her bedroom on the night of July 6, 1978, and told them how she awoke to find the defendant standing over her bed.

"There was someone on top of me with their hand over my face, completely over my face, and a sharp instrument at my throat," Fane told the jury as she placed a hand to her neck. "The person said, 'Be quiet or I'll kill you.'"

Jablonski's former landlord, Tina Montez, testified as well. It had been three years since she had talked sports and movies with the person she once pitied and considered to be lonely and fat.

"He looked different in court, like there was nobody home," Montez recalled. "I looked over at him because he had never done anything to me. I looked at him and there was no light, no nothing. No eye contact. I don't know what kind of medicine he was on, but it must have been horrendous, because there was nothing there. I was nothing to him.''

The jurors spent a month walking through Jablonski's life, seeing him go from an abused, frightened boy to a predator who used deception and brutal force to strike back at the world. As Murray had promised two months before, the panel had been led on a one-way trip into pure depravity. But the journey would not end without the dramatic summations from the opposing lawyers.

EIGHTEEN

Arguments

*"Cold-blooded. Calculating. Manipulative.
Methodical."*

"Our work is almost done," Murray told the jury as he
began his closing arguments on the morning of June 15, 1994.
"Shortly, you are going to be called upon to make the most
difficult and important decision that juries in the United States
are called upon to make. I believe in this case, your examination
of the evidence will alleviate a lot of the difficulty that some
juries have. You've examined extremely horrible crimes, and
an extremely horrible background.

"Reflect back on the kind of case you were thinking about
in the abstract," he told them, referring to the day they were
sworn in to hear the evidence. "Is the case that you imagined
nearly as bad as this case? Could you have imagined back then
that you would see and hear what you have heard about the
deaths of Eva Peterson and Carol Spadoni? Could you have
imagined the brutality, the savagery, the depravity when you
said, 'Yes, I can conceive of a case in which death is appropriate?'

"Could you have even imagined the terror in hearing about
this man working for a security service, employed by a woman
who was afraid of being raped, going over to her house, tricking
her into tying the dog up out in the backyard? Could you have
even imagined that you would hear the terror of that woman
as she began crying, as he began to mount her, to rape?

"Could you have even imagined the horror of Mrs. Carey? And this man takes her child, and puts a knife to that kid's throat and tells her, 'Strip or I kill the kid?' It goes on and on, the horror, the depravity, the evil, the violence that this man has perpetrated on society for over 20 years."

Transforming himself from advocate to teacher, Murray educated the panel about the death penalty, telling them that the subject was unpleasant, but a fact of life, and one considered necessary by the people of California. He explained how they had to consider all the evidence, the good and the bad, before determining whether Jablonski's deeds sunk him to the level of the worst of the worst.

"After hearing the evidence of the way that these women died, the brutality, the horror, the butchery, the degradation, the sexual motive, it would take a tremendous amount of mitigating evidence in someone's background to even come close to justifying life without the possibility of parole," the prosecutor lectured. "But do we have good in this man's background? No. We have more and more and more evil. Life in prison would be a gift. An unwarranted gift for this man." Murray practically scoffed at the defense's theory of the case, telling the jurors that Jablonski had already received enough breaks from the criminal justice system, which had released him from prison time and again, even as the violent nature of his crimes evolved and increased.

"The difficulty in this case is not whether the death penalty is the appropriate and justified verdict," Murray said. "The only difficulty in this case is whether each of you has the fortitude, the inner strength of a verdict of death." Murray recalled Robbins' emotional testimony as proof of how much damage Jablonski had caused to just one of his many victims, and why the defendant had no right to expect any mercy from those who sat before him in judgment.

"Can you imagine the terror that this man put that woman through?" he asked the jurors. "Twenty-two years later [and] she still can't even talk about it on the witness stand without being reduced to tears. . . . Think about the sympathy and the mercy that he showed Agnes Robbins as she lies there and starts to cry and he takes the handle of that knife and smashes her face, breaking the bone around her eye, and tells her he'll kill the kids if she doesn't shut up. Yeah, give him sympathy. Give him mercy.''

The prosecutor used each victim as a living metaphor to prove that Jablonski was a sexual sadist and a serial killer whose rightful place was beside men like Ted Bundy, and Richard Ramirez. Like each of these better-known mass killers, Jablonski had used lies and cunning to place women under his control.

Murray held the jury's full attention as he revisited the pain each victim had suffered. He reminded them of Norbert's personal humiliation and near-death experience. He shared with them the agony of Linda Kimball, who made the fatal mistake of trying to run from a man unwilling to let any victim escape his desires. ''He murdered her brutally,'' Murray reminded the jury.

The prosecutor said that he may not have known what Jablonski's mental state was at the time he killed Kimball, but reminded the jury about the actions the killer took days later, when he conned his way into another woman's home by claiming he wanted to buy her stove. Such cunning was not consistent with the acts of a raving lunatic, he argued.

''We know he wasn't an insane person during that incident,'' Murray said. ''He checks out her house, makes sure there's no man at home. Leaves and tells the woman he has to check with his wife. He has no wife! She's lying dead in the morgue. He's lying to her. Manipulating her. . . . He gets her to go into the house to look for a ruler, and when she does that and turns around and sees what has got to send a chill down your neck—the image of her two-year-old in this man's arm with a knife to his throat.

''This so-called 'insane maniac' that can't reason, that can't think . . . does he do something insane and crazy at that time? No, he tells her, 'He's my insurance.' Cold-blooded. Calculating. Manipulative. Methodical. He knows exactly what he's doing. He is in total control. . . . These are not crimes of a man with insane rages. These are crimes of a man who knows exactly what he's doing. He has this need to dominate, degrade, humiliate women. And the ultimate degradation, to take their lives."

Taken together, Murray said Jablonski's murderous legacy made him a perfect match for the death penalty, not only because of the terrible nature of his crimes, but because he was obviously lying about his hallucinations as a way to avoid punishment.

"You have not heard from one single witness that at any time before or after these crimes he exhibited any symptoms of mental illness," Murray said. "The only symptom he ever exhibited was when he goes in and lies to the psychiatrists and says, 'I'm remembering what happened to me back in Vietnam with the helicopter crash and my poor buddy dying in my arms.' Lies!"

Murray told the jurors to examine Jablonski's official military record, which indicated that he had completed a tour of duty in Korea and had been assigned to Fort Bliss, Texas. Conspicuously absent from the record is any mention of him being in Vietnam.

"He was never there," Murray said, before confronting the defense's last line of hope.

"There is a place for sympathy in this case," he began. "There is a place for pity for Phillip Jablonski in this case— sympathy and pity for Phillip Jablonski, the boy. No one deserves to be raised by an alcoholic father. No one deserves to have a father that is brutal toward his mother. No one deserves to be raised in that kind of atmosphere of violence. But I want you to take whatever sympathy and pity you feel for Phillip Jablonski, the boy, and I want you to project it 30, 35 or 40 years later to Phillip Jablonski, the man, and ask if he deserves sympathy and pity now."

Murray was not through attacking the defense's strategy, as he scolded the opposition for trying to shift blame away from their client. "It's disturbing to me to see a new trend in criminal defense these days," Murray said. "To find somebody else to blame and then your client doesn't need to be blamed. Who has the defense pointed the finger of blame at in this case?

Phillip Jablonski, Sr. He was a brutal father. . . . It does appear that he [the defendant] was beaten. [But] it doesn't excuse rape. It doesn't excuse sodomy. It doesn't excuse the kinds of crimes that this man had committed. And it really doesn't even explain them. Whatever beatings he suffered at the hands of his father were 40 years ago. He's had years of therapy in the army, Veteran's Administration, prisons and none of it explains the kind of sneaky, predatory, planned acts of rape and murder that he commits.''

Murray had lectured for most of the morning and wanted to leave jurors with doubts about what he suspected the defense would say during its closing arguments in the afternoon. In closing, the prosecutor reminded them of their promise to deliver a fair verdict. He asked them to consider how much kindness Jablonski had given his many victims.

''His lawyers will tell you he deserves lenience because of his troubled childhood,'' Murray said. ''As you listen, think of the sympathy he showed Agnes Robbins. Think of the sympathy that he showed to Sandra Norbert, Linda Kimball, Penny Carey, Fathyma Vann, Eva Peterson, Carol Spadoni, Margie Rogers. Think of those things and weigh it and balance it. . . . If the death penalty means anything in this state, it means that he gets it. . . . He does not deserve your good will. He does not deserve your sympathy. He does not deserve your pity. He does not deserve your warmth. He does not deserve your compassion. How many posterboards of dead victims do we have to fill before we decide enough is enough?''

As Judge Schwartz called the court to order at 1:30 that afternoon, Richard Keyes, a Hastings Law School-trained attorney with a deep, almost monotone voice, lifted his long and slender frame from the defense table and turned to the jury.

''In your decision, a knee-jerk reaction cannot be used by you,'' he began. ''The prosecution was suggesting that the death penalty is for this kind of case, only this case. [But] that's wrong. That is not the law. . . . Put it all together. What came first? What caused what? What's related? Where does sympathy play a role? Follow the law.''

To understand what created Jablonski, Keyes had called witnesses from his distant past, and some who were familiar with the family even before Jablonski was born. For Keyes, the elder Mr. Jablonski was the central figure in this part of the case, and he would not let the jury forget the man who he felt had molded his client into a twisted killer.

"The father is to blame for a lot of this," Keyes said. "He is to blame for the creation of a series of scarred people." During the trial, Keyes had called Orill Crum, a Jablonski family friend, who related stories that told of Jablonski Senior's stubbornness and angry ways. He had also called forward those who had grown up around the Jablonski home in the 1950s to search their childhood memories for tales of terror that centered on that Severance Street home. Each helped fill in a little piece of the story, which, when gathered together, cast light upon a dark and sinister home life for Jablonski, the boy.

As a boy, Keyes told the jury, Jablonski had been a quiet and polite child who had stood face-to-face with his drunken father in an effort to save his mother from her regular beatings. At school, young Phillip had been withdrawn, stooped-shouldered and isolated.

"Everybody you talk to about his life in the first 20 years [says he was] polite," Keyes said. "Polite to his parents. Polite to his neighbors. Obedient to his sister. Obedient to his mother." Keyes gave his own lecture on what the rules of law demanded the jury do in terms of evaluating Jablonski's life. He told them that they had to go well beyond a listing of his good and bad acts, but to also examine the limited options he had thanks to his unfortunate upbringing.

"Mitigation is not just limited to good stuff," he said. "[It's] anything about how they're raised. What chances they had, what abilities they had. What social acceptance they had or didn't have. Anything like that you can take into account as mitigation. That is why this is a life without parole situation, because for the first 20 years, this man came through a mine field of terror at a time when he's unable to understand it, unable to cope with it, and he never recovered to adequately adjust to our society. It takes a different case than this one, where he was so terrorized and stunted, degraded sexually and physically abused and beaten as a child that he ended up where he is . . . It takes more to kill somebody that has gone through childhood beatings and took those beatings—some of them to protect his mother—a mother who could not protect him.''

Keyes focused on Jablonski's life in San Bernardino, recalling for the jury the testimony of his client's relatives, who spoke about their bizarre father. He reminded them how the older man had once force-fed his granddaughter hot sauce, despite the little girl's screams. How the Jablonski children had to flee their home and hide in a ditch at night until their drunken father was done beating or sexually abusing his wife.

"What does a youngster of three or five or 10 start to learn, seeing a father like that who got away with it every time?" Keyes asked the jury to consider.

The defense attorney could not help but wonder how Jablonski's life might have turned out had he not been tossed into that home with that man as his role model.

"If any of you, any of the people we know, if they had adopted Phillip Jablonski at a young age, there would have been a tremendous difference," Keyes said. "They would have fed him spiritually and emotionally. They would not have drained his humanity from him. . . . The sympathy that you have to extend to somebody who is here because of the way he was raised has to say we're not going to kill you, but you're going to be punished forever in prison. Because we know he would have developed in a totally different way, a healthy way."

Keyes asked the jury if it was right to give his client the ultimate punishment for the sins of the man's father, and told them that it was easy to understand how Jablonski had become a cruel man since all he ever knew was brutality.

"What did he learn from his father?" Keyes asked. "Women were degraded. Bitches. Slaves. They were to be treated as second-class citizens. That they were nothing. . . . We have seen the results of his father's creation, of his own self-loathing and worthlessness into his son. If Phillip Jablonski had stumbled out of the house on Severance one day and you walked by and you had heard what was going on and you saw him crying, who among you would not have assisted him and dried his tears?

"You're being asked today to render some sympathetic look at a person who went through that. You're being asked to look at a human being. He was a unique person upon whom a personality was stamped, branded and imprinted. I am asking you to allow him to finish his life in a cell, clammy as it is, but one that would allow him to die at a natural schedule whatever that is going to be. For if you vote death, it may be an unwitting carrying out of the father's statement about his young children—that they should not have been born."

The jury began deliberations on June 16. They spent two hours discussing the evidence they had heard, then broke for the weekend. They needed only one hour the following Monday morning to agree that Jablonski's crimes called for death. Jablonski rubbed his chin but, as usual, showed no other signs of life when the death call rang out in Judge Schwartz's court. The jury foreman, Raymond Taylor, told the press that day that the evidence had been overwhelming and that jurors had reached a unanimous decision on the first vote.

"I think they did the right thing," Kres Daphne told the *San Francisco Chronicle* after the verdict was announced. "When someone had destroyed as many lives as he has, I think it's the only thing they could have done."

Even though Jablonski's audio-taped description of the killings had given the investigators chills when they first heard it, Taylor later told the media that the recording had not been the major factor against the defendant. He said jurors considered it as just another piece of evidence. "There was much more to look at," he told the *San Mateo Times*.

On August 13, 1994, Judge Schwartz passed official judgment on the defendant by calling the murders "savage and brutal," while Jablonski, now clean-shaven and chained, stared blankly and said nothing.

Carol Spadoni's brother, Michael Spadoni, never attended the trial. He had come to terms with the tragedy and did not care to look into the eyes of the man who brought death into his life. Part of his resolution may have come well before

Jablonski's conviction, when Michael gathered his mother and sister's cremated remains and drove into the desert.

"I took the ashes to where I knew there were wild burros and stuff," he recalled. "My mother had a bunch of old bowling trophies from the '50s, so I set up a little shrine on the top of this cliff. That is where the wild horses and burros are. That was one of my mother's causes, the wild horses. I mixed their remains together, because that is how they lived and I figured that's the way they should be."

In a letter he later sent to Judge Schwartz, Michael Spadoni called for a death sentence to, "ensure that there are no more victims in the future."

His two daughters also enclosed their thoughts in notes sent to the judge. "My sadness over the abrupt and humiliating end to their lives is something I will have to live with forever," Lisa Spadoni wrote. "How do I tell my children about Grandma Eva and Aunt Carol?"

NINETEEN

San Quentin 1996

"Like Sheep to the Slaughter."

Phillip Carl Jablonski is now 50 years old. He is one of more than 330 people awaiting execution on death row in the San Quentin State Prison. As with all death penalty cases in the state, Jablonski's conviction is under automatic appeal in California courts. The state appellate review process takes years to complete, and after that is done, the matter heads toward the federal system for additional review. As a death row inmate, Jablonski is technically a "dead man walking," but no one expects him to make it into the death chamber until well past the year 2000.

San Quentin State Prison sits on 440 acres of prime waterfront property that offers views of the San Francisco Bay. The prison was constructed in 1852 and has carried out state executions almost from the start. Legal executions by hanging were authorized in California in 1851. Early on, capital punishment was unpopular enough that inspectors for the state's prison at San Quentin recommended in 1855 that juries be allowed to choose, in murder cases, between sentences of death and life in prison. With time, however, the people of the state apparently lost some of their squeamishness. From 1893 to 1942, 307 men were hanged from the gallows at San Quentin and Folsom prisons.

On March 22, 1938, the State of California entered a new era. According to an account in the *San Jose Mercury News,* a small pig was placed in a cage laid across the arms of two chairs in a small, octagonal room. The doors to the room were shut. Within minutes, the state's new gas chamber—a replacement for its gallows—was christened with the vapors sent up by cyanide pellets mixed with acid. The prison warden, Court Smith, had opposed the switch to gas, saying it took too long to kill. He had even refused to allow a dog to be used to test the chamber because he thought it too cruel for a pet. An account in the *San Francisco Chronicle* noted that the little pig pulled away from the choking fumes, and bashed its head against the cage until it was overcome.

After pitched debate, the California Legislature approved lethal gas as its means of execution, effective for sentences imposed after Aug. 27, 1937. Robert Lee Cannon and Albert Kessel on Dec. 2, 1938, became the first men killed in the chamber for their roles in a Folsom riot. Eithel Leta Juanita "Dutchess" Spinelli was the first woman to die in the chamber, on Nov. 21, 1941. Spinelli, who had arranged a murder, said before her death that "my blood will burn holes in their bodies."

Police-killer Aaron Mitchell, 37, was the last person gassed before state executions were halted for more than 20 years. He died April 12, 1967. He was one of 190 to die inside the death chamber until a series of legal challenges halted executions. San Quentin began carrying out executions again in April 1992 when double-murderer Richard Alton Harris went to the gas chamber.

David Mason was the next to enter the apple-green gas chamber in August 1993. Three guards strapped him into one of the two metal chairs in the chamber and connected a cardiac monitor to his chest. Mason's last words were, "I've said all I have to say."

Since Mason's death, the gas chamber has been deemed cruel and unusual punishment. The state carried out its first lethal injection execution in 1996.

In several letters Jablonski sent to the author, the killer wrote openly about his crimes and even bragged about the killings. He claimed to have no fear of execution and expected to be led into the prison's death chamber one day in the future.

"I do feel I will be executed," he wrote in April 1996. "I sent women to their graves and I don't feel one bit sorry about doing it."

But for the present, Jablonski is enjoying life. He has several female pen pals and spends his days inside a four-by-10-foot cell that is decorated with postcards and pictures.

He claimed to spend most of his time doing artwork. He favors creating semi-nude drawings of the women who write to him. One of the ladies is fond of teddy bears, he wrote. She had even named one of the stuffed animals "P.J."

Jablonski is an avid reader. He enjoys the *New York Times,* the *Marin Independent Journal, Newsweek, Smithsonian* and *National Geographic.*

Jablonski's letters are logical and coherent, hardly the type one would expect to receive from a lunatic, as his attorney once described him. Jablonski discussed details about his crimes because he does not expect to face trial in Riverside County for the murder of Fanny Vann, and in Utah for the death of Margie Rogers. In these letters, he calls Vann "the target," while referring to Rogers as "the friendly and sweet brave lady."

Jablonski said he chose Vann for death because he needed the practice before taking on Eva and Carol. "I already planned on killing Eva and Carol," he wrote in April 1996. "But I wanted to know how close I had to be to my subject to kill them; which shots to the head and how many?"

He called Vann a "friendly, outgoing, naive person." He said it took him three months to set up her murder.

"Fanny served my purposes just great," Jablonski concluded in his letter, after he explained in graphic detail how he raped and mutilated her body.

Jablonski's recent letters also hint at the reason behind the Burlingame killings. In one letter sent on January 14, 1996, he claimed that there was a romantic link between himself and Eva Peterson.

"There was more than a son-in-law and mother-in-law relationship going," he wrote. "Eva was the one who converted [sic] Carol to marry me." In closing, Jablonski said that the women "went to their deaths willingly, like sheep to the slaughter."

In additional letters, Jablonski touched upon the murder of his common-law wife, Linda Kimball, stating that he had "the privilege of putting her in a graveyard." When musing about Linda and the other women, Jablonski took pleasure in describing their bodies. All of his letters are filled with references to the breasts and rectums of past victims.

He is a man still trapped by his own dreams and sexual fantasies. He seems to relish the memory of the women whose lives he has touched and ruined.

"Linda was the only woman I truly loved," he wrote in April 1996. "I treated her with deep respect. At times, she is the only woman I feel sorry about murdering. But the feeling doesn't last long. She got what she deserved."

Jablonski also fantasizes about how he degraded his wives. There is a sense of joy or boasting in these letters. In one, he spent time recalling Sandra Norbert, the Bible enthusiast who sought to bring him to Christ in the early 1970s, before barely escaping with her life.

"She had a real nice shape that I used for my sexual needs," Jablonski recalled.

Jablonski claims that he warned Norbert about what he intended to do to her should she visit his parents' home. He also claims she fell in love with him—a boast that seems doubtful given her court testimony.

Most of Jablonski's recent letters to the author included stories about how much control he had over his women. Jablonski also claimed to be currently engaged in pen pal friendships with several others. He wrote that at least one of the women is interested in a loving relationship.

One of the current pen pals reportedly wrote him because she was curious about life on death row. Jablonski said their friendship has grown into something deeper.

"What attracted her to me was my drawings of animals," Jablonski wrote. "Plus the portraits I have done, also the many times I have been married. So far, I have done portraits of her topless and in a negligee."

He said the woman is a 29-year-old divorcee living in England. His second pen pal is 20 and the single parent of a four-month-old boy. "Her view is that it is a shame for men to be on death row," Jablonski wrote. "That the death penalty should be abolished. . . . She wants to be my special lady."

Most of the investigators and civilians connected to the Jablonski case shake their heads upon hearing such stories. They don't understand why women write to dangerous inmates.

"The prisoner certainly has the motivation to write," said Judy Spadoni, Carol's sister-in-law. "The women who write don't seem to have very successful relationships on the 'outside' so to speak. This gives them a pathway and keeps the fantasy going that they can be anybody they want to be. Carol's physical appearance was disastrous, remember. No one would look at her and find her attractive. So this [pen pal relationship] was a way of being somebody and having a fantasy relationship. It kept her stable."

Jablonski agreed, explaining the strange power he has over woman.

"Most of the women [who write] enjoy the thrill of hearing about the women I have married," Jablonski explained in a May 1996 letter. "Plus [they enjoy] feeling the thrill of knowing I raped women and killed them. One of my pen pals asked me how it felt to rape a woman. One of my new pen pals wants to know if any of my victims screamed before I killed them.

"Women are funny; the ones I have met get a thrill out of knowing I harm other women. Maybe they think they will be next. They say women love outlaws, and I love breaking them."

Jablonski certainly planned horrible things for Shirley Thorp and Helen Blair, the two pen pals he met before beginning his 1991 killing spree. Jablonski confessed that had he not been caught in Kansas, he would have paid each woman a surprise visit. Had the visits gone off as planned, more names would have been added to his snake belt.

"The only plans I had for Shirley was the grave," Jablonski wrote in April 1996. "My plan was to enter her house, use her sexually, then while she was asleep, shoot her through the head."

He said that he planned to rape Thorp's two daughters, then escort them into their mother's room to view her body before he murdered them as well.

His had similar plans for Blair.

For now at least, Jablonski remains unchanged, housed with other killers and left to live out his days remembering the evil he brought to so many lives. Perhaps Eva Peterson's grand-daughter, Theresa Spadoni, summed him up best when she wrote Judge Schwartz following Jablonski's murder conviction, and explained that the killer haunts her nightmares.

"I find it unbelievable that I have to share this planet with someone like him," she wrote. "I can't stop him; no one can!"

APPENDIX:
The Tape

The following is a transcript of the tape-recorded message police found inside Phillip Carl Jablonski's car following his arrest for the murders of Carol Spadoni and Eva Peterson. Investigators believe he made the tape shortly after each murder and listened to it repeatedly to enhance his pleasure during masturbation.

"My first victim was Fanny N. Vann, she was five foot, born September the 4th, 1952. She's 130 pounds, brown eyes, black hair. I met her at the College of the Desert. First time I met her I didn't see much in her, bodywise anyway. Then, uh, she started working on her car. Then I seen that she had something I wanted—her body. She had, ah . . . when she wore her shorts one day, ohh, did she show off that fine little ass and those sweet legs. And I tried to look down the front of her blouse and see those fine medium-sized black breasts.

"I asked her for . . . I could take her home, 'cause she was standing around, and she said, 'Yes.' She had to go back and tell the girls [I] was gonna take her, that she had another ride.

"Well, I took her home for about three weeks. And I . . . each night I was planned on killin' her, but I didn't have everything I needed. I had a taser, but I didn't want to strangle her to death. So I got a gun. Bought a gun at the school from a guy I met there. And . . . it was 'bout a week then, uhhh,

that Monday night, 22nd of April, was her dying night and rape night.

"The friend I usually took to work didn't have to go to work that night, so I took him over to where the bar . . . Went back to the apartment I rented, got the gun, knife and taser. Went back to school, picked up the victim. We left there approximately nine o'clock headin' down Montgomery. Got to Dinah Shore, just about a block from Dinah Shore Road, when I pulled the gun on her. I turned down Dinah Shore to, to the dead end, turned around. Told her, 'Time to get raped, sweet thing.' I cocked the gun and said, 'Honey, you do it my way, or I'll do it when you're dead.'

"She took her clothes off. I asked her if she had ever sucked a dick. She says, 'No.' Ever have it up that fine black ass? And she said, 'No.' I said, 'Tonight's your lucky night, sweet thing. You're gonna get sodomized and you're gonna suck your first dick.'

"I forced her head down on my dick and first she didn't know that I put the gun to her head. And it went in like a breeze. She sucked and played with it, and squeezed my balls like I asked her to. Almost come in that sweet mouth, but I pulled her head and I says, 'Fuck, sodomy time, girl.' So I rolled her over to ride those fine black cheeks. Run the dick up in, in, wham! Right home in that big black ass.

"She let out a howl. I said, 'Ssh, ssh, be quiet girl,' and I fucked her good in that black ass. And I rolled her over saving the sperm and that sweet juicy beautiful pussy she's got housed between those beautiful legs. I made her guide it into her pussy. I sat there with it in her for awhile and I sucked on her fine full breast and I fucked the shit out of her. And squeezed her fine black breast.

"God, this woman's fine. I'm coming in her pussy. And I made her get dressed. She sit there with a tear in her eyes. Looked at her, I says, 'Sorry sweet thing, can't have no witnesses.'

"I shot her one time and she screamed, and she went, 'Ahhh.' I shot her again right in the temple. Laid her head against the window. The blood outlined that fine black breast

through her white pullover and her bra. I reached up and got me a handful of that sweet black breast. Squeezed it again and said, 'Well Fanny, I got what I wanted, you.' Yeah, you sweet little grandmother. You ain't gonna see your grandchildren, honey. At 37 she was a grandmother. Yeah, sweet thing, you're mine, all mine.

"*I took out, got on the freeway, took her out to Jefferson. Pulled her out of the car. Striped her of her jewelry. And uh, took her clothes off. Run my hands all over that gorgeous fine black ass and down her fine black legs. I turned her over, had a hard-on. I fucked her in . . . gorgeous black pussy again. Yeah, too bad she didn't feel it this time. Then I gouged out her eyes, cut ears off, cut her nipples out, stabbed her in her stomach, up her ass and her pussy. Left her there like garbage—what she was after I got done with her. Yeah, she is a sweet good-looking black woman that I finally got.*

(*The tape ends, then starts again*)

"*Back in Burlingame about noon at Carol's house. I got . . . I walked in no problem. And we talked for awhile. I got up. I hugged Carol. And I grabbed her around the waist, around the throat. Told Eva to strip. She said, 'Don't hurt . . . scare us with that gun. What are you trying to do?' I said, 'You don't strip, I'm gonna shoot ya between your beautiful breasts.' She didn't do it and I shot her right above the tit. She went, 'Uhhh,' and I just turned the gun and shot Carol through the brain, through her head. Let her drop to the floor. She curled up. I shot her mother again in the head. She dropped to the floor.*

"*Both making noises like they're breathing their last, but I make sure these girls are dead. So, I tied duct tape around Carol's mouth and nose. She's still making that noise, so I stabbed her through the throat, and I cut open her silicone tit. I stabbed her ass and pussy. Stripped her mother and fondled those fine big breasts. Rolled her over, sodomized that fine big ass she had. Ran my hands down her legs, turned her over, fucked her in that fine li'l pussy while fondling those big ole tits. I tried to take her eyes out. They wouldn't come, so I ran the knife through her throat to keep her quiet. Stabbed her in the stomach, ass and pussy.*

"Then I took, drug Carol into part of the house. Come back and drug Eva down the stairs. Then I ate some food. They made me a dinner. I ate my . . . eat their food, took a shower, shaved. Went back, took me a towel and . . . tried to muff the shot. I shot Eva through the mouth before I left. I said to her, 'Well sweet thing, believe me now. I was gonna rape you.' The old girl cost her her daughter's life. Yeah, I got them both, them bitches. Yeah, got 'em. It was so good to watch 'em fall dead.

"A few days later. I was leaving Utah about six in the morning. A sign saying gas and diesel at the truck stop ahead, so I pulled off and went in. There was an older elderly woman at the counter. I come to the door, bought me a soda, some potato chips and . . . uhhh, cased out the place. And 'yeah, uhh, this is what I want. I'm gonna have this woman,' and walked out.

"Got in the car and waited. Uhhh, there was a car pulled up and left. And uhhh, these two buses with no passengers I guess came in, turned around and left. So, I walked back in the store, gun cocked in my pants. And I got some coffee. She sat with her back to me. She got up and she says . . . she asked me if there was anything else I needed or wanted. I said, 'No.' I turned and walked around the store a little bit. Then I reached in my shirt, turned back around shot her in, guess in the body somewhere.

"She goes, 'Ahh.' I shot her in the head. She fell to the floor. I walked around, opened up the cash register and took all the bills out. Looked underneath to see if there was any extra money. Ripped open her blouse, pulled her bra up over her big gorgeous big breasts. Fondled and fondled 'em. Her eyes were rolling, it was still blinking like she was looking around. So I shot her through the temple, and the blood oozed out the side of her nose. Yeah, ole girl, I got your life.

(Tape stops again, then continues)

"Hoping this woman ahead of me is my next victim. She's got some great big ole tits, nice big ole ass. Has got a little kid with her. I'm gonna fuck this one alive if I can. As soon as these people leave—this trucker and this car ahead, she's mine if she don't leave before. God, look at that ass. Gorgeous big woman. God, would I like to fuck this. Oh, what an ass. What a set of tits. Well, I'm losing her. She's getting ready to leave. Man, would I give anything to fuck that, then kill it and fondle those big ole, big ole, big tits. God, then kill the little boy. God, [what] would I give for this woman. Come on you guys leave the fucking restroom 'fore I can have her. Shit yes. Come on guys, get out of the fucking restroom.

(Tape stops, then starts again)

"I get a chance, I'm kidnapping this woman. I'll put her in my car with the kid. Put her in the back seat. Make her lay down and shoot her. I don't care what I have to do to get this baby. She's mine.

(Tape stops, then starts again)

"Lost her, but there's two more that just went into the bathroom. These two guys would leave, I'd have these two. I'd just walk in and shoot 'em, and do what I wanted with 'em.

(Tape stops, then starts again)

Not gonna get these either. Well, I gotta move along and hope I get one soon."

THE LEGACY OF PHILLIP CARL JABLONSKI

1964: Sexual assault on sister Patsy. At age 17, Jablonski wrapped a rope around his sister's neck, pushed her on the bed and said he was going to "get something off her."

Oct. 1968: Attempted murder of Rose Ludwig Jablonski. During intercourse he would strangle his wife to unconsciousness with his hands on her throat and with a pillow. She sought medical treatment and Jablonski was arrested by army police. He received psychiatric treatment. In October or November, he traveled to California where he caught up with his estranged wife and tried to strangle her. The assault was interrupted by Jablonski's mother.

Dec. 1968: Rape of Ann Riordan; Jablonski raped victim on their first date. She did not report it. He saw her the next day and apologized. She continued to see him and became pregnant. During sex he would smother her with a pillow to the point of unconsciousness.

Jan. 1970: Sexual assault of Noreen Mitchell. Jablonski attempted to force victim, who was 17 at the time, to remove her clothes in the back room of a liquor store. He wrapped a belt around her hands and pulled her blouse over her head. She started crying and he stopped. Police concluded that the victim's report was unfounded.

Dec. 1972: Rape of Agnes Robbins. Jablonski, then employed for a guard dog service, gained access to victim's home in order to train her dog. He forced her to undress at knifepoint and grabbed her by the throat. He raped her and threatened to kill her children. Victim escaped and alerted a neighbor who captured Jablonski at gunpoint. He was paroled on Dec. 17, 1976.

March 1977: Sexual assault of Sandra Norbert. Upon Jablonski's release from prison, he telephoned a woman whom he had met through a pen pal club. Jablonski's mother sent Norbert money so she could travel to California to visit her son. Once inside the home, Jablonski attempted to smother her. He claims to have dug a grave for her. During the night, he entered her room and approached her with a razor. He shaved her pubic hair and tried to smother her with a pillow. Norbert left California, but did not report the crime.

July 1978: Attempted rape of Norma Fane. Beginning in March 1978, Fane received obscene phone calls in which the suspect threatened to rape her. On July 6, 1978, Jablonski entered her home and asked for a hug. She escaped, but did not report the crime to police.

July 1978: Murder of common-law wife, Linda Kimball. Victim was found strangled to death. Evidence found indicates she was strangled by a belt and beaten before the murder. Jablonski later said she planned to leave him. He said he strangled her then sodomized her. He pleaded guilty to a charge of second-degree murder and received a sentence of seven years in state prison.

July 1978: Attempted rape of Penny Carey. Jablonski called the victim in response to an ad she had placed in order to sell a stove. After arriving at her home, he picked up the victim's young son and put a knife to the boy's throat. He forced the woman to remove her clothes. She kicked him in the groin, but could not escape. He choked her into unconsciousness.

Jablonski later pleaded guilty to a charge of assault with great bodily injury. The sentence was imposed consecutive to the Kimball murder and gave him a total sentence of 13 years and eight months in prison.

July 1985: Assault on mother. While incarcerated at the California Men's Colony in San Luis Obispo, Jablonski attacked his mother who had come to see him on a weekend family visit. He grabbed her and tried to choke her. The assault was broken up by Jablonski's father. Jablonski pleaded guilty to a charge of battery and received a nine-year sentence. He was paroled in September of 1990.

April 22, 1991: The murder of Fathyma Vann. Jablonski murdered his classmate, then raped and mutilated her body before dumping her remains in the desert. Cause of death was a gunshot to the head.

April 23, 1991: The murders of Eva Peterson and Carol Spadoni. Jablonski met Spadoni through a pen pal club and married her in 1982. He entered Spadoni's home on April 23, 1991, and shot both women. Jablonski mutilated Spadoni's body and tried to gouge out Eva Peterson's eyes.

April 25, 1991: The attempted murder of Jacqueline Eadwine. Victim saw a man approaching her at a rest stop on Interstate 80 near Lyman, Wyoming. As Jablonski got out of his car, a gun fell from his pocket. He picked it up and continued to move toward her. She fled and notified police, who stopped Jablonski. The state trooper questioned Jablonski, who claimed the gun had accidentally fallen out of his car. The trooper told the suspect to keep the gun in the trunk of his car and let Jablonski drive off.

April 27, 1991: The murder of Margie Rogers. Jablonski entered a Utah gas station/grocery store and shot an elderly clerk in the head. He molested her body and stole about $150 from the cash register.

April 28, 1991: Jablonski was questioned by John C. Smith, an alert Kansas Highway Patrol officer, who spotted an out-of-state car stranded by a rest area. Smith talked with Jablonski and checked the car's license plates. He discovered that its owner was a suspect in three California murders. Jablonski was quickly arrested without incident and taken back to California for trial.